Pat

Praise for **Michele Hauf**

"Hauf delivers excitement, danger and romance in a way only she can!" — #1 *New York Times* bestselling author Sherrilyn Kenyon on *Her Vampire Husband*

"So sexy it will leave you breathless!" —MaryJanice Davidson, *New York Times* bestselling author of the Undead series on *Her Vampire Husband*

"Dark, delicious and sexy."
—*New York Times* bestselling author Susan Sizemore on *Her Vampire Husband*

"Adventure, intrigue, and a voice like no other—Michele Hauf is a force to be reckoned with!" — *USA TODAY* bestselling author Emma Holly

"Cleverly engrossing dialogue, overwhelming desire and intriguing paranormal situations are skillfully combined to make this an irresistible read." — *CataRomance.com* on *Moon Kissed*

"...a wicked good read!" — Kelly Mueller, *For The Love Of Books* blog on Follow The Night

Also available from Michele Hauf

HQN Books
Her Vampire Husband
Seducing the Vampire
Forever Vampire

Harlequin Nocturne
From the Dark
Familiar Stranger
Kiss Me Deadly
His Forgotten Forever
The Devil To Pay
The Highwayman
Moon Kissed
Angel Slayer
Fallen
Ashes of Angels

Harlequin Nocturne Bites
Racing The Moon
After The Kiss
Vampire's Tango
Halo Hunter
The Ninja Vampire's Girl

LUNA Books
Seraphim
Gossamyr
Rhiana

Silhouette Bombshell
Once A Thief
Flawless
Getaway Girl

Rogue Angel series (pseudonym Alex Archer)
Swordsman's Legacy
The Bone Conjurer
The Other Crowd

Self-Published
Wicked Angels
My Lady Madness
The Sin Eater's Promise

Michele Hauf

Follow The Night

ISBN-13: 978-0615500218
ISBN-10: 0615500218

FOLLOW THE NIGHT

This is a work of fiction. Names, characters, places and incidents are either the product of the author's imagination or are used fictitiously, and any resemblance to actual persons, living or dead, business establishments, events or locales is entirely coincidental.

This edition published by Swell Cat Press, LLC.

For questions and comments about the quality of this book please contact swellcatpress@gmail.com

The characters in this novel are a part of Michele Hauf's world of Beautiful Creatures. If you like Gabriel and Roxane's story, please check out their daughter, Jane Renan's story, From The Dark.

For more information on all characters in the Beautiful Creatures world, stop by Club Scarlet at: clubscarlet.michelehauf.com

ONE

Paris – 1780

"RUMOR HAS IT THE RAKE RIPPER lurks in the shadows, a demon in wait of pretty young men. He slashes their throats and dashes away, leaving the precieuse with his dignity staining his lace."

Madame de Marmonte studied the half circle of eager faces that clung to her every word. As salon hostess she made it her responsibility to report the latest rage, be it fashion, politics—even murder. But tonight concentration proved difficult. The hands on the tortoiseshell clock showed seven minutes before the midnight hour. Her star —where could he be?

"The Ripper struck again two days ago behind the Palais Royale," Chevalier de Champvillon added in a feckless whisper. The black heart patch, stuck at the edge of his lips, creased as he pursed his mouth. "The victim was, as usual, a handsome young rake of the aristocracy. When found, Monsieur Giscard's throat had been slashed. Blood had pooled about his head and stained the white roses edging his garden. And yet, a diamond pin and ruby ring remained intact. Isn't it remarkable the Ripper does not rob his victims?"

Madame de Marmonte started to reply that a life was the ultimate robbery, when she heard something over the boxy notes of the harpsichord Mademoiselle Leuze taunted to a cruel adagio—the crisp jangle of gold chains.

Diamond-encrusted watch fobs greedily clung to the final link of each sparkling chain. Two of them, if she was not mistaken—and she never was. Both tucked in a fine waistcoat of impeccable design. The wearer had introduced the fashion of double timepieces a month earlier during his debut.

Relief softened Madame de Marmonte's tense jaw. A little-girl smile parted her tight lips into a peeling giggle. *He* had arrived.

Breaking from her devotees, she called gaily, "Leo!"

Yes, the single name. The man insisted it was the only name he possessed. Deliciously mysterious, which further increased his appeal.

Finally, the night could begin.

HEARING MADAME DE MARMONTE'S contralto bellow, the muscles at the base of Leo's neck tightened, but he maintained a calm visage. Well beyond a quarter of an hour late, he knew. The woman was a stickler for promptness.

Lifting his right hand and turning his wrist toward his chest, he let his fingers fall into a graceful pose, palm up. Alençon lace spilled over the narrow cuff of his velvet frock coat. The lace was all the rage, or so he'd been coached. Excess was always in vogue. And if Queen Marie Antoinette declared it *du jour*, the more the better.

While keeping his gaze wide and his mouth not quite in a smile—broad smiles were passé—Léo took in his audience.

Madame Rigaud fluttered a lace fan before her poxed face. The fan was powdered to disguise how yellow the lace had become; the pox had found welcome breeding ground on the old bundle's flesh.

Chevalier Champvillon could not hide the strain on his face, a result of trying to suck in his tumescent gut while attempting a genial smile. Where had he found that brown striped waistcoat? Utterly vile, the color, like mud one scraped out from a horse's hooves.

The twins, Violette and Viol would never quite grasp the notion that large wigs were on their way out. A cavalcade of ships and battle cannons sat upon their heads in nautical swirls of powdered, greasy, pomaded strands.

How the women of Paris lived exclusively to be admired.

"Steady me, Toussaint," Leo muttered *soto voce* to the valet who winged him to the right.

"Not enough hard ale in France," Toussaint quipped. "But do avoid breathing Marmonte's toxic air. Best of luck, good man."

Feeling Toussaint pull back, Leo drew in a settling breath. The same feeling overcame him at every salon he attended. And he had attended far too many in the last two months. They admired him as if he were a new marvel displayed in the shop windows of the Palais Royale. A queer veneration that made him uneasy.

Truly this façade of worship and ingratiating smiles had worn thin. But it did serve a means to an end.

Morbleu, he may as well be on to it. He would only remain the fashionable fifteen minutes. All things told, every moment felt like a lifetime.

The hostess swept the intricate Aubusson carpet in a boisterous sashay toward him.

"Madame de Marmonte, do forgive me for inquiring the direction of your conversation? Certainly it must regard your exquisite selection in fabrics?" Leo drew an eye along the vulgar red and orange dress, splattered with malicious geometrical shapes. *Back*, he coached the silly grin tickling his mouth. "Indienne painted is quite the rage. Such vivid colors."

"Oh, Leo!"

Here comes the unavoidable. Steady, man.

He clamped his lips shut as Madame de Marmonte leaned in to buss both his cheeks. Unfortunately she could not hide her quest for slenderness, for her vinegar breath overwhelmed all who tread within arm's reach. A nauseating wave stirred in his nostrils.

Quickly he curled his fingers round the diamond-capped walking stick he sported. That redirected the disgraceful urge to sneeze.

"We were discussing the notorious Rake Ripper," Marmonte explained in a covert whisper designed to be loud enough for all to hear, "and trying to decide why he never robs his victims."

"A murderer's mind is a queer place," Leo offered. "Perhaps it is a lust for blood he seeks to fulfill."

The chevalier tilted his head and spoke wryly, "You speak of lusts you know nothing about, Leo."

Touché. A wince curled behind Leo's carefully controlled upper lip.

"Indeed," Madame de Marmonte added in an enthusiastic bellow. "You had best pay that valet accordingly to keep an eye in front as well as behind you, Leo."

Assuming a practiced pose, he splayed his fingers, beringed in ruby and sapphire. "Madame, you do not mean to imply *I* could become a victim?"

"Oh, come! You are the prettiest of all the rogues who stroll the Bois de Boulogne in the afternoon. I am surprised you have not yet been cut."

The wince escaped. All elegance fled Leo's stance. "I am not sure how to regard such candor, Madame."

The Rake Ripper had tallied a dozen to his count within the past few months. Indeed, all victims were *precieuses*, pretty young fops with no care beyond the latest vogue, and living the grand life thanks to a generous inheritance. Their playgrounds were the finest shops and gambling dens at the Palais Royale, and on the weekends, the gardens of Versailles.

"Forgive me, Leo." Marmonte slid a hand to rest upon his crooked arm. Vinegar dizzied his senses. "That was most uncouth."

The circle of wide-eyed sycophants nodded mechanically in agreement.

"It is only that we wish to keep you for ourselves. What would Paris do without your stunning fashion sense?"

His crowning achievement. A masterful disguise, if ever there was one. Leo's faux smile slipped. "You think I do not know of such things as the darker pleasures, Madame? I know some things."

"I am sure you do." Marmonte had a tiny grin that flickered in her pale gray eyes more than moving her mouth. "But I have never considered murder a *pleasure*."

"Nor have I." Leo slipped one of the watches from his waistcoat pocket and observed ten minutes had already passed. How time crept. "Strange bastard who's killing those men. I shudder to consider such a crime."

"Oh, but you should not. Worry pales your countenance, Leo. Do tell us about this fabulous frock coat you wear. It is as if it changes color!"

"Why, indeed, it does."

The flock of admirers gathered around him, yet his gaze slipped to where the movement of bold red velvet cast a wicked slash amongst the sea of fashionable whites and grays. The skirt of the frock coat, encrusted with thick gold lace reminiscent of Louis XIII, moved about the wearer's hips, a garish frill. Such attire had surely been excavated from the previous century. How had the man gained entry when Madame de Marmonte was noted for shutting her door in the faces of those sans fashion a la mode?

"What is the name of the color?" the chevalier entreated.

"Hmm?" Leo could not pull his gaze from the oddity. Wide cuffs could have stored a loaf of bread up each sleeve. And that soot-black wig. It swept down the man's back in a multitude of unsuitable sausage rolls. "Leo?"

He swung a look to the chevalier Champvillon, and landed on the old man's saggy jowls.

"Er?" He adjusted his straying attention. "Yes, the color is Moonlight Violets. Monsieur Bousset on the rue Saint Honoré sells it exclusively," he added rotely.

"Ah, my dear Leo," Marmonte bellowed as she noticed his distraction. "I must introduce you to Monsieur Anjou. He is from distant Provence." She led him from the mindless flock that chaffered enthusiastically about a visit to Bousset's shop on the morrow. "Though to judge from his accent one would think him merely a Normandy bourgeois."

"You admit him in such attire?"

She shrugged. "Rumor whispers he's royalty in his lineage. The Valois, I believe. As for his attire, he is merely eccentric. All the Parisian *precieuses* have their foibles, as you well know."

Yes, but Leo's foibles were necessary, and not distasteful to the eye.

Dark eyes alighting at Marmonte's beckoning, the tall stranger crossed the room in a few jaunty strides. He bowed grandly before Leo, sweeping his hand to the ground and stretching a leg out behind him in a courtly bow. Red-heeled shoes, as well—a court standard. Why, then, was he slumming at the Marmonte salon?

"Leo, I take great pleasure in introducing you to Monsieur Anjou."

No title? Could not possibly be royalty. It had been some time since Leo had appeared at court—wisely, he avoided the king's wrath. Were they admitting commoners now?

"Monsieur Anjou has been in Paris for a few months after a most adventurous excursion to the Americas."

"Such adventure." Despite its vogue, Leo cared very little for any news regarding America. He maintained interest with difficulty.

"Monsieur Anjou, this is our very own Leo, the star of my humble salon."

"Known by but a single moniker. Intriguing." The man offered a forced smile. As if he were bothered by such an introduction. Why the rude piece of anachronistic fluff!

"What is infinitely more intriguing," Leo said tersely, "is your remarkable taste in anachron— er, antique attire. Where *did* you find the gold lace, Monsieur Anjou? It looks to be real, not the gold threading currently the rage."

The man fondled the jabot coiled about his neck, though he kept a cool eye on Leo. "It is actually an heirloom." Coal eyes did not waver from Leo. Such nerve to look at him so directly. "I am not much for style, as you can see. That, as I understand, is why Madame de Marmonte displays—er, *invites* you here, yes?"

A verbal cut, but hardly enough to slice. "I suppose it is."

Madame Marmonte offered, "We've been discussing the Rake Ripper, Monsieur Anjou."

"A popular topic lately. The fellow seems intent on extinguishing every *precieuse* he can place his hands to. Quite the rake yourself, eh, Leo?"

The sudden hysteric gesture of flailing arms from behind Anjou caught Leo's attention. He tilted his head to peer around Anjou's bouffant of wig and arched a curious brow.

"If you'll excuse me," Leo said, cautioning a smirk. "It appears my valet strives to develop the newest dance."

He nodded congenially to Monsieur Anjou and Madame de Marmonte as Toussaint crept up and whispered in his ear. Unwelcome tension tightened Leo's fist. It was not anything he wished to hear. Not now, when he was engaged in the charade. How his past continued to find him, no matter the venue.

"Forgive me, Madame, Monsieur, I must beg off."

What excuse for leaving? For the truth would surely attract an audience.

A glance fixed to Toussaint, wide-eyed and waiting. Where *did* the man procure his clothing? At the Monday market in the Place de Greve? Did they not sell clothing peeled from corpses there? All the same, it would serve a useful distraction.

"Toussaint is a bit green to see Monsieur Manette dons the same Parakeet Wing as he this evening. It has become so common a color. Alas, I must hurry him away before the lackwit expires from embarrassment."

"Always so elusive you are, Leo. You will show next Sunday, as usual?"

"May the Old Lad Himself set my lace on fire should I miss it."

Marmonte chuckled behind her fan and blew giggling peals at Leo's retreating back.

WITH A JERK OF HIS HEAD, Gabriel Renan summoned the valet to his side. His alter ego, the foppish Leo, was always abandoned in the salon—Gabriel's dignity demanded it.

His strides moved him quickly, heels clicking down the cracked marble floor. Social pretense slipping as quickly as his mincing gait, his jaw tightened and his voice hardened. "Where is he?"

"Out back," Toussaint instructed. "In the courtyard between the estate and the carriage run."

Perturbed, Gabriel tugged at the itchy lace ruffled about his wrist. Leo's lace. He abhorred this fop's costume. Yet if he wished to succeed at dispersing his inheritance the disguise was necessary.

"Just the one?"

"All alone," Toussaint verified. "No one to hear his mad meanderings."

"Thank the gods for that small mercy." Gabriel turned the corner and slowed his pace. "I do hope Leo begins climbing the social ladder soon. I tire of this charade, Toussaint."

Toussaint shuffled up behind him. "Your hard work will pay off. You'll be a poor man soon enough."

"You believe so?"

"Yes, though you will save enough for living expenses?"

"Of course, Toussaint, it is only of the tainted money I wish to dispose."

Stepping outside, Gabriel stretched a look along the parking aisle that hugged the south side of the hornbeam-fenced estate. The air crackled with autumn crispness. Cypress leaves broke from their tethers and drifted to the cobblestones in fluttery winks of amber and gold. A dim oil lamp clinging to the corner of the house painted a pale sheen across the grounds.

A drunken squawk of surprise alerted him. Pale blue damask displayed runnels of burgundy wine down the left side of his coat. He stabbed the air with a finger, piercing Gabriel with an impotent dagger. His porcupine wig askew, and his wrinkled jabot undone, he spat out a spray of wine.

"You!" he managed with slippery lips and uneasy balance. "Her son. I saw you through the window! Oh," he moaned and clutched his chest. "I loved her...my Juin-Marie. Juin-Marie!"

Gabriel rolled his eyes and shook his head. "What miserable remnant from my mother's past has come to haunt me this day?"

"She was mine!" the drunk protested to the moon. "*My* Juin-Marie."

Another outburst like that and the entire salon would crowd outside to witness the spectacle. Gabriel could not have that—nor could Leo.

He twisted the diamond head of his walking stick and drew out a rapier from the cherrywood shaft.

The man stumbled across the courtyard, but saw Gabriel's intentions and, with a crooked wine-spattered grin, withdrew a rapier from the concealed folds of his sodden frock coat. Not so inebriated as he would appear then.

Gabriel tossed the walking stick to Toussaint, who expertly caught it, crossed his arms and cast an observant eye upon the match.

"She left me," the drunk spat. He stepped forward a pace, wobbled, shuffled back two steps, countering his wavering equilibrium. Yet his weapon remained on the mark for Gabriel's heart.

Not yet compelled to go en garde, Gabriel merely shook his head. He strolled a half arc, mirroring his opponent's ridiculous challenge. To face one in his cups? Hardly a man's match. And to do so in heels and lace? Bother.

"Tell me where she is! I die a new death each day that passes without my Juin-Marie!"

Yet another of his mother's discarded lovers. Did they never learn?

A thrust of his arm placed the point of Gabriel's rapier to the drunk's bobbing Adam's apple. Drawing his weapon arm straight, he looked down the blade of cold steel at his misshapen opponent. "Cease your idiot ranting. Go home. Sleep it off. If you do not, you will regret this foolishness in the morning."

"You are no challenge to me, you frimpy bit of lace!"

Frimpy? Not even on his worst days.

Steel cut steel, dashing away Gabriel's rapier. Quickly, he delivered a riposte. Sword blades clanged in the chill quiet of the night. Judging the man's skill in the slight tremor as their blades kissed, Gabriel determined insufficient challenge.

"There is only one man—" he smashed the hilt of his rapier across the man's right hand. His opponent's weapon clanged to the ground. "—in all the world—" He pressed the drunk backward, stumbling toward the hornbeam wall behind him. "—who may use that name."

"Juin-Marie?"

Gabriel prepared to deliver the coup de grâce.

The man thrust up his hands, palms out to placate. "Have mercy on a miserable sot, vicomte!"

Too late. Gabriel had touched rage. And this man had named his title correctly. He stabbed the rapier, missing the man's throat by a hair—then swung up his left fist, connecting with the man's jaw.

Gabriel toed the idiot heaped at his feet. "And that man is not you. Drunken sot."

Juin-Marie had never been overly discriminating regarding choice of lovers. But this one did give him wonder.

He tossed the rapier to his valet, who resheathed it, returning it to an unassuming walking stick.

Stepping over the fallen man's legs, Gabriel tugged at the lace about his neck and wrists. "This party has become dreadfully dull, Toussaint. Bring up the carriage, will you?"

"Of course." Toussaint skipped around the trimmed boxwood hedge.

Tension slipping away, Gabriel leaned against the wrought iron gate that barred the servants' entrance from the back courtyard. He drew in a deep breath, the exhale hissing out in a cloud of condensation. The moon expanded well beyond the half-rounded mark. No need for street lamps this night. Not that the miserly lamplighters ever filled the lamps with more oil than to serve a few hours.

A glance to the man sprawled in the thick, hornbeam shadows only raised his ire. He had named him *vicomte*. And he'd known his family. To be recognized, when he thought to remain anonymous in Paris, would not prove a boon to his covert affairs.

He went to great lengths to create a persona that the aristocracy and city officials would be willing to trust.

The click of a heel followed by a staccato of slow, heavy claps alerted Gabriel. A shadow in the shape of a man glided along the limestone wall of the carriage shed, stretching to monstrous proportions. It stopped over the fallen sot and the singular applause ended. A red-heeled shoe toed the inert body.

"I watched from inside," Monsieur Anjou said. "Impressive."

"Did anyone else see?"

"Not to worry. Your adventures were discreet. But tell me—" The man approached, hands behind his back, and dark wig obscuring all but eyes, nose and a slightly crooked mouth. "—why did you not kill him?"

With a shrug, Gabriel stated what should be obvious. "Life is precious."

"Indeed? Some lives are."

The man's soft epitaph put up Gabriel's hackles for reasons he could not touch. He was out of sorts, not thinking straight.

"It's a beautiful evening, isn't it?" Anjou paced closer. "I could not endure the stifling confines for overlong. Madame de Marmonte's salon is notorious for—"

"—fainting women and swooning men. My valet has expired on occasion."

Assuming Leo's loose stance, Gabriel leaned against the iron gate, crossing his feet at the ankle. "The woman insists all windows remain sealed for fear the latest pox or plague will seep in. Pity the old bundle's a-a-ddiction to vinegar will kill her more slowly and cruelly than any plague might."

He always stumbled on that word—addiction. His second least-favorite word. The first? Comfort.

"You give her far too much credit."

Gabriel chuckled at the man who had fixed his gaze high above the estate wall. "What is it that has captured your attention?" He scanned up two windows capped by smiling stone corbels.

"The gargoyle."

Gabriel startled to realize the man's whisper had been easily heard. Straining his peripheral vision he found Anjou stood beside him. Scent of something musty—perhaps the man's clothing—taunted his nose. A flicker of caution traced his spine.

Toussaint had walked away with his rapier.

Good sense emerged and Gabriel shook off his wariness. He was merely an old man with horrible fashion sense. "Yes, that gargoyle. Interesting creature, isn't it? Face like a mongrel and a body resembling a lion. With the damnedest set of wings."

"Surprising," Anjou rasped. "All the city's sculptures are blackened with soot, but that one is not. The beast appears frozen mid-flight."

"Fantastical notion." Gabriel could not prevent a genuine smile. The man possessed a whimsy seldom seen in the social circle he navigated.

Closing his eyes, he took in the calmness of the evening, the crisp scent of dew and the fetid straw Madame de Marmonte kept strewn before her home to muffle the racket of carriage wheels. Tendrils of night jasmine permeated his nostrils, like a ghost beckoning him to follow the night, to surrender to the unknown.

Yet so close lingered that musty shroud.

"So, you are the hero this evening, eh Leo?"

Nearby, the man on the ground groaned once, lifted his head, and then collapsed.

"Hero?" Gabriel smirked. "Just what I most desire carved onto my tombstone."

"You would prefer something else?"

"How about..." He fixed his gaze to the gargoyle. Scent of ancient dust mingled with jasmine. "He tried."

"Very well, I shall remember that, and try to see it is done. Until then—"

A wide, gloved hand squeezed about Gabriel's neck.

Reacting instinctively, he clenched his fingers and lifted his knee to connect with Anjou—right on target, yet unsuccessful in releasing the clutch. Strong and determined, his attacker.

Attacker?

The man possessed remarkable strength. Gabriel could not budge. The iron gate dug into his shoulders and elbows. He saw his own reflection in the metallic irises that held him a muffled captive.

"You see what you want, pretty one?"

The Rake Ripper attacks pretty young rakes...

He required a sword, for his strength was outmatched.

Something warm, moist, and sharp touched his neck. Anjou moved his mouth against Gabriel's neck and began to feed upon him as if a ravenous beast.

Amidst the mystifying horror, a gargoyle swept down from the roof and skimmed over their wicked embrace.

And then...

...the strange suctioning kiss at his neck began to entice.

A kiss?

Just a little kiss. Strong and demanding. Controlling in a manner that diminished further protest.

A strange compliance hazed Gabriel's mind. Rationale blurred. Enmeshed in an erotically macabre caress, he could no more resist or push away than he could call out.

You must resist. This embrace joining two men is unnatural. It must not be—

Gabriel's eyelids flickered. His palm slid down the ancient frock coat. A wanting moan spiraled up Gabriel's throat, escaping into the night on a canorous sigh. He curled his fingers, clinging to a forearm, and pulling the man closer.

He barely registered the shout of another.

"You have found the Ripper! We must call for his capture!"

His limbs numb and growing heavy, Gabriel answered the call to surrender. His body slid down the iron gate. Anjou moved with him, his tongue and lips sucking and drawing out his blood in an exquisite communion.

"Bastard!"

A heavy *clunk* preceded the tear of flesh. Teeth ripped from Gabriel's neck, the sound, as if a knife cutting through leather. He slumped into a seated position against the gate and began to shudder at the loss of warmth, the absence of control—or rather, of being controlled.

"It is the Ripper!" he heard Toussaint shout. Another loud *thunk*—wood against bones? "Get off, murderer!"

Toussaint swung a walking stick at the beast.

"Deserving!" came the shout from the drunk crawling across the cobbles.

Gabriel's head lolled upon his shoulder. He could make out blurry images of people. The swirl of red and gold. Parakeet Wing, what a ridiculous color...

A divine pulse within his veins pounded in rhythm to his heartbeats. Monsieur Anjou had awoken something deep inside his soul.

Two

ROXANE DESRUES PUSHED THE glass-paned carriage door open and jumped onto the cobblestones fronting the Marmonte estate. Thick straw frosted the cobbles, having softened the announcement of her arrival. She was late and—

"Make way!"

She withdrew from the open door just as the brass hinges split from the curved wood frame. A hand skimmed her gloved fingers. A bellowing groan erupted near her face. The source of the groan—a man running blindly—dashed off into the shadows of the rue de Temple.

"What the devil?" The driver jumped from his lofty perch and, wielding a lantern, held it high to study the damage. The carriage door hung from one bent brass hinge; the glass had cracked down the center. He swung the lamp close to Roxane's face. "Are you harmed, mademoiselle?"

She pushed the lantern away from her face and tugged down the corner of her fur-trimmed tricorn. Then, noticing the smear on her tan kid glove she pulled up the lantern and studied the side of her hand. *Losh*! Blood. Yet most certainly not hers.

"Mademoiselle?"

"Not to worry. I am safe," she assured the driver. Sliding a hand into the placket tied in the seam of her skirt she produced a silver ecu and pressed it into his palm. "*Merci.*"

A shout from the darkness alerted her. Roxane eyed the dodging shadow of the escaping man, now some distance down the street.

It is him! her instincts screamed. Her body wanted to pursue. *This is the moment you have waited for. Never have you come so close.*

However, another shout from the opposite direction vibrated through her veins. A cry for help. A familiar plea she had heard too many times since arriving in the ugly city of Paris.

Clutching her skirts, she dashed toward where she had heard the call for help.

"What is the trouble?" she yelled before rounding the corner.

What she saw around that corner stopped her cold. A sobbing man tricked out in yellow satin kneeled over a bepowdered and laced fop who bled at his neck like a holy miracle.

"Is he dead?" she called to the pair. She jerked her head around to scan the street down which the intruder had fled. She still had time to pursue if she ran right now. "Which way did he go?"

"Down!" the frantic valet insisted. "Do you see? He is down on the ground. The Rake Ripper has attacked my master. He is bleeding. Summon help!"

"H-he's alive?"

"Of course he is alive!"

Drawn from the prospect of chase, Roxane strode to the victim and plunged to kneel beside him. The fop flickered open his eyes and groped his soiled neck cloth.

Above the bloody lace sat two perfect wounds, half a finger apart.

The unthinkable had occurred. Again.

HE WAS ALIVE.

The last thing Roxane needed now was another "almost" case.

On the other hand, he was not dead. Since chase had not been possible, this may prove to her advantage. The victim may be able to provide her with important facts, such as the identity of his attacker.

Walking around the burst of color that beamed through a marvelous oculus window set into the domed bedroom ceiling, Roxane approached a lavish bed set upon a lacquered wood base. She had accompanied the victim and his valet to an elegant mansion clinging to the outskirts of the faubourg St. Honoré, and had waited while the valet put his master to bed amidst an explosion of lace, silk, satin and plumes, plumes, and more plumes.

Leo—that was his name—slept.

Roxane could not chase images of tonight's attack from her thoughts. When she had come upon him, he had not been in his right mind. Mutters of "sweet kiss" and "bring him back" had whispered from the man's lips.

She'd heard the same desperate murmurs but two months earlier. The memory cut like a machete to bone. For hours she had struggled to contain Damian's ranting, to quiet him, and to convince him it had not been a lover who had left him for dead, but something unspeakably evil.

So much she had learned of the creature called vampire in the past months. A creature that usually served a boon to her very nature had now become a vile bane to her family.

Fighting tears, she had decided she could not leave this poor fop to his own fumblings; he would never get things right. He required guidance.

And she needed bait.

Despite the viciousness of the attack, the man slept peacefully. Gleaming chestnut hair had been smoothed across the satin pillow by the valet. A trimmed moustache drew her interest to his mouth. Full lips were underscored by the shadow of a rogue Van Dyke beard. An attractive man. High cheekbones could have cut through any female's heart.

Such a thought startled Roxane. Attractive? This fop? She did not find vain, insouciant bits of lace and powder attractive.

She glared at the man's mouth, compressed in a soft line. His lips were neither full nor thin, but possibly...inviting. And pecking out at the vee of his lace-berimmed shirt, a shadow of dark chest hairs intrigued enough that she could not take her eyes from the sight.

Hmm... Perhaps meagerly attractive, she decided.

The valet slipped in and trimmed the candle wick on the bedside table with an expert squeeze of the scissor, and then tapped a heel to capture her attention.

Roxane sensed the valet's impatience with her presence. Sternly protective of his master, the trait impressed her more than bothered. "I will leave in a few moments."

"Very good." Toussaint left the room but did not close the door.

Of course, she mustn't be discovered alone in this man's home so late at night. She could be compromised in ways that would only add to her struggles.

Roxane eyed the white marble floor, focusing on the frenzy of colors the stained glass window beamed upon the cold stone. One color in particular caught her eye, a deep blue. Simple and endearing. Like Damian.

In the five months she and her brother, Damian, had been in the city her younger sibling had flourished, taking to the rakish lifestyle as a flower soaks up the rain. For the first time, she had witnessed true happiness in his pale green eyes, and had regretted refusing him all those years he had begged to leave their country cottage for Paris. She had always thought it a ploy designed by their father to corrupt Damian. Destroy yet another piece of the precious remainder of family she yet retained.

Xavier Desrues had kept his distance since his children had arrived in Paris. Roxane had not once seen him. She did not care if she ever saw him. Mostly.

Happiness had not greeted her here in this city of debauchery and decay. The Gauls had christened Paris *Lutetia*, the city of mud—a fitting title. Lutetia's dark evil had quickly caught up to Damian, snaking her dirty fingers about his neck and flashing her fangs in a most horrible way.

Do you know what happens when a swimmer stops paddling?

She smiled briefly to recall one of her brother's favorite wonders. And his positive response. *They float.* Nothing could dim the smile on his face. Until he had ceased to float.

It had been more over a week since she had last seen her brother. While he cursed her and spouted mad diatribes to the few who would listen, she continued to visit him at Bicêtre, a hospital at the edge of the city that housed the sick and insane. She would not surrender hope for Damian's sanity.

Even if hope meant befriending the enemy.

CONSCIOUSNESS SEEMED A NEW EXPERIENCE. Sounds were not immediately distinguishable, merely muffled fuzz inside his ears. Daylight filtered through the pale sheers strung before the ceiling-high windows topped with fluffs of officious crimson plumage.

Gabriel blinked at the brightness. His vision, initially blurry, slid down a hazy rainbow pouring from the massive oculus window set into the ceiling.

Cinnamon curled into his nostrils. That meant he was in bed. Toussaint instructed the laundress to use a cinnamon soap imported from India. It was one of many pleasures he entertained as part of the playacting he performed. A man's home must match his personality because one never knew when one might bring home guests or a woman.

But beneath the sweet fragrance lingered something...not right, almost vile. Musty? Yes, the smell of old things, of long forgotten and dusty attire. Yet at the same time that odor cloyed at him with a seductive invitation.

He swished his tongue across his teeth. "Toussaint, wine."

Toussaint's curly-topped head appeared above him. "Leo?" A strangely exuberant grin lifted the man's thick black moustache on one side, and quickly vanished to a worried moue. "You are finally awake."

Finally? And why did he call him by that name? Toussaint knew better. Leo was his public persona; a façade he could not abide when at home in private.

Gabriel winced and flicked his fingers toward the silver bed tray that, though he could not see it, should be within arm's reach. A clean white handkerchief landed in his palm. He pressed the linen to his mouth and drew in the scent of orange. The acrid fruit oil pierced his numb senses and wakened his muddy brain.

What had happened last night?

It was difficult to order his memories from the chaos of shadows and screams swimming in his head. Shadows shaped like armed men. Shadows shaped like flying beasts.

Why did he imagine a gargoyle taking flight from the Marmonte roof? Had he had a nightmare?

The room moved into sharper perspective. Overhead, sunlight beamed through the oculus, painting the air with dusty swashes of indigo, crimson and subdued pumpkin. To stand amidst the silent colors made him feel more right than any other place. So far from the false society that frequented the salons. So close to acceptance.

A familiar susurration steered his attention toward the end of the bed. Ells of fabric swished. Had he found a woman to debauch last night?

Why couldn't he remember?

The most remarkable female stood at the end of the bed, framed between swaths of burgundy velvet that poured from the bed canopy like waterfalls of wine. Gabriel hated all the fuss and frippery, but endured it as part of the charade.

But she was not a part of this charade.

He shoved Toussaint aside. Streams of pale red hair spilled in loose curls over the woman's narrow shoulders. Pink satin jailed in narrow brown stripes pushed a delicious bosom into enticing mounds and enhanced her petite yet curvaceous shape as exquisitely as the latest Pandora doll. A plain Pandora, for she wore no excess ribbon or lace, no hat or gloves, not even a wig.

He lowered his head near the valet's. "What—she—that woman—did I...?"

"No, Leo."

Toussaint's reply stung like a slap to the face. He had *not* slept with her? Pity. She was fetching in a fragile, pale sort of way.

Not a hint of carmine brightened her cheeks. Everything about her, from her blanched strawberry hair, to the fine milky complexion seemed washed out. Drained. And yet, an intense energy vibrated in the wide eyes fixed to him.

Not slept with her? The only instance that saw a woman in Gabriel Renan's bedchambers—or rather, *Leo's*—was that he had made love to her. But fact remained...

"She's dressed," Gabriel said, a strange sadness staining his tone.

"I said you and she"—Toussaint twirled a finger near his chest between he and Gabriel—"did *not*."

"I can hear you," a delightful female voice sang.

Toussaint winced, then straightened and turned to her. He splayed out an arm to present their guest. "Leo, might I introduce Mademoiselle Roxane Desrues."

"Roxane." Gabriel worked the name on his tongue, rolling the 'R' as he often did with his own surname. Rrrrrroxane. A tasty name.

"She accompanied you home Wednesday evening, and has been checking in on you every few hours."

"Every few—whatever for? The deuce, how long have I been asleep?"

"Two days," the woman offered with a bit more cheer than he preferred upon rising.

He gaped at Toussaint, who nodded agreement. "It is Friday, my lor—er, Leo."

A swallow etched his throat. He clutched the side of his neck. Beneath his palm a thick cloth wad had been secured to his neck.

"What has happened?"

"Do you not remember?" Toussaint turned to the wisp of a woman. "He's lost his memory?"

"Hard to believe," the velvet-smooth voice announced as she moved around the side of the bed. No, not moved, the woman floated on a swish of satin and *fraises et la crème* hair. "Loss of memory has never before been a condition of such an attack."

"Attack?"

Gabriel swallowed again, only to make a face from the pain tugging at his neck. Attacked? He was skilled in the martial arts and could go to fisticuffs with the largest of men.

Another swish of satin distracted him from his befuddlement. This woman had accompanied him home? Didn't make sense. Two days? What—oh—

Remembrance attacked with vicious accuracy. The sudden sensation that he was falling for endless parasongs pulled his thoughts from the pale beauty that leaned over him to the more troubling sensation of pain at his neck.

Shadows and screams, indeed.

Gabriel recalled the smug applause following his defeat over the idiot drunk. For but a moment he had felt uneasy about Monsieur Anjou. Ancient attire aside, the man had come off as whimsical. They had stared up at a gargoyle clinging to the edge of the Marmonte roof.

Then it had all quickly changed.

"That bastard bit me!" Gabriel struggled to sit upright.

Toussaint propped pillow after pillow behind his back and straightened the lace around his nightshirt.

"Enough, Toussaint!" He slapped at the valet's fussing fingers.

"But your lace is crinkled."

"Damn the lace!"

Gabriel touched his throat. *Morbleu.* A lecherous chill curdled at the back of his throat. Did not the Ripper kill his victims? With a blade? The man had bitten him.

The woman mustered her way between the valet and Gabriel's bedside, filling the air with the aroma of something familiar, yet he could not place the earthy scent. "You mustn't subscribe to the ridiculous rumor of a man slashing fops' throats."

"Rakes," Toussaint corrected from over her shoulder.

The woman splayed an impatient hand through the air. "Fops, rakes, they are all the same. Leo, it was a vampire—"

"A vampire?" Unbidden laughter spurted from Gabriel. He cast Toussaint a harried silent plea for sanity. "Mademoiselle, you would have me believe that a mythical creature attacked me? That is akin to saying stone gargoyles can fly."

Her eyes widened. He hadn't meant to blurt that detail.

"You saw a gargoyle fly?" she interrogated.

"No. I—it was merely an example. Who *are* you, by the by?"

"I am Roxane Desrues, as your valet has already introduced me."

"She's come to hunt the vampire," Toussaint cheerfully explained.

Gabriel pinned the valet with a scathing sneer.

Toussaint shrugged and smiled, exuding more mirth than he'd displayed for years. "I was given the details the night we brought you home."

"Mademoiselle Desrues..." Gabriel muttered the name. "You don't sound like any French woman I have ever met." A touch of brogue tinted her speech. "You're not French?"

"She's Scottish," Toussaint offered gaily. "Er, half and half. Her mother was Scottish—"

"—and my father French," she finished.

"It seems the two of you have shared much."

"Merely conversation," she replied.

"For two days," Toussaint added helpfully. "During your convalescence."

He switched his gaze between the twosome. Toussaint savored every syllable of this exchange. The servant had a penchant for the occult, the unexplained, the downright unbelievable. The valet regularly visited Mesmer's shop on the Place Vendôme. He was always so pleased to be involved in anything beyond the mundane. Poor, gullible man.

"I've come to help you."

Gabriel angled a scrutinizing eye on the woman. Why would a strange woman—albeit, a gorgeous and enticing woman and smelling like *what*?—wish to help him? He had already been attacked. Help was too late. And he knew nothing of Roxane Desrues, save she was the loveliest scoop of strawberries and cream, and he should have been in bed with her two nights ago instead of falling victim to a vampire.

Preposterous!

"You are lucky, monsieur—er, Leo. Of a sort," she said. "Few can claim their lives following an attack from the vampire."

The deuce! "Monsieur Anjou was *not* a vampire," he spat.

"Did you name the man Anjou?"

Insistent eyes riveted to his face.

"Yes, Anjou. Madame de Marmonte introduced us."

"He was *in* the salon?"

"Yes. He seemed normal, save the antiquity of his attire. He appeared as though he belonged in the seventeenth century. What do you mean I was lucky *of a sort*?"

"Bother that. You must tell me: the man introduced himself to you as Monsieur Anjou?"

Gabriel nodded. He prodded the bandage on his neck. "Toussaint, take this off me. I want to see the damage."

"I'll return shortly," Roxane called as she strolled out of the bed chamber.

"Where is she off to? Who the devil is that woman?" Gabriel twisted to follow her exit as Toussaint tugged at the bandages. A layer of lint clung to his wound and the valet picked carefully. "Has she really been here for days?"

"Mademoiselle Desrues has come and gone most discreetly. Would you sit still? And leave the shirt on."

"It's a monstrosity." He tugged at the loose neckline, scratchy with adornment. "All this lace!"

"There is a woman in the house, I will remind you."

"Why did you leave me in this awful fluff? You know I cannot abide such frippery. Leo gets left at the door."

"She would have questioned."

Gabriel sighed. Toussaint was more than just a valet; he was a capable ally who knew his weaknesses better than Gabriel did at times.

That he'd been so out of his head he must have been carried inside...? The shame.

"Very well, a fop I must remain until she leaves. She is lovely. If a trifle touched."

"She's not to be trusted, Renan."

"Why not? And she smells like what?"

"Rosemary," Toussaint stated with annoyance. He pressed a wet cloth to Gabriel's neck. "As for the vampire, I believe."

"Believe what?"

"In the myth. Or rather, the truth. Just because you've not before seen one does not mean they cannot exist."

"You are a sorry bottle of spoiled grapes, Toussaint. You've dipped your brain into Mesmer's magnetic tank one too many times."

"We do not put our heads in the tank, only our hands."

"No matter. And I will thank you to catch the Ripper next time I am—"

"Indisposed?" The valet tossed the bandages onto the silver serving tray. "Now listen, Renan, the woman would not allow me to call a surgeon after your attack. You could have bled to death."

"And yet you, an able man, a full head taller than the delicate wench, succumbed to her wishes?"

"Well, she..." Toussaint shifted his gaze up the wall to the oculus. "...touched me." A mysterious grin curled the man's lips, much as he fought it.

Gabriel lifted a brow. "Touched you?"

Toussaint leaned close to him as if to reveal a dark secret. "Yes, touched. She put her finger to my lips when I was frantic over you, and of a sudden I felt calm. Like I would do whatever it was she asked."

"I see. So she bewitched you?"

Toussaint blew out a breath of frustration. "It is just, she is different. Why not call upon the surgeon? She made it clear she wishes to keep your attack a secret."

"Why reveal that what the authorities have on their hands, instead of a throat slasher, is really a mythical vampire?" Roxane said as she entered the room with folded bandages in hand. "They would think the two of you mad, as well as me."

Gabriel crossed his arms over his chest and leveled a hard gaze on the pale beauty. "You roam about my home as if it is your own?"

"I brought supplies. I have been tending your wound for days, Monsieur Ungrateful."

He exchanged a look with Toussaint. The valet merely shrugged and mouthed the words, "Touched me."

"Now"—she set the medical accoutrements on the bed—"I've information you both will find valuable. But first, I wish to take a look at the wound. If you would allow?"

"Allow such a gorgeous pair of hands to fondle my flesh?" He spread out his arms, opening himself to her. "Charge ahead, mademoiselle. I am at your mercy.

Though it appears you've already had quite your way with me. Should I be ashamed?"

"It appears the attack has done little to staunch your charm."

"How are you aware of my charm?"

"Your valet has told me I should be honored to tread about your lair of—how did you put it—?"

Toussaint begged indifference with a tilt of his head toward the ceiling.

"Ah yes," she recalled. "Leo's lair of sensual delights."

"Just so." Though, not so much a lair as a haven, Gabriel thought, despite the surrounding fluff. He'd not lived in such elegant means for over a decade and now it reminded him of growing up. "You must know it troubles me, the two of you talking about me while I lay dying."

"Death was not to be yours," Toussaint reassured.

Yet if it had been?

Gabriel shuddered to think he'd not been on his game that evening. The duel with the sot had put him off when he should have remained alert to potential predators.

Roxane sat on the bed near his shoulder. What he wouldn't give to toss this lovely betwixt the sheets and prove to her the distinct difference between a lair and a haven. And yet, she was different, as Toussaint had pointed out. Touched? He felt inclined to tread carefully about her, lest she shatter like the pale glass she resembled.

"Tilt your head for me, please. *Losh*, what a mess." Her fingers touched up and down his neck on the left side. He might have taken pleasure from the warmth of her flesh, but the ache only reminded of the strange circumstances of his attack.

"Marvelous."

Both Roxane and Gabriel looked to the voice of fascination. Leaning over the bed, Toussaint clutched his hands gleefully to his chest.

Roxane flickered a pale look at Gabriel. "Your servant shows morbid fascination for your rather unfavorable condition."

"Disturbingly so. Toussaint?"

"Hmm? Oh, sorry." The valet straightened and took a step back, but could not disguise the glitter in his eye.

Did he not have an appointment with Mesmer, or some place more pressing to be?

Intent on her medical discovery, a curl escaped from the mass of hair queued down Roxane's back and swung across her cheek. Gabriel reached for the strand and twirled it about the tip of his finger. Not the unnatural dyed red so fashionable amongst the lie-abeds. This color belonged beneath the oculus with the rest of the muted rainbow.

She looked at him, mindlessly twirling her hair, and he leapt into her eyes. "Celadon," he decided.

"What?"

"Your eyes, mademoiselle. They are the delicate tint of celadon. Like an ice-frosted pine forest."

She smiled an unabashed smile, but too quickly her lips drew straight. "Your eyes are shot with streaks of red. Bring a mirror," she directed Toussaint. "Proof will make you believe, Monsieur—er, Leo."

He liked that she was uncomfortable calling him by the singular name. What else hid beneath the surface of this pale beauty that could stir a soft blush to her countenance?

She tilted the heavy pewter hand mirror toward him. Angry red flesh had formed a wide circle below the left side of his jaw. In the middle of that circle two swollen punctures sat like vicious boils piercing the line of his vein.

Gabriel opened his mouth in amazement

"Bite marks." Roxane said. "Do you believe me now?"

He fingered one of the wounds. A-a vampire? Impossible.

What sort of idiot did she think him?

"All men have teeth. A bite mark is not so unusual when one has been bitten. The man was an idiot. Demented. Yes, that is it. He—he *gnawed* me."

"Gnawed?" She lifted a brow. "Perhaps. But the impression leaves only the two wounds from the canine teeth?"

He flicked his tongue along his own teeth, noting the two upper teeth that did extend further than the others. No way to leave such marks without the middle front teeth also leaving an impression. And human teeth could not puncture flesh without brute force. His attacker had been disturbingly gentle.

"Did he suck blood from your body?"

The question raised bile to Gabriel's throat.

"Very well," he said resolutely. "Since you are the most delicious wench I've had in my bed chamber for a time, I will allow you your little fantasy. Not the Rake Ripper? Instead, a creature who tore his way up from a rotting grave to stalk the *precieuses* in Paris? Ancient attire aside, he looked rather tidy to me. Difficult to imagine the man sleeping in the ground."

"The Rake Ripper and the vampire are one and the same," Roxanne offered. "Paris does not know what sort

of creature the man truly is. And Monsieur Anjou did
not rise from a grave. That is a lot of nonsense. Vampires
are not dead, they are undead."

"But of course, merely undead." A burst of nervous
laughter escaped. At times like this he was thankful for
the façade Leo offered. "And what makes you so
knowledgeable, Mademoiselle Desrues?"

"I just..." The color in her cheeks brightened. As well,
her bosom colored.

Triumph curled his mouth. He enjoyed the sensual
victory. If she moved closer, he could trace his fingers
along the plump curves of her breasts.

"I have studied the vampire for a time," she said.
"Monsieur Anjou in particular."

"And yet for all that study you did not know his
name?"

"Why won't you believe me?"

"Because your claim is utter nonsense!"

Allowing his anger to emerge, Gabriel fisted the
counterpane. He'd been prepared for a duel that night,
not to have his blood sucked from him. He wouldn't
believe it. He could not.

"Vampires do not exist. Nor do giants or fairies or
mermaids. They are manifestations of a child's fairy tale.
Bogies concocted from imagination and a cruel desire to
frighten the little ones."

"What of witches?" Toussaint conjectured from the
end of the bed. "At least once a month another witch is
burned at the Place de Greve. You cannot deny their
existence."

Roxane's posture stiffened and Gabriel reacted.
"You know a witch or two, mademoiselle? Toussaint's

silly chalk markings before the front door tend to keep them from my home."

She stood from the bed and smoothed her hands over her skirts. With a pert jut of her chin, her expression segued from unsure to determined. "If you will not believe me, there is nothing I can do for you. Suffer at your own peril. I will take my leave."

"My own peril? Such dramatics!"

Gabriel crawled out from between the sheets. He wore but a linen nightshirt that flowed to below his knees. The sleeves were long and billowy, hanging over his wrists, and the blasted lace concealed his hands. Damned nuisance concoction.

"Do stay, Mademoiselle Desrues. I want to hear it all," he entreated. "I am starved for entertainment of a sort I have not known. Please, amuse me with tales of the undead."

Toussaint dashed to the door, blocking Roxane's exit. She spun to face Gabriel, anger firing her cheeks to a luscious bloom.

He crouched at the edge of his bed, easily assuming the role of predator. It felt far better than the prey of which he'd been posing lately.

"If I have—allegedly—been bitten by a vampire, why then, am *I* not stalking the night? If I recall my bedtime scaries correctly, is that not what happens when one's blood has been sucked by a creature of the night?"

"Of a sort."

"Ah." He eagle-eyed the nervous demoiselle. "Not very decisive, are you?"

"I am a very resolute person. You just—"

"I just what? Confuse you?"

"No!"

"Tempt you?" He flexed an arm, though the nightshirt hid his muscles. It wasn't a move Leo ever employed. "Do you find it difficult, mademoiselle, to be in this lair of sensual delights with my overwhelming maleness?"

"Please." She actually rolled her eyes. "You are a swish."

"Rake," he countered coolly, confident of his own masculinity.

"Same thing."

"Not at all," Toussaint corrected from the door. "One is much more concerned for fashion as compared to the other, who cares far more about the women who frequent his bed."

"Swish," she countered.

Gabriel rolled to his back and splayed out his arms in defeat. A chuckle was most appropriate, because the role he played could not be abandoned until he'd achieved his goal.

"Very well, I concede." No sense in arguing with an image he had worked months to concoct. Lifting his head, he speared Roxane with an engaging look. "Though I would not hesitate to choose you, mademoiselle, over an ell of Alençon lace."

"That impresses little," she said, following with a stifled yawn. "I must go home and rest. But before I do, you need to know what to expect."

"Expect? Beyond this damned wound healing and me getting on with my life?"

"Monsieur Leo, life as you know it will never be the same."

Three

ROXANE'S CELADON GAZE DID NOT waver from his. Where had the woman garnered such confidence? Any other time he would have sent Toussaint from the room, and seduced the woman into his bed.

The situation as it was, Gabriel drew in a contemplative sigh, spread his hands open before him, and said, "Humor me."

"Very well." Roxane paced the end of the bed, her hips swaying in delicious taunts to Gabriel's resolve.

"You have been bitten," she said. "Which means you may or may not become a vampire."

"So I have a choice?"

"The moon is waxing gibbous."

"I give the moon no regard."

"You should. Or rather you *must* from this moment forth. You've less than a week before the moon is full, Leo. And it is not so much a choice as options."

He managed a false gaiety. "Options? What man does not favor options?"

Mademoiselle Desrues strode the length of the bed. Her earthy scent was so unlike the powdered creations that normally landed on his sheets. Gabriel could not stop breathing her in. The urge to gasp, choke at a dusty, musty odor wasn't there. Because she was fresh. Alive.

Just breathe. Inhale the purity and keep it.

After a few lingering inhalations, his agitated state softened. As did Roxane's gaze, yet her pale eyes remained intense, liquid and clear. What sort of disease had planted itself in the mind of this exquisite beauty? To forge her belief in such hideous myth?

"It is rare the vampire does not kill," she explained matter-of-factly. "Since the murders have been noted, Monsieur Anjou has been meticulous—save two cases."

"Two? Another besides me?"

She nodded.

"And another who survived such an attack?"

"Survived...to an extent."

"An extent? Woman, why do you not simply speak what you mean to say? You dress up your fears in euphemisms. Of a sort. To an extent."

"Will you listen to me?"

He sighed. Another breath of rosemary filled his senses. It appealed so strongly after breathing nothing but powder and greasy hair pomade for months. Captivated against his will, Gabriel conceded. "Fine."

"Should the victim find himself in such a situation—having been bitten" she began again, "he can do one of three things. First being suicide."

Gabriel's jaw dropped open.

The valet clutched the bedpost, his knuckles growing white.

"Not a consideration, I assume," she said. "Now, the second option is that you drink blood and complete the change."

"The change? You mean *become* a vampire?"

"Yes." She blinked calmly. "Ransom your mortal soul for immortality."

"Immortality." Toussaint's eyes brightened into mystical beacons.

His mortal soul? "You really are a mad bit of work. And so are you," Gabriel shot at Toussaint.

He clutched his throat. This was not a laughable farce performed by the Comédie Française. This was reality. A sickening reality this woman somehow made more evil by the moment. Suicide or vampirism? How far would she go with this charade? He had merely been bitten by a lackwit!

On the other hand, what did he know?

Gabriel swallowed the hollowness rising in his throat. "You said I had three options?"

"Indeed. The final option is that you wait it out until the orb of night has grown tumescent."

"The orb of night," Toussaint repeated in fascinated wonder, his stance like a street charlatan seducing the crowds to buy his potions.

Gabriel sat up straight. "What sort of blather is a tumescent orb?"

With a shrug, Roxane pointed toward the oculus. "The full moon."

One could never see the midnight sky for the lantern suspended above to rain light through the colored glass. Toussaint never missed a night.

"The moon is nearly full," she said. "If you can abstain from drinking blood for the next few days you will triumph and the vampire's taint will pass through you. Your mortal soul will remain intact and you will continue to be the swish you are."

He should challenge her assessment of him, but at the moment, Gabriel had graver matters to consider.

He mined the depths of his charm and finessed a smile. "Mademoiselle, I'll have you know, of the many wonderful drinks that top my favorites list, blood is not one of them."

"It is not so simple as it sounds."

"Oh, I imagine not. I wait, engrossed, to hear your next words."

"Certainly, I shall assist you in your endeavors to overcome the blood lust."

"Blood? And—" Lust? Gabriel squared a palm flat before his face. "Do not place those words in the same sentence. It is utterly insane!"

"You need someone close by who knows what to expect," she said. "Of all the men who have attempted to fight the call to drink blood none have succeeded. Most give in to the blood hunger within a few days."

"*Give in* to drinking blood?"

"It is a powerful temptation. At least, that is what I have come to understand."

"Through your studies?"

She nodded.

What sort of person studied blood and vampires and lust, all tossed together? Much as the woman attracted, she also repelled him like no female had before. Best to put an end to this charade. "Toussaint, remove this mad scrap of satin from my home."

The valet merely stared at Roxane, his lips parted and a *yes, Mademoiselle, whatever you wish* glaze to his eyes.

"It is not I who is mad," Roxane said. "It may very well become you, Leo. For if you are determined to resist the compelling and exceedingly tempting hunger for blood then the only result can be sure madness."

"Madness," Toussaint whispered in eerie wonder.

"Indeed." She paced to the wall where a cheval mirror reflected her tense jaw and crossed arms. "Which option will you choose: madness, vampirism, or suicide?"

Those were the least appealing choices Gabriel had ever been offered. And he had been offered some horrendous choices in his lifetime.

Would a few days find him stalking innocent people in hopes to suck out their blood? He was not a man to become such a monster. Monsters did not marry or raise families. Monsters could not...have love.

"No!" He punched a fist into the plush counterpane. "This is all a spectacular lie conjured by a lone woman in need of attention."

Roxane made an objective chirp. She remained facing the mirror.

"Yes, attention," he countered, knowing well the need for such. "You appeared from out of the blue. I have no idea who you really are. You say you have come to hunt the Rake Ripper? Sounds rather dangerous for one so petite and female as you."

"It is. But I have no choice. Listen to me. What has been done to you is not finished. Know you are not safe until the full moon. As soon as Monsieur Anjou learns you survived his attack he will seek to finish what he could not complete the other night."

So now he would be pursued by a vampire as well as facing madness? "I certainly hope he does. I will be waiting for him, rapier en garde."

"He is ten times stronger than a mortal man. You will be defeated."

Shoving up a sleeve to his elbow, Gabriel punched a fist into his palm. "How can you know so much?"

"It is a guess. Anjou cannot risk creating a minion."

Morbleu, this was wrong. Was the Rake Ripper really a creature of the night? By acting the fop had Gabriel lured a monster to him?

He wanted to believe in Roxane's innocence and her sweet, seductive scent. He wanted to take her in his arms and kiss her. Kiss away the evil. Take back the night of his attack. But the evidence remained as two painful and deep punctures upon his neck.

"If I succeed..." He slid off the bed and paced the floor. "If I fight the madness, then it is sanity and a normal life that waits?"

"Sure."

That was the least convincing assurance he had ever heard.

He sought out the celadon sparkle in her expression. Only now did he notice the glass vial suspended around her neck by a fine silver chain. Why, it looked like—

"What is that?"

She held the vial between two fingers, tilting it to move the thick red liquid inside from side to side. "This is blood."

Call out the surgeons! This woman was not in her right mind.

"I feel I shall regret this, but I must ask: Why do you wear a vial of blood about your neck?"

"It is witch's blood."

Toussaint brightened from his bespelled haze. "Witches?"

"First it is vampires, and now you've added witches to the brew? Surely they do not allow such trinkets in the asylum from which you have escaped?"

"Bastard."

Gabriel followed her retreat toward the closed door. "What do you expect of me?"

She spun in a grand fury of tight fists and a blaze of strawberry tresses. "Witch's blood works like acid to a vampire. The two are mortal enemies. That is how I plan to kill the vampire who attacked you. And perhaps, with his death, the madness that awaits you will vanish."

"You know that to kill Anjou would release me from vampirism?"

"I cannot know for sure. It is only a guess."

"I see. Very well." He tapped his mouth, considering. "If I must skip along into this fantasy world of yours, my next regrettable question will be: Who elected you the vampire slayer? What stakes, if you'll pardon the pun, does a fragile slip of a woman have in pursuing this alleged vampire Anjou?"

"Is not putting an end to his murderous rampage reason enough?"

"You are quite the libertine."

"Gorgeous."

"Toussaint!" Gabriel snapped his fingers at the valet clinging to the bedpost. "Snap out of it. She has bewitched you."

"I have done nothing of the sort!" Roxane protested. "I—oh…men! Always seeing only the surface of a woman."

"And yet, you have already judged me by my surface. A swish?"

She had no answer for that, save an audible huff. Clutching her skirts in tight creases, she announced, "I am leaving."

Gabriel apprehended her, pressing her shoulders against the wall. "How do you know so much?"

Her frantic gaze darted back and forth across his face. "Th-the vampire attacked someone close to me two months ago."

"Who?"

"Someone close."

"You cannot name this victim?" he pressed, for to summon the color in Roxane's cheeks gave him a twisted sort of thrill. *Blush for me, my sweet. Reveal your lies.*

"It is not that I cannot, but that I choose not to name him. I have not wanted to go through this nightmare again, but I will, if only to ensure another man does not suffer the same pain." She made a tiny fist to punctuate her mighty words. "I will kill the bastard, that is truth. But first—" She shook her head, as if to shake away the words from her mouth. "Good eve, Leo."

With that declaration to war she pressed easily from his barricade and strode from the room, leaving Gabriel in a sensational state of anger, surprise and strange wonder.

Whom had she known who had fallen victim to the Rake Ripper?

I choose not to name him.

A lover? A husband? Whoever it was, she had been close to him. For the fire in her eyes spoke of passion and the compulsive need to seek vengeance. Truly, she suffered a great loss and had slipped from reality. To have designed the attacker as a vampire?

Gabriel turned to Toussaint. The valet pierced him with a castigating gaze. "What is it, man? You chill me with your morbidity."

The valet stiffened and twisted away from his master.

"You know so much about the woman." He punched a fist into his opposite hand, twisting it into his palm as if to wring the frustration from his being. "So much time it takes to learn about a person. And yet in two days she thinks me merely a swish."

"You have mastered the costume."

"Yes, but can I shuck it off? Anjou remains at large, despite my having him in my grasp. Had I been alert I could have ended the whole thing right there. No worry for the Ripper or vampires, for that matter."

"Are you going to pursue him now?"

"Of course." He didn't need to consider the options. "I can't have him going after another innocent."

"Very good." With a subservient nod, Toussaint left the room.

In the silence that followed, Gabriel wondered if maybe—just maybe—a morsel of truth lived in Mademoiselle Desrue's macabre claims. Could lunatics hold such a firm grip on outer rationale and calmness?

The woman was beguiling and delicate, yet intriguingly decided in her beliefs. So different from the lamps he had been around. Lamps fussed and primped so much they never did make it out before nightfall. They were weak and vapid, so much *less*.

Roxane Desrues was a lustrous blend of celadon and *fraises et al crème*. Slender as a willow branch, but, he decided, equally as strong. Something about her refusal to lower her head—to be an agreeable female—set his blood to a race. A woman who knew her own mind, and yet, she blushed so gorgeously.

She was more woman than he could hope to touch. To know. To taste. To...

No. He would not think the 'L' word. His needs would for ever go unmet—his parents had taught him that cruel truth years ago, and any attempt to move beyond his predestined misery had failed.

To close his eyes and press away the words, the thoughts, the dreams, Gabriel moved to the core physicality of his being. He felt something beyond the pulsing reminder of attack on his neck. 'Twas lower. There, in the center of his chest. An ache in his heart.

A man has to believe in something.

A long forgotten epitaph issued by his father on the last night he'd seen the man. Cecil Renan had believed in greed, of the flesh, mind, and purse, all in the pursuit of his *comfort*. And ever he sought to please his fickle Juin-Marie.

Determined to create beliefs so distant from his absent parents' licentious greed, Gabriel had striven to walk higher ground. Much as he had clung to that high path while taking the Grand Tour, upon return to Paris he had been kicked and shoved by the naysayers who could not see beyond his parents' damning legacy.

His disappointments had turned his heart cold.

A man could lose himself in the cream of Paris, floating upon the surface, mired in the thickness of it all. Mayhap he had already lost. What *did* he believe in?

Could he believe in a vampire?

He fingered the wound on his neck. *You do believe. You just don't know how to admit it.*

He drew in a breath that captured lingering tendrils of rosemary. Traces of her. A breath of freshness he had not hoped to have. Despite himself, he smiled.

"Toussaint!"

The valet's head immediately popped inside the bedroom. "Yes?"

"Bring along Leo's clothing. We will go after Mademoiselle Desrues."

Four

Toussaint knew Roxane lived in a garret not far from the Palais Royale on the rue Vivienne, for the two had talked much during Gabriel's confinement. She did not occupy a cell in Bicêtre, as he had sullenly mused. Though certainly she did display a tendency toward eccentricity, if not outright lunacy.

His attention focused inward, Gabriel stared out the carriage window at the passing building fronts. He felt oddly envious that Toussaint possessed so much knowledge of the pale beauty. Almost as if the valet had uncovered her secrets, and Gabriel was left to grope through a mire to discover any small fact.

Foolishness. He could learn the woman's secrets with but a crook of his finger and a wink. Seduction was as easy as selecting a waistcoat from one's armoire.

But to truly know a woman? That was a different challenge entirely.

Beyond mastering her physical desires, he had never really known a woman. If they were lovers he attended to her pleasures, and in turn, his own. If a lover had ever shown promise toward the future, well, lately, he'd gotten himself as far from their presence as possible. Why risk torturing himself with hope?

Because it is hope that fills your empty heart. If only for a moment.

And moments were often all he was offered.

You've but days until the full moon.

Many moments, that wait. But all in all? So little time.

Of the choices Roxane had offered him, the one she was not sure of seemed his best hope. He would kill the vampire before the full moon, thus ensuring he did not become one himself. But to find the man, he needed Roxane. Unless she was correct in her guess that Anjou would seek him.

He hoped for that. He would be waiting, stake in hand.

"She is wrong, you know."

Gabriel smoothed his fingers across the tender wounds on his neck. "Don't know what you're talking about."

"You are not a swish."

Certainly not.

"You were winded following the duel with the drunk. That is why you were not at the top of your game."

He had not needed that to be pointed out to him. But Toussaint never avoided the truth. "Winded by a skirmish with an idiot dancing in his cups," Gabriel mocked himself.

He pressed his forehead against the glass pane in the carriage door. "It doesn't matter what Mademoiselle Desrues thinks I am."

"Don't lie to yourself, man. You're already falling. I can see it in your eyes. They are seeking, searching, dreaming of Roxane."

Gabriel clicked his fingernails against the dirty glass and smirked. "Silence, Toussaint."

✦✦✦

ROXANE LIVED IN A POSITIVELY medieval neighborhood unhampered by wide streets or sanitation, to judge from the refuse piled outside doors and leaking onto the streets. No center gutters here to redirect the sewage.

Toussaint directed the driver to stop outside a three-story limestone building sandwiched between others of its like.

Gabriel stepped out onto the cobbled street and stretched his neck to look over the perimeter. Long iron brackets attached to the building fronts thrust over the street, their precious lamps dangling precariously, so that a high-seated coach driver must duck to avoid a fierce thunking. None were lit, for the increasing moonlight. High above, an assortment of chipped and heavily-sooted gargoyles stared down upon the street.

A flying chunk of stone? Truly, his mental state had taken a bruising since the night of his attack.

He untwisted the rapier from its sheath and slid it up and down.

At that moment a miserable moan preceded a creeping shadow that may have been female, but for the oddly distorted skull. Releasing his blade, he went en garde.

The woman suddenly noticed her observers as she took the steps to the same apartment building. She literally held up her head, one hand to a massive confection of wig, ribbons, curls and flour powder. The creation soared three feet into the air and would have given a giant a megrim.

"I've no interest, messieurs," she muttered weakly. Dipping her head forward to enter the building, she toppled across the threshold.

Gabriel dashed up the steps and caught her arm, preventing her from a painful landing. "Careful."

She pushed him away, but sunk to her knees and literally crawled toward a door but five strides away. The wig collapsed and folded over her forehead. "Please, monsieur, I am well."

Silently cursing a female's need to possess such extravagant hairstyles, but at the same time noting the woman wore a very plain dress—hardly a match to the wig—Gabriel stepped to her door and opened it for her. As he sheathed his rapier, she crawled inside and kicked the door shut. Sobs seeped out into the foyer like imperfect jewels discarded with a toss.

Toussaint merely shrugged and gestured they take the dark staircase.

Reluctantly, Gabriel took the first creaking wood step. "You don't think we should attempt to help?"

"Help her with what? Pry the hideous monstrosity from her head?" Toussaint snorted. "Women."

"Something was wrong," he said. "Beyond the wig. I sense it."

"Save your charity for those who need it."

"That's what I'm trying to do, but no one will touch my money."

"They'll touch Leo's money. Soon enough. This must be the place." Toussaint landed on the second floor and pointed out a plain door with a dash of gold paint swirled in a loose 'S' in the center. "What's the 'S' for?"

"Maybe from a former resident." Gabriel rapped with the head of his walking stick. "You're sure of the place? It looks dismal."

Still concerned with the woman's crying, he glanced down the darkened staircase. The sobbing could no longer be heard. Had someone hurt her? He really should—

The door opened to emit a gush of warm candlelight and Roxane's surprised face, enswathed in the faded ruffles of a night robe.

Gabriel had to catch himself from gasping. A woman en dishabille. What easy plunder she offered. The balding blue velvet robe clutched at the bottom of her face looked a night flower seeking the sun.

A nudge from Toussaint redirected his straying thoughts.

"Oh, er...yes. I've come to beg your apology, mademoiselle," he spoke the practiced lines. "My treatment of you earlier was unforgivable. I had no right to speak to you so."

"You are fearful to spend the night alone?" A lift of brow exposed her sneaky mirth.

"Of course not. I merely—"

"I talked him into it, mademoiselle," Toussaint tossed in over Gabriel's shoulder. "The two of us know little regarding my master's condition. If that is what it can be called? A condition? It would be a tremendous boon if you would see to staying a night or two and teaching us all that you know."

Gabriel flashed Toussaint a scathing look, but turned a warm smile on Roxane. "What he said."

Pity reflected in her eyes. Gabriel thought to protest her misplaced concern, but then, the charade must be maintained. Surely she thought him a vapid and utterly helpless swish.

Clutching the robe tightly, she sighed. "Apology accepted."

"Might we enter?"

"What for?"

"Certainly not to pillage," Gabriel offered at sight of her fearful eyes. "Is it a bad time?"

"No, er no. Certainly, you are welcome inside. Give me a moment to straighten things."

The door slammed shut. The clatter of furniture scraped a wood floor and clinking metal sounded.

Gabriel looked to Toussaint. The valet shrugged.

A strange whisking noise stroked behind the outer wall. Gabriel pressed a palm to the wall and again exchanged curious looks with Toussaint. "She is an interesting study, yes?"

Suddenly the door swung inward and Roxane beckoned, "Come in, messieurs."

They followed her into a wide sitting room, the walls lined in fading English paper that had seen better years— perhaps better centuries. Half a dozen thick cathedral candles placed upon the windowsill and hearth flickered.

A faded wool blanket had been pinned to the outer wall where Gabriel had heard the strange sound. As a tapestry? Or...to hide? He cautioned himself from tugging it free. A tufted chair and plain wood table furnished the room. A fieldstone hearth to his left snapped fire sparkles up the chimney.

"Settling in for the night?" He strode to the fire and spread out his palms. A scatter of chalk lines on the stone hearth took his interest. And there, next to a stack of ash wood, a piece of black cloth was draped over something. Bowls? He thought to lift the cloth, but felt Roxane's stare upon his back.

Hands spread before the blaze, the cozy warmth settled his apprehensions. *This woman is not insane.* A simple home, though oddly decorated, did not lend to a tainted mind. Besides, he liked her all snuggled into that blossom of a robe. There was no reason whatsoever he should not seek the treasures she hid beneath the faded fabric. Perhaps Toussaint could wait out in the carriage?

"So, you wish me to stay with you?"

Did he? That had been Toussaint's idea. "I'm not sure about staying, but there is a certain amount of information I'm sure—"

"There is much to consider," she replied.

And the closer this gorgeous beauty was to him, the easier it would be to seduce her.

"I do have an extra room. You've nothing to fear from me. Certainly your virtue will not be in danger. Toussaint will keep me in check." The valet did not meet Gabriel's glance. But the man's knowing smirk was, fortunately, out of Roxane's eyesight.

"Ah yes, the very same valet who keeps the lair of sensual delights in order for his master?"

Gabriel's smugness fell. "Of course, you will bring along your maid."

"I..." She shrugged a hand up the sleeve of the ruffled robe. "I have not had opportunity to employ a maid since arriving in Paris. If truth be told, it is unnecessary."

"Astounding. How do you dress?"

"I am not of the society that was born to such expectations of servitude, such as yourself. And, much as you may find this remarkable to digest, we country women are perfectly capable of dressing ourselves."

"That is quite remarkable." He cast Toussaint a knowing lift of brow.

"Ninon does stop by."

"Ninon?"

"She lives downstairs."

"The one with the wig?" Toussaint interjected.

"You've met her?"

"She seemed terribly sad." Gabriel drew his gaze up and down the dusty velvet curtains drawn before the window that looked over the stinking street. Such old things. Very little in the way of personal possessions. Not a figurine or portrait in sight. And there was the obvious, that her dress was years out of vogue.

But what were they discussing? Ah yes, the woman down the stairs. "Rather a contrast, her hair and clothing."

"She only does it for the coin."

"Does *it*?" He turned to Roxane. A flip of his lacy wrist splayed out a questioning hand. Yes, he'd mastered the fop's flip. Just when Gabriel began to sneak up on Leo an extravagant gesture reeled him into the costume. "In what delicious wonders does the bewigged creature indulge?"

"Ninon is in debt after her mother's expenses. The old woman is dreadfully ill. The coiffures pay her to experiment with new hairstyles."

"I see. I have never before heard such a thing. To pay women to use their hair?"

"It is quite miserable. Being prodded and poked and curled and burned and powdered all the day. She's a nasty burn on her ear from a careless barber. But it does pay well enough to keep her mother in laudanum."

Gabriel nodded, and muttered *laudanum* under his breath. The word worked like a snake coiling in his gut, clenching and writhing. For accompanying that word always came addiction. An addiction to comfort. *I am in my comfort now. Mustn't bother mama...*

He glanced to Toussaint, who, companion that he was, nodded that "I understand" nod.

Realizing with a start that he'd pressed the nail of his forefinger deep into his palm, Gabriel shook out his hand and mentally shrugged off the dark thoughts. "So you'll dress yourself then?"

"Of course. And if I need assistance, I am sure Toussaint can lace me up."

Toussaint gaped.

Gabriel asked, "You do not fear the lacking propriety? You could be ruined."

"I don't subscribe to malicious whispers. I know my truths, Leo. I hardly feel you will impose upon my kindness in any manner that will see me ruined. Nor would I allow such. If you'll excuse me, messieurs, I'll pack some things." She strode from the room.

The woman certainly had a mind to her. Gabriel wasn't sure how to take her bravado. She had no idea what she was walking into.

"Me?" Toussaint stabbed his chest with a thumb. "Handmaid to a woman? I don't know how to lace and primp and do whatever else it is women require."

Gabriel winced to think the valet did just that every day to him. "You'll fare well enough, old man. It's either you or leave Mademoiselle Desrues to me."

"Not a wise choice."

"At least not until she trusts me. Course, then I am sure I'll engage more in undressing than dressing, eh?"

"Remind me to ignore the next queer opportunity that arises, will you?"

"I thought you were excited for this adventure, Toussaint? You've opportunity to step beyond the mundane. You already play handmaid to a swish, what's so different about dressing a woman?"

"Oh, my soul. Laces and boning and petticoats and—" He molded the air before him. "—curves."

Gabriel smiled. Perhaps he would see to assisting the beauty himself. Pity to waste those curves on Toussaint.

LOCKING THE DOOR TO HER bed chamber, Roxane shrugged from the night robe and blew out the breath she had been holding since opening the door to discover Leo's puppy dog pout.

Shivering as the cool night air whispered across her bare flesh, she hastily wiggled into the dress she had previously worn. Tugging the laced stays to a comfortable fit, she bent her arms up and over her shoulders and tied them securely. A maid? Ha!

A mad scramble had hidden all from her visitors' wondering gazes. But the man had almost lifted the cloth from the bowl of herbs sitting before the hearth.

Leo wanted to believe in what everyone else subscribed to: the normal, the surface, the valid. Asking him to believe in vampires was asking much. Yet how difficult could it be to believe when the man sported a bite on his neck?

She would give him time to accept. Though, not much time. He had but days. And she had less.

She had surpassed fragility and haplessness weeks ago. No longer did she cry herself to sleep, cursing herself for the trouble that had found Damian. Now, she was determined to make the world right for Damian. For if all went well, her bait would attract the vampire Anjou.

Eyeing the collection of candles that sat around the ancient grimoire her grandmother had gifted her, Roxane shook her head. Mustn't risk it. Recall of the white chalk symbol traced on the limestone before Leo's home sent a shiver through her. She'd avoided the marking easily enough. As well, the chalk marks she'd drawn out on her wall had swiftly been covered to prevent suspicion.

Clasping the vial of blood suspended around her neck, she nodded, decisive. She mustn't risk revealing any more of her truth than necessary. Some truths could do more harm than good.

ℱIVE

ROXANE ALIGHTED FROM THE CARRIAGE behind the two men. The moon was growing larger. She had perhaps three or four days to either capture Anjou or watch Leo go insane.

"Roxane?"

Leo stood waiting, his hand extended. Straight shoulders and proud stance. The handsome man pranked out in lace and powder intrigued her more than she thought possible. But she mustn't subscribe to a rake's attractions.

Bait. If you consider him anything more you will lose Damian for ever to the madness.

Glancing down, she spied the chalk circle Toussaint had drawn before the door. A portent to keep away witches.

"Mustn't subscribe to my valet's superstitions," Leo offered.

"Still." Drawing her skirts close to her legs, she stepped around the circle and over the threshold. "I'd hate to smear his artwork."

"Tired?" He followed her inside and tugged at his jabot to loosen it.

"Completely puggled."

"I'll assume that means tired?"

"Yes. I should like to sleep." And avoid looking into the man's troubled eyes.

Intuition told her he was in need of comfort, of an understanding soul. How easy it would be to give him what he needed. At the sacrifice of her needs. Because what if? What if he succumbed to madness? Or what if he did not succumb, but instead became a drinker of blood?

A shudder shook her shoulders.

The only other option was that Leo could surface unscathed.

Impossible. She had not witnessed such triumph, nor had she heard of it beyond what had been written in her grandmother's grimoire, a book of knowledge passed on through the centuries, filled with practicalities, wisdom, and the occasional legend. Roxane's bible, of a sort. Unfortunately of late, the section on vampires had become worn.

The brush of Leo's fingers glided along her arm. When she had walked another step and his fingers had almost left her, she turned her wrist to catch his grip. Stopping, she turned to him. They stood palm to palm. No question in his eyes. No challenge in his pose. Defeated?

No. The man was determined. As was she.

Compelled by a part of her heart she wasn't completely sure of, she touched the dark stubble on his chin. His sharp intake of breath tempted her closer. Here, alone by the man's side, she felt his presence as a viable heat. One breath closer and she would snap to him, like a piece of metal being drawn to a magnet.

He made not a move to reciprocate her touch. But there, she scented faint cinnamon wafting from the fibers of his clothing—why, from his very being.

Pressing up onto her tiptoes, she leaned in and touched her lips to the mouth of a man she knew she mustn't think of as anything but bait. He allowed the tender kiss without grasping her. Again, his breath mingled with hers and she closed her eyes as their mouths barely touched.

Snap.

She'd been pulled to the magnet and now could not—did not want to—resist. For here, offering the man her trust with a kiss, Roxane felt the banshee screams of *Lutetia* subside, and all that remained was the soft pitter-patter of her heart.

"IT IS NOT IN HERE!" Henri Anjou thrust aside the flimsy piece of paper that purported itself the literary gem of Paris society. More truths published, it raved. Plenty of gossip, as well. The obituaries listed no less than seventy-two people, none of them the illustrious *precieuse* Leo.

Following every attack Henri always placed his victim in the obituaries. It reassured him no minions had been created. As it was, there were enough baffle-headed lickspittles under his charge. Really, he could start a tribe, but the notion of organization, and having to look after that organization, bothered him.

The man had to be dead. Yesterday's pages stated Leo had been absent from Mademoiselle de Vaine's salon.

Perhaps the fop's family sought to keep the man's death quiet?

It was useless to hope. Henri knew without doubt that had he been allowed a few more moments with the man before being whacked across the back with a stick he could have ensured a finished job.

Such sweet elixir the man's blood had been. He'd hated killing him the moment he'd begun. Of course, he hadn't succeeded, had he?

"What is the trouble?" Xavier sauntered into the mist-blurred bathing room and kicked off his embroidered Chinese slippers.

Though a hazy cloud of steam, the man's towel dropped onto the slate floor and he eased his way into the hot water across the sunken bathing pool from Henri.

Henri stretched his arms across the rim of the tub. "He is not dead."

"Who?"

"That fop Leo."

"The mishap?"

Xavier often used euphemisms. He tiptoed about his own vampirism as if it was a temporary condition and it would yet clear up if only he did not speak of it so loudly.

"I'll have to send someone out after him," Henri said, his lips dipping to touch the surface of water. "Can't risk creating yet another minion."

The look Xavier speared him with cut delicious runnels through Anjou's heart.

"My lovely Xavier, you are more than a minion," he assured.

"I don't like that word."

"It is a good word for the lackwits who do my bidding. A word dripping of evil, blood and danger—"

"Enough." Xavier leaned forward, catching his face in his palms. "Whom do you wish me to send out after the fop?"

"Try Renfeaux. He's an idiot, but for coin, he smartens up nicely. No more than five livres. The fop can't be worth any more than that. Leo should be half drained as it is. Should make an easy mark."

"Do you know where he lives?"

"That is up to Renfeaux to discover. St. Honoré, no doubt. The idle rich all live there. Now come. Let me rub your temples for you, Xavier. It'll relax you, take your mind off things like—"

"Minions?"

"Indeed."

Six

ROXANE FOUND BREAKFAST WAITING for her in the music room, a massive space, floored in black and white harlequin tiles, and stretched floor to ceiling with heavy, red velvet curtains. Only a sofa and a chair set near a pianoforte furnished the room. Toussaint escorted her in and served pastry and chocolate from a silver platter.

Alone in a rich man's home, surprisingly she was not uncomfortable. Nor did she fear for things like her virtue and propriety. She did not consider the kiss she had given Gabriel last night seduction. It had been a reaction. In that moment, they had both needed. Besides, a simple country rustic as herself could never attract the eye of a swish.

Just keep to the plan.

"Bait," she murmured.

"What was that?" Toussaint asked.

"Oh...great. This chocolate is great."

She liked Toussaint, and his casual regard for his master. Damian had considered hiring a valet but she had dissuaded him. Too expensive. Damian had only father's money to support his newly acquired habits. Roxane did not care to be beholden to anyone. Even her father. It was his way of showing emotion, she knew. I love you—can't you see that in my money?

Not wishing to spoil a perfectly marvelous morning with thoughts of her rogue father, she focused on the glide of spiced chocolate down her throat. Cinnamon flavored the drink. Truly, Leo must put out a fortune for that spice alone.

Toussaint gestured to the silver tray that displayed pastries fresh from a patisserie down the street.

"You will spoil me," she said. "I am accustomed to country fare. Simple greens and roasted fowl."

"Then it is a wonder you are not much rounder." The valet sat and popped a thumb-sized almond tart into his mouth. "Most country women wear their meals on hips and bosom."

A giggle escaped before she could suppress it. "You're not like most servants, are you?"

"Too forthright?" He smiled. "Forgive me, mademoiselle. Leo and I do not enjoy the usual servant/master relationship. I should be more respectful of company. But that giggle, it surprised you, yes?"

"What?"

"Just now." He tipped another tart to her before consuming it in one gulp. "I wager it has been a time since you've surrendered to something so easy and light."

She nodded and allowed the smile to remain. "You are perceptive."

"I do my best. Do you favor him?"

Like the sun glinting from a shiny copper roof, a lingering kiss stolen amidst a captured rainbow flashed across her thoughts. "You mean Leo?"

"Are there other rakes in this house I am not aware of? Come, you can talk to me, mademoiselle. You are all alone, yes? In need of a confidante. I'll keep our conversation private from Leo."

"I don't worry about that. You're a good man, Toussaint." She sipped the sweet chocolate.

He had guessed correctly. She desperately needed a kind ear to spill her woes. "Favor your master? When there is so much *not* to like about him?"

Toussaint raised a brow.

"Well." She set the cup on the saucer with a *tink*. "The man is arrogant."

"I'll grant you that."

"Conceited."

"To a delicious degree."

"Vain."

"Decidedly so."

"Materialistic."

Toussaint sighed.

"And worst of all..."

"Yes?"

"He's so damned..." The word teetered on the tip of her tongue. Toussaint waited eagerly. So be it. "...charming."

"Ah." He nabbed a sugar-dusted strawberry with an elegant twist of his wrist. "You've just described Leo perfectly. But really, the arrogance, the conceit, the vanity and materialism, it is merely a façade. You haven't begun to look beneath the surface."

"When one has to wade through all the lace, powder and frippery? Trust me, that man's surface is impenetrable!"

The two shared knowing laughter.

Toussaint leaned an elbow on the table. "Do tell me one thing."

"If I can."

"I've always considered charming to be a favorable trait. Why is it you do not?"

"Well, I…" She felt heat color her neck and sensed the valet had guessed far more of her mind than she wished. How many women had he had this same conversation with, perhaps following a tumble from Leo's bed? "It is a false charm. The man uses it easily. I don't believe he has a clue how artificial it is."

"Oh, he does. The veneer serves a purpose, that is all." Toussaint collected the silver tray and the cooling chocolate pot. "Promise me you'll take a look beneath the surface? There is a genuine man beneath all that frippery."

"Really?"

"Really."

GABRIEL PEERED UP THROUGH THE OCULUS. One could never see out at night for the glare of the lantern. But that was the purpose, wasn't it? The shower of color offered sanctity, not the darkness that lurked beyond the iron lamp reflectors.

Toussaint entered, linens in arm. "Would you like me to prepare your bath, Renan?"

"I'm going out, tonight, Toussaint. Let the vampire come to me."

"Ah yes, the laced fop trips into the night to face danger, wielding a walking stick and a smart patch on his brow."

Gabriel waggled his brow. "And a jaunty stake." He pulled out the stake he'd tucked in his waistband.

"When did you—?"

"Carved it myself in the stables this afternoon. You think it will serve?" He mimed a stabbing motion.

Speechless, Toussaint swallowed.

Gabriel strode to the armoire and tapped the smooth white wig sporting three sausage rolls above each ear. "This one."

"It is dangerous!"

"Come, Toussaint, if you are concerned my guardian angel will admonish me, she'll not say a thing, because I won't tell her."

"This has nothing to do with Mademoiselle Desrues."

"You don't think I can protect myself?" He spun the stake expertly.

"You are quite skilled—it is just...you've no training for this sort of opposition. I—I can't allow it."

"You forget your place, Toussaint." Gabriel tossed the valet the wig. "Quickly. The night is young. If I'm to go vampire hunting I want to meet him at his weakest."

"Don't say things like that. Besides, how can you know when the beast is at his weakest?"

A spectacular crash brought both to alert. Pulse beats pounding in his ears, Gabriel watched as a shower of glass shattered across the Aubusson rug before the window. In the wake of the deadly shower something crept through his window.

The servant clutched Gabriel's shoulder. "What is that?"

Toussaint's yelp did not dissuade him from gripping the stake and approaching the man who crouched on the floor like a predator. When the intruder turned and sprang, Gabriel dashed the air with the stake in warning.

Tattered fabric covered the man's bent body; he looked to have jumped from the rag-seller's bin. But to have jumped up two stories? Dirty black hair tangled before his eyes, but did not conceal a mouthful of yellowed teeth. Two teeth in particular were long and sharp.

"A minion!" Toussaint shouted. "We must run. Roxane!"

Irritated that his valet should run screaming for the aid of a woman, Gabriel straightened and slapped the stake in his palm. This swish was not going to cringe from any beast. Even if the thing did stink of the unholy.

Charging the intruder, he rammed his head into the stranger's gut. They crashed against the wall and landed on the litter of glass shards.

"Who sent you?" He rolled to kick, but the intruder bared his fangs and lunged for his neck. Hot spittle dripped over his chin. Fangs flashed. Gabriel succeeded in delivering a kick to the vampire's gut, sending him flying to land in a heap against the wall.

With the beast momentarily dissuaded, he raised the stake over his head.

"Stay there!" Roxane's voice.

What? He had the situation under control!

"Don't get too close," he shouted. "He is a vampire."

Roxane tramped across the broken glass toward the staggering vampire. He saw the red vial she ripped from the chain about her neck. As the vampire charged her, she uncorked the vial and with a flick of her wrist doused the bastard with a spray of red droplets.

Agony filled the room with screams to wake the dead. Clawing at his face, the minion fought against the unstoppable. His flesh literally sizzled. What had once been a solid, flesh and blood man, liquefied and dispersed into glittering droplets of scarlet.

Seven

HAVOC SCATTERED ABOUT THE ROOM with glass shards and a bloody mass upon the floor—a mass of blood that had once been a man. *Vampire.*

"That really is blood in your vial?"

Roxane nodded.

"Witches and vampires..." Gabriel gestured futilely with a hand.

"Enemies," she finished. "Vampires cannot tolerate witch's blood, as you have seen."

"Tolerate?" He tilted his head, trying to grasp that statement, but sight of the mayhem on the floor utterly horrified him. Remembering the stake, he slid it under a pillow, hoping Roxane hadn't seen the weapon he should have used before she had entered the room.

Toussaint carefully approached the bloodstain. "That's going to leave a mark."

A mark? Instinctively Gabriel clasped a hand over the scabbed wounds on his neck. He stared at the blood, seeping quickly into the thick Aubusson rug. Reality had crashed through his bedroom window. And he'd stood up to it, but not fast enough to claim the hero's role.

"It appears you are indeed the vampire slayer, mademoiselle. What poison resides in that blood?"

"None. Just the two don't mix."

"So it seems. Toussaint, fetch a bucket to clean this up. Don't alert the servants; we needn't invite unnecessary questions."

After the valet left, Gabriel ran his hands over his face and scalp. The beast had come through his second floor window. Had he leapt? "Can vampires fly?"

"Not sure." At sight of his wondering stare, Roxane elaborated. "They are very strong, and can, most likely, leap great distances so as to appear as if they have flown. I wager it was not difficult for your attacker to leap two stories."

"Why have the vampires of Paris suddenly developed a compulsion to torment me?"

"Most likely this minion was sent by Monsieur Anjou."

"A minion?" Another one of those evil words that tasted macabre on his tongue.

"He's likely aware you did not die and wants to take out his enemy before his enemy takes him out."

"Splendid. It has been my luck that I attract such ill fortune," he began, staring up at the oculus.

"Poor, pitiful swish."

At that mocking statement, he eyed the woman across the room. She shrugged as if to say, 'Well, it is true''.

"You think so poorly of me?"

He wanted to know. He needed to know. Certainly he had his favorable points. Women did admire the vicomte Renan's sexual prowess. He could make a woman think very highly of his prowess. Rather, he once could. That was until the insipid Leo had flounced onto Gabriel's territory.

But of a sudden it mattered what *this* woman thought of him. Outside the bed chamber. Even, in a nonsexual manner, despite the fact she'd kissed him last night.

"You are simply feeling sorry for yourself." She sighed. "The poor swish was attacked by a vampire. Pity, he cannot take care of himself—"

"I take very good care of myself, I'll have you know. I've this house, a full staff, and immense fortune." A fortune he was trying desperately to dispense, for he could not bear to benefit from the rewards of his parents' illicit booty.

"But your horrid luck?"

"What can one expect? A man cannot have the good without the bad. And what in your life has been so horrible? Did you send out your lace to be cleaned and have it returned in tatters?"

Oh, but the woman deserved a fine pummeling. Of the between-the-sheets sort. She wanted to know about his life? Memory painted a dreary veil over the past.

"It isn't important," he whispered. To think of his parents and their *comfort* dredged up miserable emotions. "This swish has gotten everything he has ever deserved. On the other hand, I don't know what it is I have done to deserve such a fresh breath of air as you. Thank you for saving my hide from that minion, Roxane."

"No man deserves what you are going through right now."

She approached him, and he felt his blood rise, as it had the other night when she'd kissed him of her own volition. Drawing her palm across his hair, she brushed the strands over his ear. A tingle of erotic expectation shot through him. Be damned the monsters, he wanted to think of nothing but softness.

He captured her wrists and pulled her against his body. Before he could suggest, or intimate, she kissed him. It wasn't a tentative, consoling kiss. 'Twas heated, rushed, and a bit angry. Intent in what she wanted, she threaded her fingers through his hair, her fingernails drawing skittering thrills across his skull. Did the woman realize what she was doing?

She must feel his want for her.

Deepening the kiss, he moaned as the taste of her sweetened his tongue.

"I could take you right now," he said into her mouth, as he slipped a hand beneath her skirts. The textured wool stockings she wore served a delicious tactile sensation against his surfing palm. The scent of—of something horrible disturbed him. "But I won't."

He tugged down her skirts to cover her legs, surprising himself.

A tilt of his head, regretful, spied the stain on the floor. Cursed by a revolting ability to scent blood, he left the embrace, clamping his arms over his chest and paced beneath the oculus.

"Will you leave me, please?"

"You shouldn't stay in this room tonight, Leo. Not with the blood—""

"I know that," he snapped. "I'll sleep elsewhere. But will you leave? Now."

"I'm sorry." He caught her by the waist and spun her beneath the rainbow. Vibrant orange cut a line across her face. "You wanted me to leave?"

"Yes, but not because I don't want you right here, in my arms. I want to make love to you, Roxane."

"I...I'm—yes." She touched his mouth, drawing her forefinger across his bottom lip. "I wish us to make love as well."

He nipped her finger and then sucked it into his mouth, teasing his tongue along the narrow digit. "Why, Roxane? Do you fancy me? Or is it merely that you feel sorry for this wretched swish?"

"Perhaps a bit of the two." And with that she withdrew her finger from his mouth and sashayed from the room. "But mostly," she called as she walked off, "because I wish it."

The door closed, leaving him alone and feeling much better about himself than he had moments earlier. The woman wanted him. Pitiful as he was, she wanted him. And he wanted her. But.

Hell, must there be a but?

"There should be," he muttered.

Striding from the room, he trailed his fingers down the mirrored wall, pressing his palm to Roxane's door as he passed. Yes, there was a but. He had begun to care what the woman thought about him. She was not a meaningless midnight tup. He enjoyed her company. He wanted to sit with her, to talk with her, and spend time with her.

I wish us to make love...

Yes, but so much more. Why, he could allow his imagination to place him by her side, standing in a cathedral nave.

Marry her?

You've abandoned domestic bliss, as everyone else has abandoned you. Besides, creatures *don't marry. Or could they?*

And should the worst occur...

What woman desired a husband who roomed in the lunatic asylum?

Eight

THE NEXT MORNING BEFORE THE cock announced the day, Roxane mounted a gelding she had borrowed from Leo's stable and set south for Bicêtre. The asylum sat on a hill just out of Paris, paralleled between Ville-Juif and Gentilly.

Passing an egg-man balancing a pyramid of eggs that blocked his view, she marveled that his path took him around a stack of faggots and safely to his cart, not a single cracked shell.

The pine board barrier at the St. Victor gate was closed up and a smaller door in the large gate was open to emit single-file a herd of bone-thin cattle. Fortunately she arrived as the last beast hobbled through.

Roxane had passed through these gates half a dozen times in the past few months. The bearded guard recognized her and nodded her through with a forced smile. He knew her destination.

Besides jailing thieves, debtors and beggars, the asylum also housed the sick, those the Hotel Dieu had passed on, for they either had not sufficient room or the expertise to handle those too far gone from the pox.

As well, Bicêtre was a holding cell for the insane, a last vestige for families who could not—did not have the skill to—care for those they loved.

Roxane bit her lip hard to prevent a teardrop. She had tried to tend Damian for all of a se'nnight before she realized she could not contain his madness within the small rue Vivienne apartment they had moved into months earlier. Since the attack her brother did not sleep, instead prancing the floor through the night, admonishing and taunting the moon to come out and duel with him. And when the moon surrendered to the sun, Damian would sit for hours and pound his fists against the stone hearth, leaving bloody runnels behind as he dashed, mad-eyed and raging, from one side of the room to the other.

It had been Ninon who'd finally convinced her to bring Damian to Bicêtre. Google-eyed moon hunter. Ninon had blurted out the cruel moniker the night they'd coaxed him inside from the windowsill where he had perched staring up into the darkness.

Just until he regained control of his sanity, Roxane said to herself now as the horse cantered down the pounded dirt road.

He will get back his sanity. He must.

She had only herself to blame for her brother's condition.

"FIFTY LIVRES?"

Gabriel looked up from the notes and bills. It was the first time he had heard protest from Toussaint regarding his philanthropic investments.

"Well, I just…" Toussaint tried to hold Gabriel's stare but with a huff and a sigh he accepted the coin and tucked it in his left waistcoat pocket.

"See it is delivered anonymously," Gabriel cautioned.

"I know the scenario." Toussaint hefted the full leather plackets containing notes of promise and land documents and mumbled the words Gabriel had said so often before, "Discretion is paramount for a man of such kidney."

Gabriel preferred anonymity, though a few were aware of his contributions by default. Those few were close-lipped—save Madame de Marmonte. But Gabriel kept her in check with twice-weekly visits to her pathetic salon. Of course she could never know his true identity, which also gave her knowledge little meaning.

It seemed he could not dispose of his money fast enough without the interest compounding and seeming to literally double his holdings. His inheritance, his father had explained on the eve of his departure. Gabriel had not been of age, merely eighteen, but the count had emancipated his son so that he could inherit.

A wretched inheritance it was. For it was not family money from the land holdings or the stipend the count and countess received annually. Gabriel's inheritance had been formed solely from his parents' sordid business transactions. He'd initially balked at accepting the money he viewed as unclean and vile, but he had accepted it to maintain the lifestyle he had grown accustomed to, aiming to distribute the wealth to those less fortunate.

He wondered now what the future would bring should this crazy wait for moonlight dramatically alter him. His affairs were in order, the entire sum of his legitimate wealth being divided into various hospitals and charity. Might the children's ward he had planned for Hotel Dieu, a shelter for the orphans and the abandoned to go and to be loved, become reality?

Really, man, why have you not simply built the thing? You have the funds.

So many political rings to jump through. The count and countess Renan had not left for the Americas in good standing with the king. The Renan name was shunned and spat upon. An appointment at court was unthinkable. A meeting with the King's financial secretary proved an impossible dream. Better to tread lightly, to work anonymously under Leo's moniker.

NEVER WOULD SHE FULLY ACCUSTOM herself to the stench that sweatered the pounded dirt courtyard preceding Bicêtre. From the beauty of a surrounding heather field to a festering milieu.

"Mademoiselle Desrues," the kindly clerk behind the main desk always called to her as she tentatively stepped inside.

Cracked marble tiles stretched wall to wall in the massive foyer. High above, dusty chandeliers caked with sooted candle wax held court, rarely used, far too massive and dirty to warrant care.

Skirts clutched tightly at her thighs, Roxane took a moment to adjust to the surroundings. Common stable smells, she always tried to convince herself. However stables were frequently cleaned and mucked. She dared not guess how rarely the cells and chambers within this hellhole were tended. The upper floors, she had been told, were quite clean; that was where the stable patients resided alongside the laboratories with glass-paned ceilings to let in light.

The courtyard out back provided fresh air, but Damian had not earned permission to go outside. Too unstable, the administrator had stated. Damian's humors would not accept the air so easily and may send him into fits. Can't have a wild man running about attempting escape.

Roxane had argued that surely the facility was secure. The administrator merely rolled his eyes beneath a crooked gray periwig and led her to her brother's room.

"I'll have Jean-Paul show you back," the clerk said.

"*Merci.*"

She forced herself to follow the bow-legged clerk with the grass-stained breeches. He was friendly enough, smiling and signaling she follow. He never spoke, for she had learned he had no tongue.

Thinking she might manage the shock when the guard at the door opened it into the inner bowels, she impulsively reached for the handkerchief tucked up her sleeve. The door closed behind her and the world evaporated, only to leap at her with maniacal screams and a hair-wilting miasma.

Drawing deeply of the rosemary oil, she wandered forward, following the light from the narrow windows set high into the walls. Rows of iron bars laddered but an arm's reach from her. Fortunately the spaces between the criss-crossed iron bars were too small to emit more than a finger or a—

Roxane jumped as a mangled piece of bone and fur popped out into her path. "*Losh!*"

Jean-Paul reassured with a shrug that said Roxane should be grateful and not horrified.

She skipped over the tangled offering and quickened her pace to walk down a slope. Here in the bowels of Bicêtre the noise lessened, though never completely ceased. She hated that Damian was kept so far from sunlight.

Tears rolled down her cheeks and Roxane stopped. Hearing her sniffles Jean-Paul turned back. He lifted the untied length of his jabot, silently offering a clean corner.

"Jean-Paul, you are too kind."

He shrugged and beckoned her to continue.

A wide cell housing, at any given time, from half a dozen to well over a dozen was faced with a stretch of iron bars. Roxane wondered if an emaciated man could slip through the widely spaced bars.

Jean-Paul sauntered off, his expression saying he would remain close, but at a discreet distance.

Drawing in a breath of courage, she nodded and turned to the cell.

The little hunch-backed man who wore but a loincloth and who was ever in motion paced the middle of the cell frantically. At sight of her he rushed the bars.

"I want to sit in the spinning chair!" he demanded. And with a spin he began to emulate past rides. "The spinning chair," he sang in wobbly tenor.

He sang the same lament every time. During her last visit Roxane had asked the administrator what, exactly, he'd meant by the spinning chair. It was actually a chair that spun—patients were strapped on for the ride—in hopes of jarring their brains back into proper order.

"The spinning—" The man spun face-first into the wall and staggered backward.

She winced and instinctively reached out. There was nothing she could do. Not physically. Nor dare she get too close. He didn't fall. Strange equilibrium tottered him across the room, a wide smile affixed to his face. Horrifically pleased with the results, he again made a run for the wall and landed with a loud slap. Totter and wobble. Slap.

Abhorrence was always difficult to conceal, but Roxane reined it in and searched the darkness.

There at the back wall, beating a flat palm against the stone stood a tall, slender man with long brown hair and loose damask breeches that had not seen a ball of laundering soap in weeks. His fingernails were dark half moons.

"Damian?" she called.

A scuffle of activity frightened her so she stepped back as two men scrambled to the bars and reached for her. Hungry eyes screamed silent pleads.

"Company!" the spinning man recited grandly, without losing step. "Have you come to take me to the spinning chair? Pretty swirls and dancing brains?"

Damian did not turn around. Tears rolled from her eyes at sight of the filthy breeches hanging from his narrow hips. He did not appear thinner than normal, for he had always been a slender man—Oh! But he needed to eat and to breathe fresh air and— to get back his mind.

Could she make that happen? He did have his lucid moments.

"Pretty lace," one of the long-eyed men clinging to the bars hissed. His fingers, dirtied with filth, beckoned. He darted out his tongue like a lizard in search of a fly. "She smells of fancy, she does!"

"Damian, please!" she pleaded.

"I want to sit in the spinning chair!"

"Damian."

"My liege!" One of the men pushed from the wall and swaggered toward the back wall. "My—"

Damian spun around, cutting the man's tirade with a slice of his hand before his throat.

Once tall, lithe, and ever the charmer—he would have given Leo a challenge—Damian Desrues retained a look of suave removal. Dark eyes saw nothing. Or had they seen too much? A spittle-laced mouth formed a moue.

He stared at Roxane for a long time. She could not read his expression. Did he see through her? Or did his vision stop at the bars? Always she knew her brother's moods by the merest curl of lip or a tiny crease at the corner of his eye that would signal oncoming mirth. Not a single line marred his flesh, not a hint at emotion.

Then he stepped forward, pushing aside the spinning man, who was merely diverted from his east/west course to a northeast/southwest twirl.

"I want to spin!"

"Stand back from the foyer!" Damian announced grandly, as if a palace guard.

"Yes, my liege," one of the men murmured, and scuffled into a dark corner, a spider for the shadows.

The one who wished to swirl his brains stood five paces behind her brother, his attention keen and maniacal.

"Roxane," Damian said in a tone that sounded so normal.

"Damian, I love you." She reached for him. His hands were warm but the right was slippery with his own blood. She lifted her skirt and pressed it to his bruised knuckles. "You should not harm yourself so. You've such pretty hands. Don't you want to wear fine gloves and peel them slowly from your fingers to catch a lady's eye?"

"I have caught your eye, lovely lady." He dipped his head. Thick clumps of greasy hair swept his face. Lifting her hand to his mouth he kissed it, so gently—she might swoon were he a lover—then held it against his lips. "You taste of the meadows. Of a time I cannot recall."

"Of course you can remember, Damian. It wasn't less than a few months ago we lived in the parish. Remember how every morning you strolled through the fields to bring me a bouquet of wildflowers? Bright yellow coltsfoot and those white daisies that always made me sneeze. I-I want to take you home, Damian. I want things to be the way they were."

His clutch grew tighter and Roxane impulsively pulled away.

But one eye was revealed between clumps of Damian's hair. Was it pale celadon, the color of a fop's whimsy, or had the madness muddied it to seaweed? No sparkle, not a single glint. Indeed, his face had grown gaunt. Roxane sensed it was not from hunger, but the insanity that taxed his soul. "You dare to take me away from here?"

"When you are better—"

Malice curled Damian's thin mouth. "I see. When they have finally spun my brains into position? Is that the way of it?"

"Damian, I am doing what I can to help you."

"A little late for that."

His sneering retort cut to her bones. She did not deserve forgiveness. But had he chosen the other option would she have regretted the monster?

Why should it have been your *choice?*

Indeed, it should not have been.

He's a google-eyed moon hunter. Ever gazing to the sky. No hope for him, love.

"I've met someone," she said, hoping to make Damian smile. To let him think of things other than the bars and the filth and whatever hells infested his mind. "Of a sort."

"Is he pretty?"

She lifted her head at his interest. The charming rogue wanted to hear some gossip. "Yes, he is handsome. A fop, but—"

"Oh, oh, oh! A pretty man for my pitiful, penniless whore of a sister!" Damian announced grandly. A splay of his arms was silently mimicked by the man standing behind him. "Triumph! Triumph!"

The spinner spun into a new dance of mumbles and pleas for his favorite pleasure.

"Damian, please," she pleaded over the idiots' rants. "It is not like that. It is...he is in trouble. I have been following the creature that did this to you. This man...he may be the key to attracting the enemy. I feel it, Damian. As soon as I've the vampire—"

As she spoke the word, Damian's head jerked violently. He flung himself backward, as if to splash into a pond. The man behind him caught him with an expert lunge and a gleeful giggle.

"My liege!" the one huddling in the corner rushed forth. "He has taken ill!"

"He is not your liege!" Roxane's anger unloosed. "Let go of him. Don't tear at his clothes! Step away, dotterels!"

She pressed her forehead against the bars and concentrated. Mental magic was difficult for her without preparation, and she could use very little, but success came and she managed to part the two imbeciles from her brother with sheer will power.

Damian landed on the stone floor, and curled into a ball of limbs but two feet from the iron bars. She slid down to squat and stretched an arm through the cold iron.

"I'm sorry, Damian. It was my fault."

"It *was* your fault," he hissed, his head tucked into a curled arm. He began to rock back and forth. "Do not touch the royal flesh!" he snapped at the idiot crawling closer. He lifted his head and pierced Roxane with a flat stare. "Wait for the moon? Ha! You should have run a dagger through my heart."

"No!" And yet, she wondered now if perhaps she should have. "This man I've met, he was bitten, like you."

Damian twisted his head inside the curve of his arm. A cruel smile taunted her like no spoken admonishment could.

"He did not die," she offered. "His valet rescued him before the vampire could finish. He has but days before the full moon."

"You've done it AGAIN," Damian growled in a voice that clutched her heart. "You've DONE it again." His rocking increased pace and he moved up to his hands and knees. "The bitch has done IT again. Dancing between death and madness, she spins a mighty reel! Dance with me, my loyal subjects! Whirl me upon my spinning chair."

He sprang up and his long legs skipped like a spider dancing across its web. The two men joined him. Every time they collided with the spinning man his path was redirected, which he assumed without protest.

Roxane pressed her back to the opposite wall.

"Come, my subjects!" Damian called, "Let us dance for the witch. Follow me, skip and twirl! Spin, spin, spin!"

She *had* done it again.

NINE

BREAKFAST WITHOUT ROXANE felt peculiar. In two days, Gabriel had grown accustomed to the pale beauty's presence. Odd. He knew the dangers of establishing emotions for women. To summon hope. He hadn't the time or luxury for that with Roxane. So why did he already notice when she was absent?

Perhaps because he missed her kisses?

"You are too soft, Renan." He slunk in the vanity chair, stretching out a leg and staring at his lazy sneer in the mirror. "Take it like a man. Stand up and show it your teeth." He leaned forward and bared his teeth.

"You would make a splendid creature, yes?"

His reflection snarled back.

Certainly well dressed, but hardly frightening.

"What a pitiful madman you would make, pacing your cell in tattered lace and obsessively counting the minutes on your cracked gold watch."

He sighed and bent forward, placing his forehead on the vanity, and stared down at his feet, slippered in indigo damask. Only the finest for Leo. When taking on the role of Leo, he'd thought enhancing the façade would prove himself more attractive to the upper echelon Gabriel so hoped to crack. How difficult must it be to give away money? Tainted or not, it could only help others.

"I am..." Another sigh forced his private confession. "Frightened. I don't want to change. Yes, yes," he defied his reflection, "I know that is all I have dreamed of for years. Change. A life of domesticity. Someone to care for, to spoil, and to make happy. Someone to cherish, as I have never before been cherished. Someone to"—a swallow lodged in his throat— "*see* me."

Toussaint entered the room with a tray of shaving utensils.

Gabriel tilted his head, studying the damage on his neck. "They haven't begun to heal. Don't you find that odd?"

"Maybe." Toussaint glanced at Gabriel's neck, then, with a double take, really looked at the wounds.

He read the valet's surprise. "You do find it odd."

"Do you think you will change? That you will suck another person's blood and become immortal?"

"Must you be so bloody morbid?"

"Forgive me, but is not immortality a marvelous future to imagine?"

"Your mind dabbles with strange ideas far from my imagination. To drink another man's blood can only be a curse."

"Of course." Toussaint's tone did not at all agree with his agreement. "But if it is to survive and if you did not murder..."

Gabriel caught his forehead in his palm and closed his eyes. "As pitiful as it sounds, I have begun to question that very thing, Toussaint." He picked up the stake and spun it round between his fingers. "What could be so terrible about immortality? It would be a hell of a lot more favorable than Bicêtre."

"You would make an exquisite hunter of the night, Gabriel. Elegant and mysterious; you could lure women to a ravishing swoon. And just think—to walk through the ages, witnessing the world as it changes."

"That would be a remarkable feat." Something he'd not considered. What a joy to witness the changing times. To experience different cultures and lifestyles because he had been afforded the time to do so? On the other hand... "You forget one thing, Toussaint, the vampire kills. Murder is not my mien."

"Monsieur Anjou did not kill you."

"And look where that has gotten me. If I should not kill I would leave a trail of helpless lackwits in my wake. Mad minions roaming the city in search of blood. I could not justify that."

"You're the furthest thing from a lackwit, vicomte."

"Madness yet threatens," he muttered.

"What if there was a way to drink blood without killing and without risk of creating a minion?"

"Do you know of such ways?" Tapping the stake against his jaw, he peered into Toussaint's reflected eyes. "Does Mesmer know things about the vampire?"

"Would you consider it if there was a way?"

Gabriel stared at the vicomte in the mirror. He *would* make a delicious creature. He certainly had the finances to afford a long life. And to experience the centuries....

Travel, adventure, and education called to him. He could learn so much. Grasp new ideas and see them through. And the women, ever a new supply to slake his lustful thirst.

But wouldn't loss be all the more painful to carry it so long? And what of the domesticity he craved? If he were ever to marry, his wife would die while he lived on. Could he fathom such a life?

A man has to believe in something.

"I don't know, Toussaint. I want this to all be done, one way or the other."

"Then I will go to Mesmer this afternoon and see if he can answer some of your questions, yes?"

"Fine, but do not allow Mademoiselle Desrues to know what you are up to."

The last thing he wanted was for Roxane to learn his fortitude had begun to falter. Because he knew without doubt, such a fine woman could never love a creature.

IT WAS A RELIEF TO RETURN TO THE vicomte's home. Roxane needed to be with someone mentally sound. Someone male and charming, and capable of seducing her up from the bitter emotions that yet clung to her soul.

Toussaint directed her to the music room where Leo was seated before the pianoforte, using it as a desk as he paged through a stack of documents. He covered them with a leather folio as she strode in.

"Ah, the vampire slayer returns to her nest."

"Sarcasm does not suit you, vicomte."

"But the autumn air suits you, mademoiselle. Have you heard the term blowsabella?"

"Can't say that I have."

"Italian, I think. Your cheeks are flushed and you are radiant. Gorgeous."

Yes, a male's charming presence; just the thing to feed her starving soul.

"Where were you all day?"

"I stopped by my apartment this morning to visit Ninon." Partial truth, for she had stopped by before coming here. "She has no other friends in the city. As well, I enjoy her company. She seemed a trifle...changed."

"How so?"

"I'm not sure." She thought about Ninon's cotton dress and the lightness with which she had carried herself. As if the world had been lifted from her shoulders, or rather, a really big wig. "She offered me fine pastries. I was surprised because she has so little. I wonder if she's been to the coiffures again?"

"What did her hair look like?"

"That is the surprise, it looked rather plain. As though it hadn't seen curling rod or pins and powder in weeks."

"Did you ask her about it?"

"I did, but she merely shrugged."

"Then you mustn't worry for her."

Roxane admired the pianoforte. White lacquer sported pastoral scenes in oval vignettes around the sides. On top sat a dusty blue violin.

"So you only went there this morning?" he prompted.

"Er...yes."

Please don't ask about the remainder of the day. It wasn't that she couldn't reveal her troubles; it was that she wanted distance right now. The seduction.

She leaned over and studied the violin. "This is lovely—"

"Don't touch it!"

The violin's hollow body echoed as it teetered. She pressed her fingers to her mouth as if she'd been singed. A narrow fingerprint on the belly of the stringed instrument disclosed her folly.

"Sorry." Leo stood and eyed the instrument. "Too damned many memories in that violin. I'm not sure why I don't have Toussaint pack the thing away."

Dare she delve into his horribly masked emotions? She wanted to learn more about him, the enigma. The man who could change her heart with but a kiss. And yet his future spoke sure tragedy.

"Time for a conversation switch," he tossed out. "Beyond your penchant for chasing creatures of the night, I know little about you. How long have you been in Paris, Roxane?"

"Four months." She slid into an armed chair. The chair wrapped its damask arms about her, a lush repose within a boudoir.

Leo twisted around on the stool before the pianoforte, catching his palms on his knees. "You came from Scotland?"

"Never been there."

"And yet, you've a definite brogue. Did not Toussaint learn you've Scottish ancestors?"

"Yes." She dipped her head in a sweet blush. "I long to visit someday. I grew up listening to stories told by my granny MacTavish. Tales of Scottish highlanders, fierce, brawny warriors. My granddaddy used to wear his plaid, be damned the regulations, he'd say."

"I've never seen a Scotsman in plaid."

"Plaids have been banned for decades. I don't understand why. It is a fine look on any man."

"You fancy a man in plaid?"

She shrugged. "Why wouldn't I?"

"Hmm... Well, I hope you find your tartan-draped Highlander someday."

"I won't hold my breath. But I don't dislike frock coats and lace."

Leo tugged at his lacey sleeve. "Just not quite so much lace, eh? No swishes for this lady?"

She didn't reply because the man was not a swish, and he certainly landed on her interesting list. Not that there was a list. He was the first man she'd had a relationship with, so everything about him fascinated and intrigued.

"Where did you live before Paris?"

"Villers-Cotterets, a village at the edge of the forest."

"About an hour out of Paris?"

"Yes, you know it?"

He shrugged. "I have passed by to and from Versailles. What drew you to Paris?"

"I moved here with my brother. He's always been drawn to this society of riches and manner. He is a gentle man by nature, yet loves elegance and propriety."

"A man of my own heart?"

"A swish in training, you might say."

"*I* would never say."

"Yes, well..." Her smile fell as quickly as it had formed and images of the man spinning about her brother's figure returned. "Damian had been easily tempted by our father's spectacular description of Paris. The city tainted father, and drew him away from mama. We've lived alone, just the two of us, for half a decade now. Much as Damian desired Paris, I would not allow that same taint to harm him. I was successful in swaying his desires for years. Until this year."

"He convinced you to move to the city?" Leo said softly.

"After much begging. Each summer after father's visit Damian would say, 'Let's be off for Paris. Father already has an apartment for us; we've only to claim it.' He would finger the tatty lace that circled his threadbare shirt and say in the most wrenching plea: 'I must go, Roxane. Paris calls.'

"And I would refuse. Someone had to maintain a level head. We did not live in poverty. The fieldstone parish the Desrues family has lived in for centuries was large and spacious, and the gardens out back were shaded by walls of hornbeam. But this year, after I had refused and turned to my gardening of simple herbs, thinking that was it for the summer pleading, Damian resolutely pulled back his shoulders and stated, 'Very well, I will go to Paris myself.'"

Leo offered a consoling nod and smile.

"And I knew he would." She traced the curve of the chair arm with a fingertip. "My heart speeding with apprehension, I packed up my belongings—very little— and journeyed to Paris at my brother's side.

"Immediately upon our arrival he took our inheritance and bought himself fine clothing, wigs and pretty jewels. He was so happy."

"Was?"

She nodded and glanced toward the paned window, not eager to go on.

"You wish to return."

Was her sadness so obvious? "Enough of my family. I have not had opportunity to ask how you fare today?"

"Me? I am a bit tired, but all in all, I feel rather well. Madness be damned, eh?"

"Was Toussaint able to clean the floor in your bed chamber?"

"He scrubbed away the smell." Almost. "Terrible how I can scent blood from across the room. Yours is sweet, by the by."

"You—you can smell it from there?"

He nodded. Her posture stiffened upon the chair.

"Don't worry, I won't attack. At least, I don't think I will. Roxane, I was making fun. I promise I will not bite you."

"What if the madness won't allow you that choice?"

"You think I am going insane?" He pressed forefingers to his temple, and, closing his eyes, rubbed in circles. "I don't feel it." He flashed open his eyes to look at her. "Does it strike so quickly, then?"

"I cannot know."

"You didn't witness it with this other survivor you will not name?"

She had witnessed a wrenching gradual madness, for Damian had three weeks to wail at the moon.

"You are right; I don't see any signs that your composure is changing. Perhaps you are a bit dry with your humor. But I've not known you long enough to determine if it is just your way."

He flicked his wrist, dancing the long lace across his knuckles. "Leo is—er, well, we swishes are not much for boldness, bravery or heroics."

"You are heroic. You went after that vampire minion armed with no more than courage."

He lifted a brow, and Roxane so fiercely wanted him to believe in himself.

Twisting on the stool to face the pianoforte, he touched the feather quill, rolling it across the leather folio in crisp crackles. "I have ever strived to be what others wish to see. And now it is too late to be myself. For soon this bloody moon will decide for me."

"You are a good man, Leo. Beneath the frippery your heart is bold and brave, and I honestly believe that cannot be altered."

His heavy sigh burrowed into her heart. So much troubled him.

"There is something I must tell you. About Leo."

"You speak of yourself in the third person?"

He nodded, looking down. "Because Leo isn't me." He met her gaze and his eyes were wide with truth. "Leo is a creation."

"I...don't understand?"

"A disguise I have assumed in order to serve a higher purpose, if you can buy into such a thing."

She had no idea what he was talking about. He was not Leo, the foppish rake? "What higher purpose?"

"It's to do with my fortune. I wish to disperse it to charity and yet my true identity has been stained by my family history. Please, I don't wish to elaborate. I only wish I had been honest with you from the start. But I hadn't the opportunity because I woke from the vampire's bite after Toussaint had already firmly ensconced you in my lies."

She stood and, fluffing out her skirts, strolled over to him and touched his jaw. Lingering there in his whiskey gaze she fell. Into hope. Into trust. "What is your name?"

"Gabriel Baptiste Renan. Vicomte."

"A vicomte?" She gasped.

"My title changes nothing between us."

She nodded. He was of the aristocracy. What had she been doing these past days? Staying under his roof? Speaking with him so casually?

"There is an us, Roxane. Can there be an us?" He slipped his fingers through hers. "I want the man beneath the surface to rise. The man who has ransomed hope for abandonment."

"But you are a vicomte, and I..."

He tugged her to him and spread his fingers through her hair. The intensity in his gaze stifled all reluctance in her heart and Roxane nodded. Giving him her trust completely.

"I want us," he said. "No matter what the moon brings."

She felt so small, so overwhelmed at this moment. And then she was not, because she stood in the arms of Leo—Gabriel, a man who trusted her enough to share his secrets.

Perhaps you should share yours?

"I've stymied you," he said.

"No. I want us, too, the moon be damned."

"Look at me! I am the picture of health. Is it possible you could be wrong? That a mere bite will not render me a madman who howls for the moon?"

"I believe it is the *loup garou* that howls at the moon."

"Indeed, the werewolf." He tapped a finger on her nose. "You are far too knowledgeable of the occult for my comfort, Roxane. Where and why did you pick up such information? Why this compulsion to *hunt* a vampire?"

"I merely wish you to be well," she murmured.

"And well I am. I have no hunger for blood, so do not worry your pretty head."

She nodded, lowering her head quickly.

"What is it? You won't meet my eyes. Mademoiselle?"

"I—I have spoken to him," she blurt out.

"Him? The vampire?"

She shook her head no. "The man who survived. The one who succumbed to madness."

"You did? When? Where is he?"

"He sits in a foul cell at Bicêtre, pounding the walls until his fists are bloody."

She could not prevent the tears that slid down her cheeks. Shuddering in Gabriel's embrace, she melted against his chest. A vicomte. Oh, but her world had toppled heel over head.

"You tell me true? Anjou's other victim is in the asylum?"

She nodded against his shoulder and sniffled tears. "I visit a few times a week."

"Take me to him."

"What?"

Gabriel smoothed away tendrils of hair from the tears on her cheeks. "I want to talk to the man who survived the vampire's bite."

"No, you cannot. He—he did not survive—he is mad!"

"I must!" He released her and paced before the pianoforte.

"You would look upon your own future? Is it not enough that I tell you madness waits, that you yet desire to see it and touch it?"

"Yes."

Decided, Gabriel pulled his frock coat from the chair and swung his arms into it. "I need to know what I must fight, Roxane. I have mere days. Will you help me?"

"But I cannot return so soon. Please, I...you don't know him. He's—"

"Violent? A lunatic? You needn't accompany me if it pains you to visit him. I'll go myself."

"You don't understand."

"But I do, Roxane. I promise you." He gripped her forearms. "Your heart balks. Someone close to you suffers. Yet I need to learn, to know the future I must fight."

"He's my brother," she gasped.

TEN

THE ROAD BEYOND GENTILLY, a village sitting at the edge of Paris, offered little more than a dirt line carved from the bumps and grasses by carriage wheels. Nothing was flat. The horse had a hard time of it, even centered between the tracks. They made Bicêtre in under an hour and dismounted, tying up the horse.

Gabriel looked over the burnt-grass grounds before him but Roxane stepped into view and his thoughts lightened.

A gorgeous libertine, she defied every definition he'd ever conjured of a country rustic. She was neither simple nor uneducated. Kindness had compelled her to help a stranger, and it continued to show in her sacrifice now by agreeing to bring him with her.

And her kisses, well, they were exquisite. Never before had he been satisfied merely with kisses. Always his affairs had been rushed, unemotional, and fleeting. He wanted to spend time with Roxane, all the time she would give him.

But would she ever have a madman? Or worse, a vampire?

Couldn't work, that pairing. He'd have her drained of blood in less than a fortnight. *But you may enjoy it.*

Shaking his head at the disturbing thought, he stepped up beside her to stare at the darkened façade of Bicêtre. Three stories high and stretching across a barren field, the limestone structure greeted visitors with barred windows. Few trees dotted the landscape, save the bare-branched elms behind the facility. Morbid, their blackened silhouettes like a hangman's tree.

The wind swept a wretched perfume across his face. Gabriel squeezed Roxane's hand. "You remain out here."

"He is *my* brother," she insisted.

"Exactly why you mustn't continue to torture yourself. Your frequent visits only widen the ache in your heart. Give me his name. I can find him."

"Doubtful. It took all of two hours the first time I visited. Not much for order or records here."

She strode forward, and Gabriel followed, thankful that she accompanied him, and fearful of what he would see this day—his future.

A QUIET, HUMP-SHOULDERED MAN who smiled sweetly at Roxane accompanied them into the lower cells. Gabriel threaded his hand through hers protectively. The fetid smell clung to his clothes and hair. Agony and loneliness had never before felt so tactile, so present in his soul. He felt every whimpered emotion, every raging cry for sanity.

Could he divine the riddle to his own freedom from a man who had succumbed to madness? Whatever Roxane's brother had done in an attempt to overcome the vampire's taint had been wrong. Surely, Gabriel need only take a different approach.

With a guttural cry, he bent double in reaction to a sudden streak of pain. Drums beat at his temples. A heady gush of liquid flowed through his thoughts, a raging torrent of pulsing temptation.

"What is it?" Gentle fingers traced his brow, then touched his shoulder. "Gabriel?"

"Can you not hear it? It is like...pounding blood," he whispered. "*Mon Dieu*, it is so loud!"

At his outburst a scuffle from behind the iron bars erupted into moans of pain. The silver reflection of a mirror, a single shard thrust out from between bars, sought out Gabriel and greedily witnessed his pain.

"This is horrible," he said. Pressing the heels of his hands to his eyes, he plugged his ears with his fingers in an attempt to alleviate the noise.

"We will leave."

"No." He pulled from Roxane's grasp. "I have come this far. I just need to wait until it subsides."

The pounding pace thickened, drumming in his ears. Was this the blood hunger? Here he stood surrounded by so many, enclosed in cages, cells and filthy little rooms.

A veritable feast! Take the blood. It will be good then. No worry of madness.

No! He did not want to feed upon these people. He was a human being, not a monster.

"Just concentrate." He felt Roxane move close to him and press her palms to his cheeks. Bless the coolness of her flesh. Her body limned his. The soft plush of her gown married to his stiff damask frock coat.

In her arms, he could be any man he wished to become. Confident. Not badgered by a ridiculous costume. The pulse beats softened. A new surge of sensation coursed through his body as her hip pressed against his, and he felt the womanly curves beneath her skirts. His body reacted.

He clutched her wrists. "I want you."

"Good," she whispered. "Look into my eyes, Gabriel. Redirect your focus from the pain. What do you see?"

"Ce-celadon." Indeed, the pain had lessened, but only because he'd grown randy.

"What do you feel? Tell me."

He chuckled. Some of the anxiety loosed and flowed away. "You don't feel it?" He tilted his hips, pressing his erection against her skirts. "You make me want you, Roxane."

"Is the pounding in your head gone?"

"Redirected. It has moved to my breeches."

"Even better. A diversion." She leaned in and kissed his forehead. A faery morsel, so fleeting, yet powerful. It chased away the fear, the angry hunger. "You feel able to move on?"

He nodded. "Tricky wench."

With a clever smile, she moved ahead and gained a long hall walled on one side with soot-blackened bars. She had explained her brother shared a cell with three other men.

Somewhere along their trek to Hell the silent guard had abandoned them. Gabriel scanned whence he had come and down another dim hallway. Abandoned with a silence that hurt.

"Damian?"

Compelled by a beckon of Roxane's fingers, he moved to her side and she clutched his hand. Indeed, the drum of hunger had subsided. But in its wake he had gotten an erection. What strange thing had he become that to stand in the bowels of hell and caress a beautiful woman appealed to him? Made him randy?

As he joined her in searching the darkness all lustful thoughts melted. A jitter of anticipation returned.

Gabriel spied three figures moving about in the shadows of the large cell. Overhead, a line of narrow windows—no wider than a man's arm—cast white morning light over their shoulders and sliced through the bars before him.

"I can't see him," she whispered. "I wonder if he has been moved."

"My liege!"

From around the corner a figure leapt to the bars. Wide green eyes glittered. The miasma of rot, of indifference, doubled in an awful assault. The man tilted his head, an insect scenting out Gabriel. "What have you brought with you today, sister?"

"A friend." She stepped forward. "This is the vicomte Gabriel Renan, Damian, he wanted to meet—"

"What is it?" The man behind the bars stretched his arms wide, displaying a shoddy blanket across his thin limbs as if a grand cape.

"Not an it; he is a man, Damian. Just like you. He is a vicomte," she repeated with a glance to Gabriel. She had accepted his truth easily. Even more reason to adore her.

The man tilted his head, studying Gabriel. Thin and looking more the rag and bone man than the real ones, his eyes were sunk inside two dark shadows. Dirty breeches hung at his hips, exposing the sharp slash of bones. Gabriel could not find the words to speak. He should bow, offer a proper salutation—he could but stare.

"He dresses like a vicomte," Damian said. "But he doesn't smell right. He is neither man nor beast. Aha! Like *moi*!"

Loud, unhinged laughter burst from Damian's mouth. He spun round, lifting his tattered cloak, heeding his subjects to bow. The cruel cacophony, a portent of his future, ached in Gabriel's soul.

"My sister," Damian announced grandly, "is starting a collection?"

"Do not speak of her so!" Gabriel clutched Roxane's hand. "I'm sorry for making you bring me here."

"Ah, so it is you who wanted to look upon your future?" Damian pressed his face between the bars and eyed Gabriel up and down. The bars pulled back his flesh and stretched his eye sockets into narrow slits. "Yes, I see now. Young. Pretty. Isn't that what the vampire seeks, the pretties?" He spun and did a little jig with his bare feet. "Pretty, pretty! Spin me silly!"

"Damian, please," Roxane pleaded.

The man stretched his arms wide and thrust out his thin chest. "Is this what you want, vicomte? To join me in my royal quarters? I've servants, as you can see."

A plump man, in what appeared a loincloth, spun in wobbly circles around the room, and the eyes of the others, dark and sunken, crept along Gabriel's flesh from the filthy shadows.

"Such splendid madness is my own. She has convinced you to fight that damnable hunger, yes?" Gabriel jumped as Damian leapt and gripped the bars. He clung with toes and fingers, as if an ape caged in the Jardins du Plantes. "Take the blood!"

"Damian," Roxane whispered.

"You favor my sister, vicomte?"

"I—"

"She is the mouse that roars, be cautious her sting."

Gabriel felt her tremble against his body. What a fool mission to come here. He was repulsed, and yet, sickened that he should feel so at the sight of another human suffering. Madness ruled Damian Desrues's mind. Had it seeped into his very soul? Could the man have salvation?

The bars clanged as Damian threw himself against them. Framed by cold iron, his pale green eyes sought Gabriel. Silently he reached out, his fingers grabbing at air—not close enough to touch. So far from a kind touch!

Gabriel stepped forward, but Roxane's tug at his arm stayed him. She would know better than he, so he relented.

"Pretty," Damian said. A child-like tilt of his head. "Can you float, vicomte?"

"Damian—"

Gabriel reassured Roxane's tension with a squeeze of her hand. "Float? I don't understand."

"If you cannot float, you will sink."

The background idiots had ceased to chant. Gabriel could feel Roxane's hand tremble. Her brother stood alone in the world, torn from the love and comfort he must have once felt.

Gabriel knew the feeling. So well.

Damian whispered seductively, "Take the blood."

The vicomte stared into the celadon gaze that matched Roxane's. The sadness, the pitiful repose, had been replaced by a tightened jaw.

"Take my blood, bleed me dead. If you cannot," Damian hissed, "pass me your dagger and I will do it myself. Take my blood! Bleed me to death so I am no longer a slave to madness. Take the blood! Take the blood!"

One of the idiots who bowed on the floor pounded the stone with his fist, "Take the blood!" The other imbeciles joined in. "Take the blood, take the blood!"

Damian's face grew livid, yet his smile widened lecherously as he spread his arms and thrust back his head, silently reveling in the macabre jubilation.

Gabriel remained fixed to the lithe man who stood like a deity in the midst of filth and madness, and knew, without doubt, that he spoke the truth.

Soon he would join Damian Desrues in his kingdom of madness.

Unless he partook of the blood.

ELEVEN

THEY PAUSED IN GENTILLY TO WATER the horse and seek refreshment. Gabriel settled onto a wobbly half-timber bench outside the tavern and hung his head. Exhaustion stretched between his shoulders and down his back. He was thankful he'd had the forethought to bring along the blue-lensed spectacles. His eyes ached, felt shrunken in their sockets.

He was thirsty, angry and confused. And horrified. He was so close to the asylum. Mentally, but a step away.

Roxane lingered by the horse, perhaps sensing his need for quiet. She was so strong. *He* had requested she take him to Bicêtre. Much as she had not wanted to return, she had agreed to help him try to understand the madness that waited. She had explained his options. Gabriel knew that to drink blood would grant him freedom from life in a filthy cell, ever spinning and giddily pleased to do so.

Hell, he could take a rapier to his heart and be free of it all. But he'd had to see, to observe the other option. And it wasn't a pretty one.

That look in Damian's eyes—the man had wanted, and had been denied. He hadn't been able to fight the madness for the blood.

Gabriel clenched his shirt, fingers digging into his ribs. How did one fight an attack to his very soul?

Roxane's brother was now sentenced to eternal unrest. Much like a vampire?

"Please, Roxane, sit by me."

"I'd rather stand and stretch my legs. Walk with me?"

He could refuse her nothing. Gabriel stood and walked her down the hoof-pounded street under the blessed shade of a row of cypress boughs, horse following behind.

"Do you think I am slipping?" he asked. "Tell me true, Roxane. I must know."

"You face a strange future. One you did not ask for." Not an answer. So she did think as much.

"Your brother," he said. "Was his slip...noticeable?"

"Yes."

"He was determined to avoid vampirism?"

"He didn't think much on it. I—he trusted me. Oh, Gabriel, haven't you figured it out? It was I who encouraged Damian to endure the wait for the moon. I influenced him. Perhaps I was wrong. Perhaps I am wrong to suggest the same for you."

She strode ahead, grasping the air near her head. Struggling with something that wanted to break free from her soul.

"A remarkable suggestion, my lady. Do you want to exchange the vicomte Renan for the vampire Renan?"

"It is not my place to say. And I will not!"

"You think vampirism a better choice than mortality?"

"What if the madness strikes? I want you to be safe. No matter what happens."

He stopped near a closed hawker's cart and leaned against it. Ragged red flags decorated the four corners and a sign scrawled in fading chalk advertised oranges.

He swallowed but tasted only dryness and the lingering reminder of the stinking cells.

He touched her wrist, and when she did not flinch he curled her fingers into his. "I value your opinion. You are the only friend I have."

"What of Toussaint?"

"Yes, well, you are the only friend I desire to kiss."

She lifted a brow.

"Looking at you makes me hungry."

She blushed, the color in her cheeks frothing to a delightful bloom.

He sensed the inner stirring, the craving for more than a simple kiss, and fought it back. *What if the madness strikes suddenly?*

Caution must be abandoned now, before it was too late.

"I need to kiss you, Roxane."

"Your kisses are rather favorable."

"I give them freely."

He swept an arm around her waist and pulled her against him. As he kissed her, her throaty moans fed the desire, the passion, the need to hold and touch. He dove deep into her mouth, feeding upon her taste, upon her willingness to look beyond the evil that loomed over his head. He held life in his arms, he mustn't stain it, mustn't damage the innocence.

But certainly he must own it.

"You taste like goodness," he murmured into her mouth. "More." He wanted to own her, to possess her.

Take the blood.

The thunder of her heartbeat bellowed inside his skull. Taste, sound and smell combined in a heady miasma that shrouded him like a rain-heavy cloud. The satin dress curved out from her waist and he followed the rounded swell down and squeezed her bottom.

She pushed against him. "You hold me too tightly. Relax, Gabriel, I'll not run off."

"Would that you did, and I could chase you."

Her lips were hot. Swollen and slippery, succulent fruits to be plucked and devoured. The taste of her made him want more. The thick sweet wine of life.

"No," she said. "You mustn't, Gabriel!"

The tear of her nails across his neck jerked his senses to the moment. Roxane stumbled away from him. He touched a finger to his neck, the opposite side of his bite wounds. Blood. So red and lucid. Even pretty.

Hmm... Impulsively, he raised the blood-stained finger to his lips.

Roxane tore his hand away. "Don't do that!"

"It is my blood. It should not count to the change, should it?"

He resisted as she tried to wipe his neck with the lace scarf she tugged from around her bosom. In that moment he noticed, in the generous swell of her bosom, a red mark. Or was it a blush?

"I do not know what is required for the change," she said, pressing a palm over her breasts, effectively concealing the telling color. "Your blood, someone else's blood, you cannot know until it is too late."

A red smear imbued the whorls of his fingers. Such a marvelous red, so full of life. He'd stained the innocence. Didn't feel a whit of guilt about it either.

"Please," she said, touching his hand. "Trust me."

"In other words" —he wiped the blood across his coat hem—"choose madness?"

"No, that's—"

"Exactly what you asked your brother to do?"

"Oh!" She caught her forehead in her palms.

He paced before her. Rationally he knew the hunger was winning. But he yet could determine the difference between need and mere want.

"Forgive me, too easily I jump to cruelties against you. *Morbleu*, I really am going insane. I would never treat a woman so horribly. To frighten her so. There is no excuse. Not even the blood hunger will suffice."

"Don't be so hard on yourself. Take things as they come. Trust me."

"I will trust you. For as long as I am able. But should the madness arrive, all wagers are off. Do you understand?"

Tears painted trails through her road-dusted flesh. "I do. It is your life, you must choose of your free will."

He touched her cheek, brushing away a tear. Unaware of her exposed décolletage, she still breathed heavily. Each breath lifted that interesting red mark into view for but a moment. It was a pattern, yes?

"If I did change..." He trailed a finger down her chin and across the fine silver chain about her neck. "Would you chase after me with this vial of witch's blood?"

She clutched the vial, which, he noticed, had been refilled. "I don't want to think of such things."

"But you may have to. If I become a creature you will want to destroy me to protect others from falling to such a curse. In fact, you must."

"Please don't make me choose."

In other words, *Don't do it, for I* will *pursue you*.

What a match the two of them would make: the vampire and a vampire slayer.

"I'll try not to, Roxane. I favor you. Hell, to be truthful, I desire you. I want you. I know that I could..."

Love you.

Incessant hope could never completely be set aside. Could a man become addicted to a woman? To rosemary and strawberries and long lingering kisses?

"For some reason it matters very much that you see me in the best light possible. I want you to want me, Roxane. *Morbleu*, that sounds so needy."

"It's what everyone wants, isn't it?"

"Indeed. Roxane, know that I want to fight this. Because..." He removed the blue spectacles and looked her full in the eyes. "Because I want you to have a chance to love a man, not a beast."

So he had put it into words. He did want this woman. To *see* him. To know the real Gabriel Renan.

And who the hell was that? What fool had he become? *Madness is yours if you believe this country rustic could ever love you.*

She leaned in and kissed him, and all doubt fled Gabriel's heart.

TWELVE

GABRIEL SLIPPED HIS ARMS INTO A damask night robe and sat before the vanity to allow Toussaint to unroll the paisley turban wrapped about his head. Wet hair spilled onto his shoulders releasing the aroma of cinnamon. It felt good to bathe and wash away the remnants of Bicêtre. Though parts of the day's adventure yet clung to his soul. What that poor woman must feel to know her brother suffered so.

He stared into the etched vanity mirror. His eyes were drawn and tired, his downturned mouth pale beneath his moustache. Exhaustion, or perhaps age? Did vampires age? What an elixir of youth they must possess. But at a dreadful price.

He thought of Anjou, dressed in an ancient frock coat. Had it been his own? How long had he walked this earth? Surely the man adjusted to the changing fashions so as not to draw attention? Or did he seek attention for an ancient and wanting heart, as only Gabriel could understand?

He leaned onto his elbows and asked, "Mesmer know of the vampire?"

"Oh yes, I was able to learn a few things. He once staked one, and then escaped a rabid band of minions by forging through the treacherous Carpathian mountains."

"Really? So stakes are the thing?"

"Yes, and garlic, wild roses, and holy water. It is all true." Toussaint's eyes glittered with proud possession of a remarkable knowledge. "Wild roses laid across the coffins of suspected vampires keep them down should they try to rise as a night creature. And garlic repels."

"Well, that covers the killing part. What of the living? Must a vampire lurk in the shadows? Follow the night?"

"Unnecessary. They are fully capable of moving about during the day, though weaker and more susceptible to defeat. The females rely on the males for sustenance. Call them patrons."

Gabriel glanced at the blue spectacles. "And their eyes?"

"What about their eyes?"

It was not imagination that his eyes had been light sensitive today. Though why it should matter—he was not a vampire—bothered him. "Never mind. What of their powers, if they have any?"

"Supernatural strength and the ability to enthrall their victims."

"Enthrall? Hmm... So does Mesmer concur that vampires don't need to kill?"

"I did not think to ask. Sorry. He doesn't much favor them. Though he did explain a bit about the witch/vampire relationship. Mademoiselle Desrues's vial of blood is an excellent deterrent due to the two species being enemies.

"Seems in order to obtain immortality a witch must perform a ritual of blood and fire," Toussaint explained. "It takes blood provided by an unfortunate vampire. She must drink the warm blood from a vampire's heart, then offer herself to the flame."

Their eyes met in the mirror and Toussaint nodded. "You heard correctly. Said blood being ripped from the vampire's chest leaving him, er...well, dead. The witch then bares herself to the flame and is marked by some goddess. Because the witch's blood has been tainted through the centuries with vampire blood it seems their blood has become poisonous to the very life that provides them immortality."

"Like acid," Gabriel muttered, recalling the horrendous death of the vampire minion. "Has the vampire no recourse against the witch?"

"Oh, indeed. To enthrall a witch will draw away her immortality."

"Hardly compares to literally exploding to death."

Toussaint shrugged. "It involves blood sex magic. Mesmer explained."

Gabriel lifted a brow.

"An enslavement thing involving sex, blood and magic. If you decide to accept the change you might find a way to dispose of Roxane's little trinket."

Toussaint's casual suggestion that he accept the change shuddered up Gabriel's spine.

Could he do it? He'd had but a few warning pangs so far, accompanied by the sensation that he could actually see and smell the blood of any person, or creature, close by. Surely by now he should be suffering greatly? Did not madness require suffering? Or did one simply wake one morning in a strange and macabre mind?

It made little sense. And yet, what in the past days had made sense? He had almost completely secluded himself from society. There was a young, beautiful, unmarried woman living under the same roof as he. And he'd spent the entire day on a trip to an asylum to stare into the eyes of his future.

What is becoming of you, man? You've but a few days to live your life. To mine passion. To step beyond all that has held you back, shivering for fear of addiction, of being discarded and abandoned.

He was not an idiot confined behind bars; his life shone in comparison. Life felt precious. The correct choice could either extend it for an eternity, or cut it abruptly short.

Gabriel did not want to wager on the odds that everything would turn out fine—that he could successfully fight the blood hunger and retain his sanity—for Roxanne had made it apparent such an outcome was not likely.

When you stop floating...you sink.

The look in Damian Desrues' eyes—the man had known freedom, had made the wrong choice, and now wanted death.

Only a fool would waste his final moments, yes?

A decisive nod reflected at him.

"Toussaint, is the mademoiselle bathing?"

"Yes, I requested the maid make her bath water extra hot because I know the ladies like to linger and soak. Do you wish me to shave you?"

Gabriel turned his head side to side before the mirror. "I don't think I need it."

"No, perhaps not. Strange."

"How long has it been?"

"Since your last shave? Every Wednesday."

"And today is Sunday. No stubble whatsoever. Hmm..." And still the bite marks had not healed, or even formed a scab. How curious.

"Do you think you are becoming the vampire?"

He glared at Toussaint's eager reflection. The man's macabre curiosity would be the death of him.

On the other hand...

Gabriel opened his mouth and Toussaint leaned over his shoulder. Both searched the mirror for pointed or elongated canines and found none.

"Foolishness. I need blood for the change," he said.

He recalled Roxane's attempt to stop his aggressive kiss in Gentilly. He had been so close to tasting blood. At that moment, he would have done so without second thought. No regrets. Forge on into the future.

He must not dwell on the unforeseeable future.

Time was precious. Life must be lived.

Decided, he stood and shook his fingers through his wet hair. "I think I will check on our guest, Toussaint."

Determined strides moved him silently down the hall. Live your life, his conscious hummed. Before it is too late. He may never again have a woman. At least, not in his sanc mind.

ROXANE PRESSED THE SLIPPERY BALL of soap to her nose and drew in the heady lavender. Her plan to use Gabriel as bait had proven useless. It was back to deciphering Anjou's trail. Could she pick up his scent again? Decisive, she nodded.

The door to the guest bedchamber swung open and in marched Gabriel bedecked in striped satin robe and pointed Turkish slippers. A devil-may-care smile curled lazily below his seeking eyes. Whiskey eyes slowly took her in as if to draw her in his thoughts.

She sunk into the bath water, dreadfully aware that the clear water hid nothing from the man who stopped directly above her with a triumphant grin.

"Mademoiselle Desrues."

"What in hell are you doing?"

He mocked a pout at her abrupt tone. "I wanted to ensure my guest was enjoying herself. See that you had everything you need. You are pleased with the bath?"

"Stand back, will you? Or hand me a towel." She pressed both palms over her breasts. "You are a cad, Renan."

"I thought I was a swish?"

He turned and paced away, but remained within a leap of the tub. The cocky bastard.

"I am accustomed to such a sight," Renan drawled sweetly. "You needn't be a prude."

"I am not a prude. Nor am I an exhibitionist. Don't stare!"

"Why not? If you've seen one naked female, you've seen them all. Don't worry, I won't bite. At least, I don't believe I will. There is always a chance..."

"Sit!" she demanded.

He plopped onto the wing-backed chair five paces from the tub, lazily dragging up one leg to prop over the padded arm. Dark-haired legs were revealed as his robe parted, so masculine so...bare.

Roxane realized he could be naked beneath the robe. Heat rushed to her bosom and cheeks. The water was not cool enough to bring down the flush. And whenever she blushed it only brought up the telltale mark. She could not risk him seeing the mark. He would have questions she wasn't prepared to answer.

"It would be better if you would leave."

"You just commanded I sit. Do you wish me to sit or leave? Sort out your mind, woman."

"Leave." From the corner of her eye she saw him consider her request—for but a moment.

"Not a chance."

Losh! He was making her uncomfortable, and reveling in it. "You are a voyeur! Where is that towel?"

A small hand cloth plopped into the water. She pressed it over her breasts. "What do you want?"

Closing his eyes and pinching the air with his forefingers, Gabriel expressed a fine impatience. "I want to do something."

"Right now? With...with me?"

"Such as making love?"

How to respond? The situation absolutely screamed for seduction with both of them bare of clothing and she so vulnerable.

A finger to his temples, eyes closed tight, and Gabriel announced, "No, that's not it. Well, yes, I do wish to make love with you. But as well..." He grasped the air before him in an attempt to capture the elusive something that haunted his desires. "I've but a few days before my life will be drastically tipped on end. I have had the sudden notion that until that moment I should be living life fully. Do you not agree?"

"I thought you did live to the fullest. Wenching, wine and gambling? Or was that Leo?"

"A bit of us both, actually. That was not living life, that was merely wallowing in one's place. A comfortable position."

"I hadn't thought to hear you admit such."

"Believe me, I've reduced wallowing to a fine art. And if it is bedecked in lace, all the better."

"I thought that was Leo's act?"

"So did I. Don't you see? I want to dredge myself up from the depths of selfishness and really experience. No longer must I worry that I will be left standing alone. I *am* alone. I always have been; I must get on with life."

"What had you in mind?"

He shrugged and shifted on the chair. The movement parted his robe to reveal a tuft of dark hairs centered on his chest. Roxane fixed to the sight, until his laughter startled her.

"Perhaps the same thing you have in mind." He slid from the chair and walked on his knees to kneel by the tub. Dropping an arm into the water, he again granted her that wicked smile that belonged to a misfit child who had spilled the whitewash over a new rug. "Can vampires make love to women?"

She stiffened as his hand slipped over her ankle and slapped a palm over the wet cloth, hoping to conceal her chest. "I don't know. Take your hand from my bath. Please?"

"No." He propped his chin upon the edge of the copper tub, which, at the moment, was feeling very small to Roxane. "Don't worry, I don't intend to ravish you. But I do wish to make you uncomfortable."

"You succeeded the moment you walked through that door uninvited. Why do you want to torment me?"

"So you will react." He lifted the hand he had submerged. "I want to see what you do when challenged, Roxane. You've a fire in your eyes."

"I thought they were pale green? Now they've a flame in them?"

"A brilliant fluorescence of fire," he murmured as if tasting the words before speaking them. "I could make love to you right now. Be damned propriety." He looked to her for reply, but again she couldn't summon a response to save her virtue. "I would have expected a vampire slayer to invite the adventure."

"Oh, I do, it is just—"

"What did your brother mean when he spoke of floating?"

Relieved at the sudden conversation switch, she said, "It's something we've said to one another in the past."

"Which means?"

"Floating, skimming the surface of life. Trying to keep one's head above water. It is what Damian and I have done since father's disappearance and mother's death."

"I see."

She knew Gabriel floated as well. Why or how, she was not yet sure. But float he did. "Please, don't look at me." He had fixed his gaze to what seemed her neck, caught in a stare. "I have never...had a man look upon me, er...my naked body."

Gabriel turned and leaning against the tub, gifting her with the back of his head. "Sorry. I thought you—I've no desire to deflower a virgin."

"You assumed I was *not* a virgin?"

"Yes." He slapped his forehead with a wet palm. "No. Well, I didn't consider it. The women I frequent are the furthest step from virtuous. Of course you must be an innocent, all fresh and new from the family parish, eh?"

"What is wrong with virgins?"

He shook his head of lustrous dark hair, still glistening with moisture. Roxane tensed her arm to keep the towel from slipping.

"Not a damned thing. Except that I have no time for one. They require utmost skill, a tenderness I've never possessed."

"You speak as if I am glass that will shatter under your touch."

"It is simply that I've not the time to teach you the ways required to please me."

"Ah. So when Gabriel Renan makes love it is for his own gratification, not the woman's?"

"Of course not." He turned and leaned his elbow on the copper edge, fitting his chin on his arm. "I am a master at bringing a woman to her pleasure. In fact I insist on the woman being first satisfied before seeking my own pleasure."

"Such a generous man."

"I should think so."

"But virgins scare the hell out of you?"

"Yes. No! Hell, I don't know." He dandled his forefinger upon the surface of the water. She sensed his frustration; it was brought on by a hell of a lot more than her virginity. "To be honest, I've never had one. I wouldn't know the first thing to do with one."

"Perhaps it isn't that you must *do* something with them, but rather that you must take your time with them. I will have you know I am always up for a new experience."

"Sex?"

"I—right now?"

He smirked. "You weren't listening to me, fair Roxane."

"I heard you—no virgins. What if—in the spirit of making your *final days* an adventure—I expressed an interest in making love with you?"

"You would?"

She found herself shrugging and nodding at the same time. *Losh*, but the man's honeyed eyes danced a double-step into her heart. For the first time in her life Roxane knew the feeling of beguilement. 'Twas a floating freeness, not unlike flying.

"I've already said I've no time to teach a virgin."

"I'm a fast learner," her mouth said without direction from her better judgment. Be damned judgment. Flight was not to be ignored. It was better than sinking to the depths.

"You do tempt me, Roxane. Oh, but you do." He smirked and shook his head. "This water is getting cold. Don't you want to get out?"

"Not with you in here."

"Not up for the challenge?"

"It is not I who seeks adventure, vicomte."

Oh yes, it is, her conscious cheered.

"Indeed." He sighed and turned again to slump against the tub. "You simply want to watch over me. Or rather, you think to use me as bait to lure the vampire into your grasp."

"Where did you get that idea?"

"A guess." He tilted a look toward her. Candlelight shadowed his face, gifting it a subtle, devilish allure. "How else will you find the man who delivered your brother to madness?"

"I *am* protecting you."

"With your vial of blood? How do you know it is from a witch?" He spied the pile of her clothes by the tub and leaned over to snatch the silver chain and vial from the top. "Do you even know it is blood? Where *did* you get this?"

She gasped. "Don't toy with that, Renan."

"Why?" He fingered the cork stopper. "Do you fear I'll drink it and change into a blood-sucking beast? What then would you do? You'd be at my mercy. Do you think I could spare you my thirst?"

He winced, scenting the liquid inside the vial.

Roxane snatched the vial and replaced the cork stopper. "The hunger is speaking, Gabriel. Don't you see that?"

He pressed his fingers to his forehead and rubbed. "Perhaps you are right. Forgive me." He pushed up and strode to the door. "I should not be such an imposition on you. I'll leave you in peace for the evening."

"What of your irresistible urge to do something? To live life?"

He sighed. "I imagine it will remain for the days I have left."

She didn't want to lose him. Not yet. Such sadness coated his being. He wanted to be out and about. She needed to concentrate on the mission at hand. There was a way to satisfy them both.

"It is rather early..." she stated.

"Not even ten."

"It would be a pity for Leo to turn in so early when all of society is about. Are you not expected somewhere, some salon?"

"Leo generally attends the theatre on Sunday. Would you...care to accompany me?"

"I would enjoy that."

He smiled warmly.

"Do you think we'll gain admittance so late?"

"Mademoiselle, Leo has a box."

THIRTEEN

LA FEMME WAS PLAYING AT THE Comédie Française on the rue de Richelieu. Gabriel estimated he and Roxane slipped into his box halfway through the second act. The contralto, pranked out in red damask and gilded eyelashes, bellowed about her infatuation for the burly tenor. He, in turn, offered all his worldly goods to impress and win her. She was not having it. The tenor threatened death if he could not have love.

Gabriel handed a tortoiseshell lorgnette he'd retrieved from a locked box beside the seat to Roxane, who eagerly looked over the crowd of attendees. He'd seen it all before, marveled at the fine fabrics and jewels and the indiscretions that took place for all eyes to witness. Developing *désintéressé* for this crowd had been less a challenge than a relief. Mingled scents of dusty hair powder, citrus oil, mud cleaved to shoes, perspiration and hen droppings (for the owner allowed his pet hens the run of the theatre during the off hours) briefly infused Gabriel's senses. All of it, the singing, whispering and violin trills, segued to background.

Tonight, he found the most interesting view sat beside him.

During a quick stop by her apartment, Roxane had changed into a red velvet gown that bared her alabaster shoulders and accentuated high, exquisite breasts displayed as if delicious sweets upon a buffet. How the woman dressed without a maid perplexed him. No wig graced strawberry curls. She fit well with the current rage. Yet amongst the dyed masses Roxane sparkled like a jewel.

But not to touch, no, mustn't mess with the lovely arrangement. He enjoyed the sweet torture of restraint. Though he did ache to pull away the soft white scarf rimming her décolletage. Had he imagined a red mark upon her breasts earlier? He'd not gotten a look behind the towel she'd clutched.

Propriety demanded he exercise restraint. Besides, the niggling reminder that a virgin sat next to him discomfited. Yet the thrill of debauchery skittered through his system. Dare he mar the easy friendship they had developed? Was it worth the pain he was sure to bring to both himself and Roxane after madness arrived?

Rosemary poked tendrils into his thoughts. A fragrance that put in mind that of the common, the passé. But on Roxane the perfume blossomed into a heady trap of unfurling, sticky pink petals. He closed his eyes and the scent overwhelmed.

Even with the chaffering below he could hear her. Every pretty little bit of her. Beyond the soft rustle of the red velvet that elegantly folded and creased with each turn of her head to peer over the crowd, and beyond the crinkle of lace that etched over her breasts, protecting and beckoning at the same time, he heard the gush, the soft runnels, the busy pace of her being. It purled lusciously, swimming, swirling, sparkling with life.

Curiosity inspired, he modestly leaned to the side until his damask cuff brushed red velvet. *Schush*, the gentle contact. He quieted his breaths. The song of violins and jarring contralto segued into the garish scenery. Bustle of skirts, shoes and whispering lips hushed. The air vibrated about him, focusing his senses to Roxane.

Her pulse fluttered inside his head like a winged insect. Parting his lips and drawing in a breath coated his tongue with an empyrean treat. Indeed, heaven had alighted aside him.

He reached out, and eyes still closed—but instinctively seeing—touched Roxane's wrist. He drew a curve across her flesh, a slight rise. Back again. She did not resist as he lifted her hand and pressed his nose there, upon her pulse. A rush of luscious red liquid flowing and feeding as a stream draws from the river. A kiss placed right there—yes, catch the flutter of a pulse beat— summoned the minute rise, the movement of blood against his mouth.

Roxane's sigh chimed in his brain, shushing softly against his skull. Tracing his lip with the tip of his tongue, he tasted salt and the sharp edge of Valenciennes lace. Rosemary filled his senses until he felt sure to drown from the fragrance did he not do something immediately.

And so he did.

He stretched his mouth across the fragile wrist in his hand. Carefully. Slowly. Drawing out the pleasure of the moment.

The tip of his tongue dallied with the rush of life enclosed within the plump vein. He felt her tug, but a feminine sigh replaced resistance. Yes, like a sigh, this moment of delicious exploration, to be carried out, lingering, until it wisped to but a pleasant memory.

You can have this. Take the blood!

He pressed his teeth to flesh. His tongue teased at the backs of his teeth, languorously wetting Roxane's flesh as if anointing the sacrifice.

A female cry alerted him, ripping him from his sensory reverie. A bass violin spat out a bellicose note. The sweltering essence of sensuality lifted.

Gabriel looked up into wide celadon eyes. A finger was pressed to parted red lips stuck in an 'O' of shock. And below, using his peripheral vision, the entire pit had turned to seek the origin of the shriek.

Morbleu. Such indiscretion was not Leo's forte.

He managed a cocky grin at the staring eyes, the tilted wigs spotted with semi-hardened wax fallen from the crystal chandeliers, and the curious lorgnettes that sought out scandal. Whispers rose like a swarm.

A shrug and a roguish wink answered their burning questions. One by one they turned back to the play.

Still clutching Roxane's wrist, he moved to adjust the lace that rimmed her sleeve below the elbow. Absent of vulgarity he discreetly re-entered the civilized.

"Sorry." He released hold of her wrist. "Wasn't thinking."

She nodded silently, smoothing her fingers where he had held her. He noticed red marks where his teeth had been and a glisten of his saliva.

Had he bitten her? It was not possible. He would not— But he could see the faint marks, thin angry lines from his front teeth impressed upon her flesh. *Morbleu.*

"Perhaps we should leave," she managed in a shaky tone.

He nodded and led her out into the hallway, a cove of plush sapphire velvet and fathomless cream marble. He walked her a short way down the hall, angling his steps until Roxane could not walk further without colliding against the wall. Insinuating himself before her, Gabriel encircled her waist with an arm. Red velvet cushed beneath his ultra-sensitive fingertips. He felt her resistance, but as well, he sensed she wanted to remain. Tight and stiff in his arms—trapped—as unsure of freedom as a day-old starling, her celadon gaze yielded.

"The temptation will only increase if we return to my home where we will be alone," he whispered, leaning in to sketch the curve of her ear with the tip of his nose. Strands of her hair traced his mouth. The shiver of contact shimmied through his extremities. Resistance was unthinkable. "I want you, Roxane."

Her heavy exhale hushed across his chin. The heat of her being touched him, coating him with a tantalizing invitation.

"You want my blood, Renan, not me. Remember, I am but a stumbling virgin."

"I may have been hasty in my declaration to forego virgins."

"Is that Leo or Gabriel speaking?"

"Damn Leo. Perhaps there is a thing or two the vicomte Renan could teach you before my time is up."

"You speak as if death was a given."

"Either that or a cell next to His Liege, your brother." She winced, and he regretted the remark. "Sorry, I didn't mean that. It was—"

"The blood hunger speaking. I know."

Again that damned excuse. It was as if he were not of his mind, a slave to the blood hunger. Why was it so easy for her to forgive him? Where was the kernel of fear, the good sense to beware? He needed that resistance!

She trusted him far more than he trusted himself.

✧✧✧

ELABORATE PLASTER MOULDING circled the base of the massive oculus window that mastered the dome cresting Gabriel's bedroom. Convex, the bowl could house a team of blood-horses surely. A border of red and yellow roses surrounded the design that swirled into a forest of vivid blossoms, vines and starbursts. So many colors. Surely there were not names for every piece of colored glass. The rose window in Nôtre Dame would be envious.

"Are you lost yet?" Gabriel inquired softly.

Smiling at his whispered appeal, Roxane nodded. "I like the color in the center of that flower. Such a brilliant golden yellow. What is your favorite?"

"All of them." He tilted his head and closed his eyes.

Having torn Leo's gray bagwig from his head the moment he set foot inside, his natural dark locks tumbled across the high lace jabot. Green vines and pink and orange flowers painted across his forehead, nose and cheeks. His lips curled to a satisfied smile. "I suppose celadon is my current favorite."

Bowing her head, Roxane searched the white marble floor, following the wash of colors. Though unaccustomed to such attention from a man, she liked it. She did not fear his playful entreaty to sex. Nor did she balk from his kisses. But something about him still kept her on alert. It was not because he was a swish. There was nothing frightening about lace and powder.

Gabriel Renan was not the man he appeared to be. That was what frightened her about him. An accidental fop, he. Or rather, a creation. His insides did not conform to his outer shell. At the same time, it was that very complication of the man's veneer that compelled her to remain beside him, to look up through the colored glass and divine the inner workings of a soul he hid from the world.

She craved a piece of his being. To truly know the man beneath the mask. Before that mask was replaced with the darkest mask of all.

"Renan!"

Both spun at Toussaint's sudden and erratic entrance. The valet literally skidded into the bedroom, a white-knuckled clutch groping the doorframe.

"What the hell is it, man? You look as if you've seen a ghost."

"A gargoyle!" Toussaint punctuated his high nervous tones with fluttering hands. "On the roof!"

Gabriel chuckled. He shot Roxane a sly wink before turning to the agitated valet. "There are all of four gargling drain spouts up on the roof, Toussaint. Did they frighten you?"

"Th—" Toussaint gaped and swallowed a lungful of air. "I was lighting the lantern and— Th-there's a new one."

"What?"

Roxane fixed herself to the wall, palms flat. Working her way toward escape, she slid a foot out the doorway behind Toussaint.

"A new one?" Again Gabriel chuckled. "You are a barmy one, Toussaint. And here I thought it was I who should be showing signs of madness."

Roxane started down the hallway, intent on the roof access stairs. She listened for the conversation she had left. The worst could not happen. Not now.

"If you don't believe me, have a look for yourself," Toussaint's voice shivered down the hallway.

So soon comes the worst? She rounded the corner and scrambled up the stairs.

"Roxane? She must have gone to investigate. To the roof!"

Pushing open the roof door and scrambling up the last stairs, Roxane arrived first. The night swooped upon her with a chill that lodged in her throat. Gasping at her racing heartbeats she pressed a hand to her chest. Distant clops of horse hooves echoed out in dull thuds below. She did not spy the 'extra' gargoyle. A scan of the surrounding rooftops and the gray cloud-striped sky found nothing.

She let out a breath of relief and plopped onto the roof ledge.

Toussaint's head plunged up from the stairway as if a ground rodent emerging from his burrow.

Gabriel followed, a god arising from the depths. Frockcoat tails blowing out behind him and hair listing in the breeze, he winked at Roxane. Just humoring the valet, he conveyed.

"I see nothing but the usual gargoyles," he said as he bent over the roof edges to study the stone drain spouts, each extending out two feet. All four matched— extended lizards more like, with curled forepaws and gaping maws—save the one with a chip to its nose. Soot had darkened the heads and talons of them all. "Are you sure you haven't been imbibing in the champagne I purchased this summer, Toussaint? Those bubbles tend to go straight to one's head."

"But it was right here!" The valet splayed out his hands, bewilderment toggling his voice up an octave. "I swear to it! It was huge and had wings and a monstrous body. I saw it." He turned to Roxane. "It was there."

She shrugged and eyed Gabriel. *Play this one carefully.* A scan of the surrounding rooftops yielded nothing unusual. Church spires and red-tiled roofs. Small lamplights glittered about the Palais Royale like a frenzied constellation that leaked toward the river and onto the island.

"I think you should retire early, good man." Gabriel walked Toussaint to the stairs, an arm about his shoulder. The valet conceded, arms hanging limply at his sides and head bowed. "The lantern throws off such shadows. You were simply mistaken. Yes?"

Toussaint nodded. With a final preening sweep of the roof, he descended the stairs.

Gabriel turned to Roxane and extended a hand. "Come."

"Let's stay up here a while," she suggested.

"Very well. It is a lovely evening."

He held out a hand, entreating her. She placed her palm on his. Spinning her, he drew her against his chest and spread his hands around her waist.

He smelled divine—cinnamon, fresh air and a trace of masculine musk. The hard planes of his body moving subtly against her hips worked an exquisite tease. In Gabriel's arms she felt safe.

If only she could keep him safe.

From no one but you, my dear. No one but you...

"The fresh air reminds me of home," she said, and couldn't help a sigh.

"You'll get back to your parish some day. You've told me your mother is dead. What of your father? Is he alive?"

"My father is here in Paris. Somewhere." Ask me no more, she silently pleaded.

"It is good to have family."

Shoulders nesting against his chest, her head fell back against his shoulder. What divine pleasure: falling into Gabriel Renan.

"What of yours?"

She felt him shrug against her body, but his embrace deepened.

"Long gone to the Americas," he said. "Good of father to emancipate his son so I could inherit without waiting for my twenty-fifth birthday. About the only kindness he ever showed me. Cecil and Juin-Marie both had their obsessions. Rather, addiction. Opium took them away from me long before they physically moved."

Roxane clasped his hand against her breast. He'd shown her a piece of his soul—finally.

"Were they ill?"

"You mean to take the opium in the first place? Not at all. But illness soon arrived, a cruel malady that blinds the user to life."

"I'm so sorry."

"I learned to fend for myself at a young age."

"You were left alone?"

"Abandoned to my own discretions. I'm no worse for the wear. At least not on the surface. Money can pretty up any man, hide him safely away. As you've seen, Leo is my armor."

"Why do you wish to hide, Gabriel?"

He touched her neck and drew a line to the cleavage she carefully disguised. "I'll tell you my secrets if you tell me yours."

She tilted her head and gazed across the horizon. "Some secrets are not meant to be shared."

"Then your secret must be evil," he said, with a winking grin.

"No, just personal."

"Wouldn't you share it with a dying man?"

"You will not die, Gabriel."

"Most likely not. But you do concede life will not be the same once Mistress Luna has grown full."

He had her there. And why couldn't she tell him everything? It might deepen their relationship. On the other hand, it could threaten the fragile bond they had created. "I have secrets, but I'm not ready to share them. I don't know how."

"Just speak them."

"Soon. I promise."

He nodded. "I won't rush you. It means the world that you trust me, Roxane. I'm so glad you came into my life."

ᏭOURTEEN

Around two A.M., the creaks of an ill-sprung equipage passing below his window startled Gabriel awake. He rubbed a hand over his face and through the sweat that coated his flesh. Odd. It wasn't at all hot, and the window was open—

He flashed a look to the window. The white sheer flitted in and out on a gentle breeze.

He jumped from the bed and pulled down the sash, securing the brass lock with a flick. He scanned the room. The moon let in enough multi-colored light to reassure that all the shadows were of inanimate objects.

Then he caught himself. "Hell, what is becoming of me? I'm jumping at shadows and shivering over an open window."

He glanced outside and up into the sky at the white moon. "Bitch," he hissed. "You control my life? I will not let you win." Striding to the vanity he tipped the dregs of a wine bottle into a goblet and tossed it back. Warm but rich, the bouquet and— "Ouch! This wine has bite."

Gabriel touched his lower lip. The crimson dot staining his fingertip was not wine—too thick. Examination of the goblet showed a sliver had been chipped from the rim, imperceptible, but sharp.

You cannot know if it is your blood that will make the change.

He licked his lip.

Morbidly curious, he stood in his night shirt before the cheval mirror. Waiting. Wondering. He separated the taste of wine at the back of his tongue from the metallic taste of blood, barely detectable at the tip of his tongue. Such a small drop could not possibly— "Ah!"

With a snap of his head, he bent double. Staring at his bare feet, he grimaced as a streak of pain ripped through his gut and shot up his spine. He tumbled forward, landing on his hands and knees. Huffing to dispel the sudden shriek of rage that danced upon his spine, he gasped against the dryness in his mouth. Crawling on all fours he gripped the edge of the bed and pulled himself up.

Was this it? Had he stupidly succumbed?

The silver water pitcher on the bedside table was empty. He slashed a hand over the table, upsetting the crystal goblet so it landed on the floor with a spectacular crash.

Crawling forward, he scented the minion's blood still locked within the floor boards and anticipated the taste of—of what? Darkness, sin and passion.

Just a little kiss...

Another wave of pain doubled him. Something inside of him shouted, clamoring to rise and float upon the surface of these sudden dark desires.

Resist.

Dragging himself up by the bedpost, he staggered to the door. He needed something to drink, something to quell the hunger that dried his throat and made his heart pound.

Take the blood.

Guttered candles oozed over the silver sconces. Eerie shapes of light moved across the mirrors. Toussaint slept below next to the kitchen in a cozy room far too small for the man. As much as Gabriel insisted he take a room on the upper level, the valet refused.

Running his hands across the smooth, cool mirrors, he navigated the darkness.

It was madness that he so needed a drink.

Needed to *drink...*

He straightened and pressed his bare back to the mirrored wall. Perspiration ran in zigzagging rivulets down his stomach.

What did he want? What did he need?

Blood.

Twisting his head to fight the inner cries, he banged his skull against the mirror. Refocus the pain. Don't think of the visceral desires grasping for relief. It was not the madness!

The door across the hall swung open and out popped Roxane's head. Illuminated from behind by a beam of moonlight she appeared a goddess, all *fraises et al crème* and palest skin. The darkness would not allow colors but he could verily taste the icy forest in her eyes.

"Gabriel?" She stepped into the hallway. One of his long damask night robes swaddled her shoulders and lithe body. With each step her white chemise slipped in and out of the opening. "What is it?"

When she touched his face he flinched. Seizing her wrist, he pulled her to his body. "Kiss me," he growled. "Quench my thirst."

She didn't twist from his grip, but instead answered his demand for her taste, her mouth, her tongue. So she desired as well. Wicked libertine disguised in virginal white, so demanding corruption.

He drew aside the robe openings and slid a hand over the crisp Holland chemise. Sliding his mouth down her jaw and to her neck, he found the thick vein pulsed madly. Another tease, always a tease.

"No, Gabriel!" Even as she protested she pulled him closer, gripping his shoulders, her fingernails impressing into his flesh.

He clamped a palm softly over her mouth. "I won't bite." He managed a roguish smile. "Trust me?"

She shook her head behind his hand.

"Let me feel you. Smell you." A deep inhale coated his senses with rosemary. "The hunger demands satisfaction. I crave sensation, the sensual, your scent— *mon Dieu*—it makes me mad."

"Don't say that," she whispered.

"Mad for you," he reassured. "You've the scent of the oranges from the theatre on your flesh. Your hands." He licked her palm and reveled in her tiny moan. Not a sound of fear, but of want. "Your throat pulses in salty waves." He slicked his tongue across her throat, over the vein where he forced himself not to pause, to wonder. If he could focus his attention on the woman, the very essence of her, he could overcome the urge to taste darkness on his tongue.

The mirrors amplified their shadowed liaison as he pinned her to the wall outside her open chamber door. He lifted the chemise to her hips and curled his hand toward her mons, which caused her to clamp her thighs to him.

"Gabriel!"

"Don't tell me no." The nest of her curls tickled his wrist. Heat seeped from her body. "Please. I need you, Roxane. I want you."

"I...I want this—but—"

"Don't resist," he whispered into her ear. "Let me play, Roxane. It keeps my mind from other things."

"I am to be but your plaything?"

"No, my wicked vampire slayer. The sensual play."

She gasped as he manipulated a finger into her hot, womanly folds. *Drown here. Bury yourself in her passion, her untapped desire.*

"Oh. What are you doing? Gabriel?"

"Giving you pleasure. Taking my own." He bowed his head and kissed her breasts through the white fabric, all while manipulating that delicious jewel of womanhood that promised maddeningly erotic delights. "Don't ask me to stop."

"I don't want you to stop. Oh, that feels—"

"Good?"

She nodded. "Splendid. But you must not take my blood."

Take the blood!

"Whatever happens, remember that, Gabriel. You cannot drink my blood. Do you promise me?"

"Promises are passé."

"Please!" She gripped his shoulder, steadying herself against his machinations. A slide of his finger deep within her stirred an unbidden whimper from her lips. "You must not."

"You'll allow me to play?"

Her nod sweetened the intensity of his cravings.

"The invitation is implied?"

"Yes. Please. I like what you are doing. I...want more."

He lifted her in his arms and strode into her bedchamber, laying her across the bed. She stretched out across the striped counterpane. Tresses spilled across her décolletage. Illuminated by the moonlight, the white chemise barely covered her mons. Wickedly, she pulled it high to her stomach. He slid a finger into her, working an alchemist's move that promised transformation. Her body reacted by surging up toward him. Her slender legs spread and her knees bent.

"I think we'll dispense with the virginity dilemma this night. What say you?" He flicked out his tongue and touched the pinnacle of her moist folds.

"Oh, Gabriel!"

"I'll take that as an agreement."

The scent of her sex drew him to sup. And her moans clued him that she intended to enjoy his sensory feast.

WAKENED BY THE BRIGHTNESS of morning, Gabriel rolled over and slid his hand to cup the heavy sphere of Roxane's breast. Her nipple hardened as he teased the ruched raspberry morsel. He sucked it into his mouth. Tender ridges hardened against his tongue. The female breast was an exquisite thing, soft, full and tempting, so changing and always touchable. It was a nice thing to place in one's mouth, to lick, to suckle, to nip. He could play with it endlessly and never become bored.

Roxane stirred, stretching an arm and flexing her back, a feline move that lifted her breasts high.

"Thank you," he muttered around her nipple.

"For sacrificing my virginity in the name of your sanity?"

He had pounced upon her in an attempt to quell the aching hunger. Naughty boy. "If truth be told, yes. Regrets?"

"None." She threaded her fingers through his hair. "You are a master, Renan. Your rumored prowess with women has been proven."

"Not so much the swish you suspected?"

"Not in the least."

He blew a hot breath across her breasts and admired the fullness, the beauty of her—*mon Dieu*, but there was a mark between the curves of her breasts. He touched the design. Barely raised, the flesh, like a bruise but not so angry.

Her eyes still closed, Roxane was unaware of his observations as she stretched out a leg and wrapped it across his thighs. "Make love to me again, Gabriel."

This discovery made him uneasy. Should he question? Surely she was not averse to explaining when she lay so exposed before him?

"Lover?"

Perhaps later he would ask. For his thickening cock did not plead for conversation. "I'll have you know that morning usually brings my quick escape from a woman's bed. I find myself in a quandary. How to escape my own house?"

"You wouldn't dare."

"Look what you've done to this infamous rake, you've brought me to heel."

"If that be so then why are you not supping between my legs, rake?"

"The virgin becomes a whore overnight. I love it."

"Perhaps you've unearthed the wanton that was always there? Just waiting for release?"

"You mean like a man waiting for the release of his monster?"

"Don't speak of that. Not now."

"We cannot avoid the inevitable."

"There will be time later to worry, when we are dressed and sipping our morning chocolate."

Yes, and time to speak of this remarkable design dashing between her breasts.

Roxane strolled her fingers down his back, igniting his every sensory reaction. "When I am naked and you are lying next to me I wish only your worship."

"Indeed, she has become a wanton. Your wish is my command, mistress. Do you like this?" He lashed his tongue between her legs.

She moaned with delight, and he returned to feeding his appetite. But this morn was very different than last night. Then he had been trying to quench a different kind of ache. This day, he hungered only for more, more, and more of Roxane Desrues.

GOOD THINGS SO OFTEN MUST END. When Gabriel finally rolled from bed and excused himself to tend a business meeting—creditors to attend—Roxane lingered, trailing her fingers across the cooling sheets where moments earlier he had lain. Turning her head aside she breathed in the aroma of their coupling.

She had made love to the vicomte Gabriel Renan.

Drawing a finger along her thigh she realized the ache between her legs was not simple exhaustion. He had pushed inside of her and claimed her as his own. They had been one. Memory of him above her revisited the heady thrill of orgasm. Her nipples hardened and she spread a hand up her stomach and between her breasts—

"Oh no." She sat abruptly. The mark. He had seen! She hadn't thought to conceal it, so lost in passion she had been.

He hadn't questioned. Was it possible he'd not noticed for the darkness? No, surely this morning he had seen.

"What do you suspect, Gabriel?"

She must tell him. All. Before he made assumptions. But how to do it gently?

AFTER DRESSING AND COMBING HER hair into soft waves, Roxane strolled in to the music room where Toussaint worked on an assortment of items spread out on the floor. He pointed out a porcelain cup on the table, likely placed there in anticipation of her arrival.

Roxane settled in the arm chair and sipped. The warm chocolate was pleasant but a dull comparison to the taste of her lover's kisses. Despite her realization that Gabriel could very well have seen her fire-forged mark, she couldn't get too upset because memory of him, deep inside her body, chased away worry. The image of their embrace throughout the night tingled at her core, and reignited a tiny hum in her mons.

Brazen, she admonished inwardly. *Do not let the valet wonder about your thoughts.*

She observed Toussaint sort through various items he'd lain on the floor before the curvy red velvet divan that sat opposite the piano at the edge of a vast rug. Amorous thoughts of last night fizzled at sight of the inventory.

A massive net, which she could only imagine was used for netting fish—did they throw nets on the Seine? A small iron cross impressed with a fleur de lys, a white linen, which Toussaint sniffed, then with an approving nod folded neatly. The braid of dried garlic gave away his plans.

Did he actually think to repel the vampire? Or to fight him off?

Setting down the cup of chocolate, she knelt on the carpet over Toussaint's cache. No one must interfere. It was imperative that *she* capture Anjou. Alive. "I thought I was the one hunting the vampire?"

"Certainly you are," he said, intent on the items. "It doesn't pay to be unprepared though. Garlic?"

She veered from the proffered bunch of crinkly bulbs. "How do you know these will be effective in repelling the vampire?"

"I am an enthusiast on the occult. Also, I spoke to Mesmer the other day."

She had heard of the charlatan. What could a man who claimed to cure people with magnetism know about vampires? She glanced over Toussaint's array. Apparently, quite a bit.

"See this?" He spread out the netting. "It will drive that bastard silly with vexation."

Granny's grimoire made no mention of the sort. Roxane assumed the vampire Anjou was far too nimble to be netted.

"You won't attempt to approach the vampire without my being there?"

"You think he'll find Gabriel? Come here?"

"He obviously knows one of his victims still walks this earth. That is apparent from the large stain on Gabriel's bedroom floor."

Toussaint swallowed a gulp. "Vex me, but I cannot figure how to remove blood stains. But if the minion is dead—"

"The master yet lives. I am sure he will continue to stalk Gabriel."

"What of your brother?"

Roxane gasped in a breath. "I'm sure Anjou feels no fear from a madman—er, Damian."

"Do you think..." He set down the net and caught his chin in a thoughtful pose. "My soul, I should not ask, but I do wonder."

"Yes?"

"Your brother. You say he resisted the call to drink blood? But do you ever wonder if he drank blood now, if he might..."

Become a vampire? Achieve sanity? One of the two. Preferably the latter.

Roxane clasped her arms across her chest. "I think about it every day, Toussaint."

"You've been through much. And now to have volunteered to keep watch over Gabriel, well, you are quite the woman."

"Perhaps a bit lunatic myself."

"Gabriel does appreciate having you here, I know. He may not show it—"

"Oh, he's shown it." All night long. Backwards, forwards, and a few contortions that now brought a blush to her cheeks. That she had not the mind to realize the ceremonial mark had been exposed! "He is a charmer, that man."

What sort of vampire would Gabriel become? Charming his victims into his arms with a flash of those whiskey brown eyes and a purse of his lips. Bedecked in lace and mystery, he would make an exquisite creature.

And such an inelegant mad man.

"He cares for you."

"I care for him."

"Really?" Toussaint seated himself next to her on the carpet and toed aside the net with a smartly polished leather shoe.

"I...well, there is more beneath the lace and frippery."

"Didn't I tell you?"

"You did."

"He's quite the philanthropist as well."

This information was new. "Philanthropy?"

"Oh yes, your friend Ninon, oh—"

Why that wily rogue! Roxane guessed what Toussaint would not finish. "He's sent money to Ninon, yes? I had thought she looked more cheerful. And she wore a fine dress the last time I saw her."

"I have said too much."

"Why doesn't Gabriel want me to know about his charity?"

"He's very protective of his private matters. A bit to do with his parents' indiscretions."

"He's told me little about them. Has it to do with the opium?"

"Er, yes. Well. He has told you more than usual. The vicomte really does trust you."

"Not enough to reveal more than bits and pieces. Charity is a noble calling. He should not be so humble."

"It's to do with the Leo costume. If those he wished to contribute to knew he was the vicomte Renan, they would reject his money."

"Why?"

"His parents. And don't ask me more. That is for Renan to tell you. He is good, Roxane. But Gabriel has never had anyone tell him he is good."

She rubbed her arms, feeling the shiver bumps rise. Abandoned by parents addicted to a powerful substance. Certainly he must crave attention. And not the vapid, false attention he received through fashion and socializing. How cruel that the vicomte had lost hold of the inner goodness. And now he was trying to be charitable under a guise? Truly, his parents must have been despicable.

"He is a good man," she agreed.

"Then tell him," Toussaint pleaded.

If only she could be completely honest with him. She had initially held back information about herself because she hadn't foreseen a relationship between the two of them. No need to tell one's life story to a man she'd pinned as bait.

The vicomte had become so much more.

"I want this to be over." She toed the iron cross lying on the floor. Small, the size of her palm, a fleur de lys was impressed upon the center of it. Pretty, in an industrial sort of way. "As soon as I've the vampire Anjou in hand, and can—"

"Stake him?"

"—er...yes." First, make him do her bidding. "After."

"After?"

She squeezed her eyelids tightly. She so needed to tell someone. To feel less alone in this mission.

Words spilled from her more quickly than her thoughts. "I need him, Toussaint."

"Gabriel?"

"No, the vampire Anjou."

ᵀFIFTEEN

"I INTEND TO STAKE THE BASTARD through the heart and put an end to his bloody murdering rampage. But first, I need him to help me."

"What?" Toussaint's mouth gaped. "You don't mean to say you're going to *befriend* the fiend?"

"I must if I am to convince him to do what I require."

A grotesque artist could not have carved his stunned look. "And what is it you require?"

"You won't tell Gabriel?"

"Why must it be so secret?"

"I don't want to cause Gabriel any more pain. He's this horrible...condition."

"It's not a condition, it's—"

"Why add another worry to that list?"

Toussaint looked around the room. His eyes widened as he focused on the door behind her, then he looked her directly. "Very well. Tell me, what is it?"

Roxane fingered the braid of garlic. "As you have intimated, I have a suspicion my brother's madness may be reversed if the vampire again bites him and this time Damian accepts the change."

"Is that so?"

She nodded. "It is a horrible thing to put Damian through. Again. But if it will lure him back from madness I must try it. I will trade his insanity for the blood thirst."

Toussaint worried his lower lip. He flashed a look up at Roxane. "Should that not be your brother's choice?"

"Of course it *should* be. But he's not rational enough to make that choice now. I don't want him to suffer in that asylum any longer. It was my fault, Toussaint. If only I had not encouraged him to wait for the full moon."

"But you've done the same with Gabriel—"

"Damian is not the same as Gabriel. My brother had three weeks to wait. As the final days approached he had not the mental strength to endure the trial."

"Roxane, you are playing with evil. That bastard Anjou kills. And to even think to—you are beautiful, yes—but you cannot beguile evil."

"I don't intend to beguile. I will simply befriend it for a day or so."

"How do you think to convince this vampire to travel with you to Bicêtre so he can once again attack your brother?"

"Toussaint."

"I only wish you to face the cold facts. Mademoiselle, this is an immense challenge."

"I'm always up for a challenge."

"Gabriel will not like this."

"He will never know. Toussaint, you promised."

"You don't believe having Gabriel on your side would increase your chances for success?"

"That would be placing the mouse before the lion, Toussaint. I cannot risk Gabriel's life—" She caught herself, her words working faster than her thoughts.

Her original plan had been to use Gabriel to lure Anjou to her. Yet now she could not comprehend using the man as bait. She did not want Anjou to harm her lover. She must continue to protect him from her own stupid plans!

"I have made a bungle of things, Toussaint. Trust that the only way to end it is by myself. I started this. I must finish it."

GABRIEL TIPTOED CAREFULLY from the doorway where he had stood listening to the conversation between the valet and Mademoiselle Desrues. Difficult to believe she had such clandestine plans.

On the other hand, it should not surprise him that Roxane had all this time been using him as a lure to draw Monsieur Anjou closer. So she could befriend him?

Truly, madness had touched not only the brother, but the sister as well.

He pressed at the ache in his temple. He wasn't sure if he was upset because Roxane had been using him, or because a woman he had come to care for had plans to put herself in great danger.

She thought to save her brother by reintroducing the vampire's bite? It seemed a possibility. But Roxane had made no mention of the reasoning behind her plan. What was to guarantee sanity would also be restored with vampirism?

The shuffle of skirts clued him that they had risen. Toussaint's footsteps were comically loud.

Gabriel rushed toward his bed chamber and closed the door behind him as he heard Roxane's voice enter the mirrored hallway.

It was certain the woman would not be detoured from attempting to save her brother's sanity. She would place herself in danger by seeking the vampire Anjou. He could not allow that to happen.

There must be someone else who could help Damian.

He tilted his head and closed his eyes to the shimmer of color beaming in from above. Immediately, the answer came to him. He knew who could help Damian.

Another vampire.

"YOU CANNOT GO OUT, RENAN!"

Gabriel dodged Toussaint's efforts to tug the frockcoat from his shoulders with a deft bend of knee and a skip to the door. "Give it up, Toussaint. I'm leaving. Now stop that. I need to get out. To be alone."

"To put the vampire Anjou on your scent?"

"Come, man! What are the chances of me running into one vampire in a city the size of Paris?"

He slid on smooth kidskin gloves and tugged down the lace rimming his shirt sleeves.

"He knows your haunts. You did hear my conversation with Mademoiselle Desrues earlier, yes?"

"Indeed, I am bait."

"It is not like that."

"Oh? I believe it is very much like that, Toussaint. You heard the woman. She wants to use me to lure the vampire to her, so she can—of all things—*befriend* him."

"So she can then kill him!"

"But not before she risks her neck attempting a foolish rescue of her brother. The vampire will kill her faster than she can blink."

"I believe Mademoiselle Desrues knows what she is doing."

"Do you now? Hell, my own valet has turned against me. That woman, she—No, I won't speak of her anymore. I might wander to the Greve—"

"That is too far!"

"Don't worry, I have protection." He slid aside his coat to reveal the stake, then spread his fingers over the waistcoat he'd chosen, stitched around the hem with crimson and silver threading. "The design is wild roses. Yet another vampire deterrent."

"Yes, but those are merely stitches, not the actual thorn. I don't know..."

"Doesn't matter what you do or do not know, Toussaint, I am off."

"Wait!"

Gabriel strode down the hall and the valet skipped ahead into the kitchen. He reappeared with a bundle of something in his hands and tossed it at him. "At least, take this. It's all I can think of to keep you safe."

He held the knotted ropes up before him. The entirety dropped to his knees in length and stretched as wide as his body. "Fishing net? You plan to net a few fish?" He studied the fine mesh, his interest growing. "Fascinating craftsmanship. How many knots do you suppose are in here?" He began to count.

"Exactly." Toussaint tugged the net from him, balled it up, and stuffed it inside Gabriel's inner coat pocket. "Legend tells vampires are notorious counters."

"This information from Mesmer, as well?"

"Yes. Give them something to tally and they'll forget everything else until all has been counted. Like stones, or beans, or...knots."

"You are brilliant, Toussaint." He tugged a chunk of the net out and ran his fingers over the knots. "One, two..."

"Just go for your walk. And don't get sidetracked by the damned netting. You are *not* a vampire, Renan."

Gabriel tilted a wink at the valet. "Not yet."

GOOD EVENING, MADEMOISELLE. Pardon me while I make an adjustment to the lace about your neck. Ah, there. Just a little nip now...

Gabriel shook his head, obliterating the idiotic thought.

How did a vampire go about attracting victims?

Certainly tact was required. As well, a taste for blood. He didn't think it possible to consider such a palate. On the other hand, of late the strangest things attracted him, such as the rush of blood through a person's veins, or the scent of their fear. *Mon Dieu*, he had gotten hard holding Roxane amongst the pitiful moans and stench of Bicêtre. And he'd taken her last night initially as a means to counteract the insistent cravings.

Did the vampire go about with such heightened perception? Could he instinctively pick out those who would taste the best? Why must the vampire be so cruel? To kill? Was death necessary?

Kicking a stone with the toe of his damask shoe, he wandered aimlessly down the cobbled street. St. Honoré was a quiet, old neighborhood that sat on the edge of the bustling theatre quarter. A notice board, fringed with the remnants of previous posts, advertised nostrums, police orders and a marionette show. Marionettes had appealed to him as a child. He had been fascinated at their dull unblinking stares. Zombies controlled by their masters.

Leave me, Gabriel, mama is in her comfort.

His parents and their comfort. Hell, they were the marionettes that had danced awkwardly through his childhood, wide-eyed and controlled by opium.

After one trip to China the count had returned with a cache of the heinous substance. Juin-Marie had quickly taken to it. *"My Juin-Marie,"* he recalled his father always singing as he'd prance through the estate, his shirt tails untucked and his wig askew. *"I met her in June; I married her in June; I fucked her in June."*

His parents were victims of their addiction. Leave it at that. Put a new foot forward, remember? His life was not miserable. It must not be.

Gold moonlight illuminated the moist cobbles and managed to make the streets a trifle elegant, as if littered with shards from fallen stars.

Skipping across the center gutter glutted with refuse, he made for the Place de Greve, the massive square in front of the city hall.

Well after midnight, the theatre goers had all settled either in salons or were at home packing up their monstrous hairstyles. Lovers were likely engaged in sweaty embraces. It was rumored a majority of children were conceived during the half hour time period when the opera let out, for the sudden swell of noise roused many to a sleepy conjugal coupling.

Such a coupling flashed in his thoughts. He and Roxane had not been sleepy last evening. Rather spirited. He should not have been so worried about deflowering a virgin. She had taken to love making as a well-seasoned courtesan. He enjoyed a woman who did not balk, one who was unafraid to discover the pleasures her body could give her. Or a man's body, for that matter. She had touched him, tentatively, and then more boldly. By sunrise she had been comfortable stroking him, licking him, and nibbling at various rigid body parts.

Pity his affectionate feelings for her had been cooled by the overheard conversation. Was she so callous to use him? Did she not feel anything toward him? Not a morsel of attraction? Or were the feelings so separate that she was unaware she might emotionally wound him with her indifference?

He was hurt. But he was also in for the count—last night had cemented his determination to keep Roxane in his life. How to do that seemed to involve her brother. And the return of Damian's sanity.

The square was quiet. He strode the wide cobbles to the bare gallows erected at the north end. Executions occurred once or twice a week here; it was the ideal location since the city hall looked down upon the square, and it opened onto the Seine and the island. People unable to get close on foot could still have a decent view of the macabre events, even when standing across the river on the island.

Rapping his knuckles on the wooden platform that would bear many guilty—as it had in the past—Gabriel lifted a hip and slid onto the edge, his legs dangling. He leaned back, remarking the absence of a noose hanging from the wooden crossbar overhead. He supposed it wasn't wise to leave the thing hanging when not in use.

Smirking, he stared into the sky. Gray velvet clouds did not touch the moon, as if fearful of her icy glow.

"Bitch," he muttered. "It is all your fault. I lie in wait of your pleasure, fearing, wondering, hating. But soon, yes?"

His pitiful plea went unanswered. Though in his head, he heard Roxane's voice shushing him to a tender silence. *Kiss me again, Gabriel. Make love to me. Touch me there.*

Was he insane to surrender to her allure when he was so close to the end?

Or was it a beginning? He could not decide. Did not want to think on the results should he give in to the blood hunger. It seemed evil. On the other hand, who was he to recognize such?

An ache bit into his ribs. Rolling to his side, he fought against the pain shimmering through his veins. The wooden planks that had seen many a trembling bare foot caressed his cheek. How many hogsheads of blood had been spilled...

He sniffed, scenting the odor that had become his nemesis. *Morbleu*, but he could smell the blood soaked into the boards. He slid his hand across the warped planks and reveled in the bouquet.

The ache in his body burgeoned to a gentle but insistent want. Delicious seduction coiled into his veins with the sure touch of a seasoned courtesan. He relaxed, released a sigh.

Why must he wait out the moon? Why not surrender to this delicious ache? He had no such religious morals that would keep him from a fall. Cecil and Juin-Marie had never been concerned for his salvation. Now was too late to seek divine intervention, not when the call to hunger echoed so sweetly within his being.

"It is truly divine, yes?"

Startled upright, Gabriel jerked his head around to spy the man who had approached without sound. Scrambling for protection, he pulled the stake from inside his coat.

"Back off, Anjou."

The vampire bowed grandly and took a graceful step back. Courtly, yes, but sans wig this evening. Coal-dark curls capped his head and spilled across red velvet shoulders.

"You can scent the blood of centuries past, yes? Does not death smell rich to you? Like fruiting bodies buried within the fibers of the wood their souls breed and live on, attracting—"

Gabriel jumped from the gallows and, wielding the stake as if a spear, approached the man. "How did you find me?"

"You are not difficult to track. Especially with my essence coursing through your veins."

He winced at such a notion. Had this man marked him? *He had wanted to swoon.* If only the bite had not had such mixed sexual connotations, perhaps it would be easier to accept his fate.

"Why didn't you finish with me?" he asked. "Why leave me this terrible choice between madness and murder?"

"I wasn't given a choice." Still wearing the extravagant red frockcoat littered with stiff gold threading, Anjou toed the base of the gallows. "If you'll remember, that damned valet of yours beat me away with a stick. I should have torn out the man's throat, but there was too great a risk."

"And so now you've come to finish me?"

Gabriel lowered the stake. Surrender would obliterate the difficult choice he faced. Could he do it?

The future offered much to one who possessed immortality.

With a decisive nod, he tossed the makeshift weapon and it clattered hollowly across the cobbles. Spreading his arms out, he revealed himself, opening wide to the future he wanted to face. But only if *she* loved him.

Can you love someone you cannot trust with the truth?

"Do it then," he said.

Anjou strolled before the empty gallows. Moonlight and mirth glittered in his eyes. "Sorry to disappoint, but I prefer a challenge. A fight, you see. Struggle draws the blood to the surface and brews it to a delicious bubble, much like champagne."

"Damn you!" Gabriel shuffled in his pockets for another weapon—why had he not brought Leo's walking stick—but produced only the tangle of netting. "This idiot net!"

"What is that?"

He flung it at Anjou, perturbed that he'd allowed Toussaint to send the thing with him. The vampire caught it and held it above his head.

"Oh, you are a cruel one, vicomte. One, two, three..."

Nothing more. No threat, no cruel command over his soul. Not even a lunge for his neck. The vampire stood there, running his fingers over the mesh of knots.

"That really works?"

The vampire nodded. "Damn you!"

Compelled by the twist of knots, so many of them, and all uncounted, Gabriel lifted an end of the netting and lowered his head to the task beside Anjou. "It is a lovely bit of knotwork, isn't it?"

"Don't interrupt, I'm on...damn, now I have to start over. Why are you out alone this night? My spies report you have the woman guarding your every footstep. One..."

"...seventeen, eighteen— I needed some time to think about my choices. Nineteen. Must you kill? Can a vampire be good? Twenty, twenty-one..."

Anjou propped a hip against the gallows, his fingers moving precisely over the network of knots. "Goodness and evil are two like things."

"Blasphemy. Thirty. Oh hell, what am I doing? I don't need to count this!" He flung away his end of the net and shoved up to sit on the edge of the gallows. His heels beat the base of the wooden structure. "You murder your victims. Is it necessary? Why not drink from them and leave?"

"I could. But I prefer a long drink. Reduces the need to feed frequently. Generally one does not survive after having so much blood extracted. I once seduced then left. Now, I do my pretties a favor by completing the transaction."

"But if a vampire were not to kill..." Gabriel leaned back and pressed his palms to the platform. "How to ensure you do not leave those victims like me, ready to change?"

"There are ways to drink and not taint the victim with the vampire's saliva."

"Saliva? That is what facilitates the change?"

"I guess."

"You guess?"

"There is not a course in basic vampire function. I had not a mentor, nor would I have desired one. I do as I wish. I serve the addiction exactly as it demands."

Gabriel jerked his head up at that word. "Addiction? T-to the blood?"

"Oh dear no, to love, my good man. The love!"

"Love?" He winced. Addiction and love were two words that should never be paired. Why was it every step he took led him to a place of addiction? He wanted to be far away from the debilitating loveless condition!

Anjou muttered a string of numbers. "You will be loved."

Impossible.

But he could not resist hearing the vampire's reasoning. "How so?"

Anjou shrugged and rattled off another number. "The look in their eyes. The pining. That is love in the moment, pulsing with need. Irrefutable. Immediate. Love."

"You speak nonsense."

Dark eyes void of sparkle turned on Gabriel. "You loved me, yes?"

"No."

"Truth."

"I thought you..."

"Yes?" He leaned toward him. Gold threading scraped Gabriel's knee. "I felt you pull me closer, vicomte."

"It wasn't like that."

"Not sexual, no, but real. For that moment, you loved me."

There was a difference between romantic love and an abiding love for friends and family. He could buy into the nonsexual love excuse. "Maybe so."

What power the vampire had, to harvest love with but a kiss? Could it really be so close at hand? The love he had always desired?

"One hundred and seven, one hundred and eight..."

To gain such emotion—such as Gabriel had felt at the moment of his attack—would that appease the emptiness in his heart? What of the trade? The good for the bad?

"So, feasibly—" he started, "A vampire could take blood from someone, and that person would not be at risk to become a creature himself?"

"Yes, yes." Anjou waved off the remark. "But why bother? Why dilute the glory? The vampire is not a saint; he is a creature. A splendid beast."

"You must kill so many."

"A few a month," Anjou offered with a shrug. "They are not missed."

"They are certainly missed. The *Mercure de France* reports their absences. You choose young, aristocratic men who have families. Why not a beggar or an orphan?"

Anjou shrugged. "I like them pretty. And clean."

Gabriel cringed at the reference. "I am not pretty."

"Oh yes, you are. Your face beholds an elegant bone structure and your eyes speak without words. Noble, most definitely, though I do know you've not a drop of noble blood in your body. The Countess Renan pandered her title from the king."

All of Paris knew as much. Another reason Gabriel kept far from court, for the king no longer held Juin-Marie in high accord. The man knew his true identity? Damn.

"Those sad, glittering eyes," Anjou said. "Your gaze literally does pierce, *mon ami*." Net in hand, he beat a fist against his chest. "Straight to the heart."

"Enough. I do not subscribe to your penchant for the equal sex."

"Oh, I do not limit myself. Women, men, they are much the same when it comes to the delicious red elixir flowing in their veins. You..." Anjou reached to touch Gabriel's chin "...were too pretty to resist. Oh!" He recoiled and redirected his attention. "Lost count again! Damned bloody net! One, two..."

Gabriel stroked the spot where Anjou had touched him and recalled the intense desire to pull the man close, to surrender to his commands when he'd been bitten. A hideous twist on his sexual leanings. *You wear my scent.* It made him shudder.

"Do it," Anjou said quickly between counts. "Take a woman. Use a dagger and slash a fine cut along her throat to drink from her. Leave her in a swoon to awake without memory of your visit."

"That will suffice? She won't remember I've been there?"

"Seems to be the case in my experience. Without the bite, the toxins that begin the change are not introduced. Or that is my determination. But once you sink your teeth into them, there is no turning back. Unless you seal the wound with your saliva. Thirty-two, thirty-three..." He paced before Gabriel, meticulously fingering the net. "There is also the thrall."

"Thrall?" Mesmer had told Toussaint a vampire could enthrall a witch.

"If you put your victim in a thrall they wake with no memory of your..." Anjou looked up from his counting to smear a greasy smile across his face— "...extraction."

"How does this thrall work? Tell me."

"Why? Have you plans to make any *changes* soon?"

"No. I—tell me or I will stake you."

"You do not threaten me, vicomte. Of course, the pretty ones never do."

Gabriel stopped Anjou's pace with the end of the stake to his chin. "This thrall. Explain."

"Very well." He clutched the netting and tilted it toward Gabriel as if to say *do you mind? I must tend to this.* "It is a mind thing. You step into the victim's thoughts and...relax them. Make them promises you don't intend to keep. It is not so much that I can explain how it is done; one simply needs to attempt it. I believe it is an innate vampire quality. You couldn't do it as you are. A mere pretty mortal."

Anjou turned and strode to the side of the gallows where the dark concealed the steps up to Hell, but also away from interruption.

"Why are you suggesting this? I thought you wanted me dead?"

"I do! Damn it!"

So long as Anjou held the netting he could not attempt a murder, so compelled he was to count. The notion was ludicrous, yet effective.

"How would you do it?"

"Do what?" Anjou spat, his fingers twisting into the net.

"Kill me."

The vampire jerked up his head. Rage tightened his features. He flung away the net, then dove for it, clutching and tugging at the nemesis he could not shuck.

"I would break your bloody neck!" he hissed. "No." His voice softened and his rage slipped as if rain from his shoulders. "First, I would drink from your succulent neck. I would drink so much you would slip close to death, dance a quadrille with the Old Lad Himself in your dreams." He twisted a look at Gabriel, smiling the death's head grin that only evil could smile. "I would tease you. Play with your life. Then..." He straightened, his concentration fixed to the net, but his thoughts obviously on rich plans. "...I would make you mine. A delicious partner of the night. Damn you!"

Gabriel backed from the simmering beast.

"I love you," came out on a sigh, and the vampire worked a few knots across his fingertips. "You must do it. Take the blood. Then come to me."

Shaking his head, Gabriel could not summon resistance. His body repulsed against the antics of this creature, but his mind, well, that was something else entirely.

"The advantages," Anjou explained calmly, "far outweigh the evils. How old do you think I am?"

Much as he should forego further conversation with a bloodthirsty creature, the compulsion to learn as much as he could riveted him there.

Gabriel splayed a hand up and down the man's attire. "Is that horrid frockcoat yours?"

"Culled from a victim many decades past my prime. I was born in 1551."

"Impossible."

"Over two centuries, boy. You mark my words. I have lived and I have learned. And what I have learned is that living is better than dying."

The man lied. Immortality did not exist. It fell into the same category as witchcraft—a fantasy concocted by an unhealthy mind. Gabriel dismissed the idiot with a wave of his hand. "Insane."

"No—Twenty-three..." Anjou nodded upward. "She is the only one to grant insanity. The blood gives life, get that straight. Dare you risk a showdown with *la Luna*? Why not surrender to my offer? I will make you such a delicious *mignon*."

"Be gone with you. Kill me now or be killed!"

"Think of what the centuries can give you, vicomte. I live. You haven't begun to scratch the surface of life. You've experienced the enhanced senses?"

He nodded.

"It is always like that. You can hear their blood, and taste it on your tongue before it spills from their veins. There are other things. Tricks. Skills."

"Like what?"

Anjou turned down to his counting, beginning again with one. This time he simply did not answer.

Vampirism, splendid? Perhaps. He'd considered as much, especially if it would allow him to walk through the centuries.

I've been using him as bait.

What else had Roxane protected him from for naught? Protecting him as a means to rescue her brother.

He strode past Anjou, his path for home.

I want to help my brother. Only the vampire can do that.

A decision came to him in the final strides that took him up the stairs to his house and down the mirrored hallway past Roxane's room. Tonight he would take control of his own destiny.

HALF AN HOUR AFTER THE VICOMTE had stridden out of the Place de Greve those living in the apartments that bordered the execution square were woken from restful sleep by the sudden and joyous outburst, "Six hundred and seventy two!"

Sixteen

A VIOLENT STITCH IGNITED IN GABRIEL'S side as he dashed toward the house. Swaying, he landed sprawled before the door, cringing against the peculiar sensation. Blood pounded in his ears and veins. It moved through his body as if fire, stabbing from within, swinging at him with Satan's spiked mace.

The stone step, cold and moist from evening dew, ground into his forehead. He'd fallen in the center of the chalk hex mark. Pawing at his jabot he managed to loosen what had become a choking hold of Alençon lace. *Morbleu*, but he'd never wear the stuff again. Croaking out a gasp, he tugged at the ties and opened his shirt wide. He shrugged off his frockcoat from one arm, but another spasm rocked him. Slapping his palms on the stone he closed his eyes tight against the pain.

Not the madness. I do not want that. I cannot. I will not. I will...

...take the blood!

And when he opened his eyes and breathed out a heavy exhale the world grew silent. Overhead, the sooted drain spouts dripped moisture. The moon moved steadily to her zenith. Still, and now pain free, he stared at the chalk design beneath his palms. His struggles had marred the white patterns. Squinting to study the design, he wondered: Similar to the pattern on Roxane's breasts? Curious. She had crossed this threshold many a time. A witch could not— Not that he gave any credence to Toussaint's silly ravings.

He touched a line of the hex mark. It had been there so long it had become as if paint on the stone. No shock of repulsion, nor did he feel like cringing and scampering off. The symbol had no power over him. It merely served a means to comfort a superstitious soul.

Above him loomed his nemesis.

"You think a little pain is going to defeat me?" he spat at the wide white moon.

Another spasm coiled his belly tight, twisting his innards until finally a shriek of surrender escaped.

"Very well," he huffed, defeated. "Very fucking well."

He could endure the pain. But...did he want to?

You think you are so miserable? You haven't begun to scratch the surface of life.

No, he had not. And now? Was there time to begin?

A vampire? Him?

"Everyone expects me to be bad. To be the rake. To make the wrong choices."

He turned and sat, his back against the door. He wanted time. He wanted...life. He wanted to help Damian Desrues.

Should he?

"*Aux grands maux les grands remedies,*" he whispered. To desperate evils, desperate remedies.

"Vampirism *is* a deliciously bad choice."

But he could not forget that Anjou had labeled it an addiction. He did not want what his parents had.

You can have love.

How he desired love, attention.

Just...*see me*, he thought. *I don't want to stand in the shadows.* Life as a night creature would pound the cruelest nail to his desires.

Though Roxane had said vampires could walk in the daylight.

Roxane. Celadon and strawberries and cream. He wanted her to be happy. Yet she could not rise above sadness so long as Damian remained locked up. Gabriel could not guess if Roxane's plan to have her brother re-bitten would be successful. But it made a strange sort of sense.

An acute flare of pain in his breast burned as if a poker withdrawn from his heart. Growls curdled in his throat, but he did not care, in fact he howled like a wild beast, feeding his courage the demand to continue.

This night he would seize Fate by the throat, crack it in two, and suck out the blood.

Standing, he kicked open the front door and strode inside.

"Renan?" Toussaint stood on the bottom stair, silver candle snuffer in hand and a wisp of smoke curling out from its bell-shaped head. Panic widened his eyes. "Is something wrong?"

"Nothing at all." He shrugged the frockcoat from his shoulder and let it fall at his feet. Kicking it aside, he raked his fingers through his hair and strode forward. He needed sustenance. He needed—to take control of his life. "Where is she?"

Toussaint stepped aside to allow him a wide berth. The valet shook the frockcoat and sorted through the inner pockets. "Your stake? It is gone."

"Dropped it," he called down as he made way up the stairs. Then a thought occurred. The valet should be elsewhere. He turned back and approached Toussaint.

"The fishing net as well?"

"Too damned frustrating," he replied. Taking the coat and tossing it over his arm, Gabriel draped the other arm around Toussaint's shoulder. "She is home?"

"Yes, but—"

"Marvelous. I've a favor to ask of you, Toussaint. It needs to be done immediately, and I won't take no for an answer."

Inside the office a lacquered set of drawers held the business papers for the estate. He pulled open a drawer and drew out the key to his money box.

"Take two thousand livres from the safe and carry it to Monsieur LaLoux tonight."

"But—"

"No protests. You'll find him at the Palais Royale—"

"It is well after midnight!"

"I know for a fact the gambling den in the dungeon is open into the wee morning hours. The whores arrive and depart as if it is their own private boudoir."

"Why the urgency? You've owed Monsieur LaLoux for months. I thought you'd decided the Dutch investment wasn't sound?"

Gabriel shrugged and gifted Toussaint with a genial smile. "I have decided to put my affairs in order. There is not much time left."

"Don't say things like that. Can't this wait until morning?"

He smirked at the valet's resistance. "Like it or not, Toussaint, I may have mere hours before things drastically change."

"The moon is nearly full. By tomorrow night for sure. You will succeed!"

"Success has no definition for me. Survival is more important. Now go. I will not abide your returning until Monsieur LaLoux holds the coin in his hand."

Toussaint stared at the key in Gabriel's palm. "That is a very lot of coin to travel the streets—"

"I trust you will be safe."

"What of you, Renan?"

He hooked his hands at his hips. "I know you worry for me, Toussaint; there is no need. Whatever should come of my morbid situation, I am prepared."

"Y-you are?"

"I am." And he spoke the truth. Every fiber of his being felt it. His conversation with Anjou had introduced a new perspective. "Be on to the task, Toussaint. Do not set foot in this house until I am two thousand livres poorer, understand?"

Toussaint nodded, and with a sigh, began to count out coin.

Gabriel spun to catch a palm against the wall by the stairs. He closed his eyes, fighting the blaze of hunger that rippled through his heart. Clutching his chest he clenched his teeth. His heart? What an odd place for the sensation. And yet, where else should the craving for blood birth?

He could smell her. To the right and four long strides down the hall. Her scent teased as if he'd opened a perfume bottle beneath his nose.

Biting the inside of his cheek, he redirected the pain. But the scent of blood sweetened his decision. He wanted more. And he would have it.

The front door closed and Gabriel did not wait for the click of Toussaint's heels down the steps. He strode down the hallway and spied the light in the music room.

Moonlight flooded the room, illuminating it with a magical white glow. A stage set, waiting for prancing actors.

The audience would not be bored this night.

Roxane had commandeered a candle and lay sprawled across the red velvet divan, a heavy volume of Diderot's Encyclopedia open on her lap. So intent in the book, she did not look up to acknowledge his presence.

Perturbed, he bit back a demand. *See me.*

Quieted by the eerie lighting, he strolled forward, noting moonlight splashed the pianoforte, the violin, the crystal candelabra centre of the arched ceiling. He scanned the darkened perimeter of the room for faces, the audience. Did anyone see him?

They will love you.

Mischievousness sprung loose, and he landed gracefully at the end of the divan, settling upon the hem of Roxane's green skirt. She did not move. And so he leaned forward. Her peripheral vision could not disregard him.

"I am jealous."

"Of what?" she said. A delicious smile tickled her soft pink mouth. She saw him.

"The moonlight romances you," he said. "You have never looked more gorgeous than now." Perhaps it was that moonlight flooded his senses, teasing him with its power. "*La Luna* beautifies you and only torments me." He stared across the expanse of marble glittering beneath his feet. A sigh opened the emotion so oft fettered. "I am concerned, Roxane."

"How so?"

"With the fact this madness you claim will be mine has yet to even tickle my senses. Are you so sure of yourself? What proof have you beyond your brother? Might he have been a lark? Perhaps the madness had been lurking in Damian's soul for ages?"

"How dare you!"

"And with the vampire's bite it was released?" He turned and placing a knee between her legs hovered over her, pinning her from struggling free. The book slid to the floor. Blood coursed through his system, firing his vigor and emboldening his manner. "Perhaps you want what the vampire can give you? Everlasting life. Is that what you want from me, my pretty country rustic?"

"Gabriel, you are mad!"

He caught her wrist. "You are the mad one, woman."

"You are hurting me! Please," she managed. Her bare foot slid along his leg, the fine silk hose would not allow her purchase.

He tightened his grip on her wrist. The pain distorting her face fascinated him. Intention drew his study to her mouth, tight and slightly parted.

"You tremble, lover. Is it me you fear?"

She shook her head negatively, but gasped when he squeezed her wrist. The sound of her pain—small and contained—intrigued. He drew closer, lingering but a kiss from her face. Pants hushed across his chin, his nose. Her eyes flickered between his. He could feel her heartbeats racing madly in the palm of his hand. The scent of life—so frightened—shimmered upon his tongue.

"Gabriel..."

Gripping her other wrist, he pinned them both high over her head upon the arm of the divan.

"You give that damned book more regard than you do me. You did not even lift your head when I entered the room. Why is that?"

"I assumed it was Toussaint," she gasped. "Forgive me—"

"You were in your comfort," he spat.

"No. I—Gabriel, please!"

The volume of her shriek snapped a twig inside his brain. *Wrong. Pain. No.*

He released her wrists and pushed up. Turning and pacing he scrubbed fingers over his scalp, fighting at the inner call to leap, to simply...succumb.

Distance yourself. Avoid yet another woman's comfort.

His pace echoed across the marble floor. Passing the pianoforte, he pounded his fist upon the surface, setting the blue violin to a teeter and a boxy metallic chord vibrating into the moonlit air. Absently sliding his palm along the sensuous line of the massive instrument, he moved around the curved end, leering at the woman who clutched her wrist. A leap would place him upon her.

A bite would make her his.

He turned and pressed his forehead to the lacquered pianoforte. It felt as though tears poured from his eyes, but he could not cry. He had never cried. He did not know how. Tears never won attention; he had learned that early on.

The soft *schush* of satin brushed his calf. A gentle touch slid down his arm and traced the top of his palm.

Why did she care? Why did she not run from the room, abandoning him to his misery?

Why was this woman so difficult to expel to the ranks of his miserable past?

"Don't tell me it is because of the moon that I rage," he said, his head still down.

"Will you let me hold you?"

She was blind to the beast inside him. Thank God.

Surrendering an overwhelming need to pour out his pain, Gabriel lifted himself from the pianoforte, and going to his knees before Roxane, pressed the side of his face to her belly. Rosemary and a trace of cinnamon. Already she belonged to his soul, like a favorite scent that he ever relied on for security. He wrapped his arms about her hips and clung like a man lashed to the mast in a storm. He pressed against her body, wanting to step inside the woman and lose himself.

And he began to shake, his shoulders trembling and his body hiccupping as he cried a tearless storm into her embrace.

She did not say a word. She did not coo or whisper soft reassurances, as a loving mother should. Not that Gabriel would know the mien of a loving mother; he could only guess. Instead she stood there, tall, straight, her hands upon his shoulders, accepting his pain. Without question.

And for that moment he did not scent the cloying odor of temptation, nor did he gauge the beats of life pulsing her veins. He merely was. And the feeling, so different, so unique to his history, lightened him.

She did not want to use him for her own gain. She wanted to save another man who desperately needed that help. And only a vampire could provide the catalyst.

This woman is nothing like you have ever known.

Nor would he know anything like her again. He mustn't lose her.

"Forgive my accusation. You would never ignore me for your comfort. It is just that I am accustomed to the like."

"Tell me about it, Gabriel." Her hand stroked his forehead, soothing. "Release it. Is it your parents?"

He nuzzled into her skirts. A sigh released memories. "They called it their comfort. The result of eating opium. The high that sailed them to the clouds, and then nestled them in a languorous reverie. Cecile and Juin-Marie were addicted. Nothing in the world mattered, save their precious comfort. Not even their son."

Roxane's fingers strode softly over his forehead and he turned his face into her palm. *Safe here.*

"She tried, my mother. In this very room. She would recline on that daybed, so oblivious—as you were just now. The opium took hold quickly, capturing her no matter my attempts to win her attention."

"The violin?" she whispered.

He nodded. "I used to imagine, as I played, that the smile on mother's lips was for my music. I possess the keen ability to fool myself into believing most anything."

"I am sure they loved you."

"Yes. So much so, that they left me. Abandoned for the quest. They could no longer remain in Paris, for father had insulted the king. Far as I know they are in the Americas, lost somewhere in the dregs of their comfort."

"How old were you?"

"Old enough. I had returned from the Grand Tour. You may think I should have been capable of seeing to myself. Hell, they left me a fortune gained from the sale of opium overseas. That is why I try to every day give it away. Impossible though. The Renan name is spat upon in respectable circles. No one of import will associate with me, not even for my parents' money. The salons I attend as Leo? Outcasts and former courtiers who have fallen from grace, yet still live for the fantasy of acceptance."

Pressing his cheek against her stomach he held her endlessly. To have spilled it so quickly, and neatly, shocked and surprised. Was it so easy as that to release the past?

But that day, the last day he'd ever looked into his mother's eyes, was not easily put into words. How long had he stood before the closed door following his parents' cold and final retreat? Stiff and stunned, he could precisely recall the tightness of his fists, balled at his thighs, as he stared at the door.

"*Adieu*, my son," Juin-Marie had said, then kissed him on the forehead.

Adieu. Go with God. A final parting.

When Toussaint had finally roused him from his frozen state, Gabriel had literally fallen into the valet's arms and allowed him to walk him upstairs to his bed chamber. He had not heard from either since. He did not care. Did he?

"Roxane, I have to ask you something."

"Gabriel, I—"

"I want to know, I need to know—Can you love me?"

"What?"

Levering up by the pianoforte, he cupped her chin in his palm. "I must know."

"Well, I...oh."

He swept his tongue across her lips, tasting red wine. From the Renan private vintage, bottled deep in the lush valleys of Provence. He could taste the raspberries that had pushed up from the soil before grapevines had ever been planted in the field. The earth, rich and moist, and the spring rain that plundered the hard grape buds and the sun that sweetened and ripened them to a fat, rich fruit.

But the wine did not come close to the taste of Roxane's blood. It could not.

You put them in a thrall. It is a mind thing...

He must know.

"You want me to love you?" she whispered against his mouth. Celadon crinkled to concern and she touched his mouth with a finger.

He licked her skin. The acrid taste of the glue used between the book's pages lingered, and beneath that a saltiness. And underlying that the pulse of hot, thick blood. Tension coiled in his chest. The hunger would not be so easily put aside.

The moon is soon full. You've but to wait it out. You do want a normal life.

Yes, normality. Domesticity. This woman by his side. Constancy.

You have finished a marvelous rage and you think now of simple pleasures?

"C-could you love me if I was a madman?" The curve gracing her lips smoothed. "Could you? Would you visit me every day at Bicêtre?"

"Don't say things like that, Gabriel."

"It is what the imminent future holds."

"No, you are strong. You will—"

"And what if I am not strong? What if I succumb? You see I slip into the rage so easily." She pushed from his embrace but he skipped around in front of her. "Roxane, could you love a vampire? A man who craves your blood and cannot be happy unless he is sucking at your neck?" Again he pulled her into a tight embrace. Tension made her curves hard against him; she did not want to surrender, to fit into him. "Can you imagine what it must be like? Two people sharing their blood. Like a sort of dark communion of the souls."

"Gabriel, don't, you cannot—"

"I can do whatever I please, Roxane. Do you love me? Tell me true."

"I...could..."

He pushed his fingers through her hair. Illuminated in paleness, those thick satin lips parted in a weak cry. Trailing kisses down her chin and neck, he kissed hard at the pulsing vein.

"Don't be foolish, Gabriel. You will make it to the moon. You can do it."

"What if I prefer to follow the night?"

"F-follow the night?" With but a twist of her shoulders she freed herself from his hold. Roxane started toward the door, backwards, facing him to—keep the predator in sight? "You romanticize the vampire!"

"Where are you going? Do you flee from me?"

She stopped in the doorway, her fingers clinging to the gilded chair rail. "You have no idea what it will be like to become a killer—"

"Where do you obtain your information on vampires? Tell me." He stalked across the room. Each step pushed her out and into the hallway. She was fleeing him!

He rushed forward. "You believe they are evil and wicked. Do you imagine I could become so evil? Look at me, Roxane. My veins are lined in lace!" And comprehension voiced itself. "I would make the most incredible vampire."

To finally voice it gave power to the entreaty. Yes. The vicomte Gabriel Baptiste Renan, a vampire.

Shuffling up the steps to the mirrored hallway, Roxane pressed herself to the wall.

Gabriel followed at a sure pace.

"You overwhelm me, Gabriel. I cannot imagine things like that. I only want to—"

"To hide from me?"

Dare he bring up the overheard conversation? It would force her to be truthful with him.

"I do want to love you, but I cannot consider it until Damian is—"

"Is what?"

"Shows signs of recovery."

"You honestly believe your brother can recover from madness?" Could he find her truth in the depths of those moistened eyes? *I want to be the ice king, reigning within her ice-forest eyes.*

"Damian is the world to me, Gabriel."

"Indeed."

No crown of icicles for him this day. A strong and determined woman, Roxane would not bring him into her plot to befriend the vampire Anjou.

But he could be stronger for her.

He rushed ahead of her and opened the door to her bed chamber. Her eyes darted from the doorway, a dash to her sanctity. Sensing her trepidation he stepped from the doorway. She slid around and inside.

She was frightened of him!

You do not want to frighten, you want to seduce.

Roxane stood inside the doorway. The guest chamber was dark, the velvet curtains pulled before the windows to keep away the moon, the vicious temptress. Gabriel literally swayed with the rage. A violent rage. A pitiful rage. A tempting rage of madness, sadness, and desperation she could not disregard.

He hadn't moved from the spot outside her door. He remained, listening, waiting. She could verily feel his wicked desire current through the air.

He'd frightened her. Her wrist ached—by morning a bruise would show. But she could not close the door. The vicomte's parents had abandoned him in the quest for unnatural satisfaction. No wonder he desperately craved attention.

Drawing in a deep breath, she exhaled. With that breath she released apprehension and fear. And found deep within, the desire. This man struggled with a force far greater than the two of them combined.

Lifting her head, she nodded. Gabriel's hand slid across hers and she led him inside her room. Into the darkness, and into her soul.

Seventeen

GABRIEL FOLLOWED ROXANE TO the bedside where she lifted the tinder box to light a candle. He placed a hand over hers. "No."

The action of them setting the box on the table together upset a crystal vase of flowers. He bent to pluck up a shard of clear glass and set it on the table.

"I'll help you."

"No need. Toussaint will get it in the morning. Just step carefully."

Her breaths came quickly. Gabriel relaxed as well as a man can relax when his heart was pounding and the inner screams for blood tormented. Fisting one hand to his stomach he strained against the cries for relief. *Concentrate on the woman.* Scent of rosemary. Eyes so pleading and open.

She slid onto the bed and extended her arms to invite him. Tugging the shirt over his head, he dropped it over the glass shards and the scattered flowers, and climbed onto the bed.

Intent in her own desires, Roxane's fingers worked the buttons on his breeches. His cock strained for release. As did the hunger. His head tucked to the curve of her neck, Gabriel gritted his jaw.

"Put it from your thoughts," she whispered. Buttons released, his heavy organ thumped upon her stomach. "Think only of now. The two of us." She kissed the side of his forehead and lured him to kiss her mouth. He bulleted kisses down her jaw and along her soft as talcum neck. *Beware the pulse.* He did not veer where he knew the thick vein pulsed close to the surface. As well, beware the tiny vial suspended on the delicate chain. It slipped over her shoulder and landed on the sheets. The urge to toss it across the room, dispel any hint of danger, was not there. Bring on the challenge!

So hot, her flesh, oozing rosemary, woman, and the sweetest taste of perspiration. He dashed his tongue along the crisp lace that guarded her treasures like a crenellated battlement. There were no ties in front of this stiffened bodice, a trap of satin and stitches.

"Turn over," he urged, and pressed a trail of fervent kisses over her shoulder and back of her neck, as he worked at the laces paralleling her spine.

Ribbons zinged through threaded grommets as he hastily unloosed her restraints, unstringing an instrument so he may command her song. The final grommet set free the laces and the whole bodice slid from her body. Roxane slipped her arms from the sleeves and rolled to her back. Flushed cheeks and parted lips drew him to drink from her mouth. Heaven on earth. Drown within this woman. Float? No, not if it meant a struggle. He must release, surrender to her allure.

Pulling open the ties of her thin chemise revealed her breasts. Pebbled nipples teased his fingers to pinch and roll. So hard, his cock. He adjusted his hips, allowing it to slide between her legs, all heat, moist and inviting.

"So luscious." He cupped her breasts. With an expert move, she directed his cock into her moist folds. Enveloped by hot woman, Gabriel knew he should be concerned with something—ah, his climax approached swiftly.

Roxane seduced him without suspecting his inner torment. Hunger called strongly. It demanded to be fed. And as his seed filled her, he fought the urge to take her body—and blood.

MOONLIGHT PAINTED A COLORLESS swath across Roxane's stomach. She lay, eyes closed, arms splayed carelessly above her head, nested in the pillows. Relaxed, unfettered by concern. Basking.

Gabriel gauged the tension tracing his muscles. He had come and so had she. But while he should be basking alongside her, the hunger had only grown.

"You are an exquisite lover, Gabriel. You own me with your kisses."

"I like the sound of that—owning you." Gripping the sheets in tight fists, he glanced at the night table. A shard of glass sparkled beneath the candle glow. "I must own you again."

"Yes." She touched his hand. "Here," she whispered, and placed his hand over her mons. He slid his finger over her delicate folds to the exquisite peak of her pleasure. Hot and plump, it was primed for command. And so he instructed her body to follow, deeper into the bliss and the darkness that would shield her eyes from the truth of the moment.

Gasps and moans quickened his pulse. Wicked, he who sought to deceive, to disguise. *To take the blood.*

Slave to his manipulations, Roxanne shivered, close to release. At that moment he held her in a sexual vice surely unlike the vampire's thrall. Or was it similar?

A glint of moonlight alerted. He picked up a shard and pressed the glass inside his palm to judge the edge sharp—

—then tore it across Roxane's wrist.

He bent and pressed his mouth over the gash. Blood oozed between his lips. Sweeter than he had imagined. Not at all foul.

"What...what are you—no!" Roxane's struggles upset his hold, but he persisted. Her fingers clasped his hand. "Gabriel, no, this is folly!"

He licked the blood from his lips. "There is no other I choose to help me change. Don't struggle, Roxane, I won't harm you." He pinned down her shoulder. Her bloody fingers clutched at the satin counterpane. "Relax. You're so close. Come into me. Let me take you over the edge."

"No, Gabriel, you must not!"

He persisted in stroking her, coaxing her. She struggled between surrender and the fight that would not be defeated.

Bending her hand down and lifting her wrist he fastened his mouth to her life. A delicious future waited. The vicomte Renan would follow the night.

Roxane's blood harbored sweetness, yet it also tasted like he'd bitten the rim of a copper platter, and of pain and sorrow, and so much darkness. He drew it in like a desert wanderer in need of moisture.

"You cannot..."

While he took he also gave. Her body jerked violently, answering the call of his sensual command. Orgasm surfed through her, stiffening every limb, then, as quickly, relaxing her into oblivion.

"My blood," she murmured.

He moved his hand over her mouth, not wanting to hurt, only to chase away her protests. She bit his finger. He pressed harder. "Trust I will not harm you. I love you."

And all the while he sucked at her wrist, drinking full and deep from her life. And in a moment of lucid awareness he realized that if he drank too much she might die.

"I am..." Roxane whispered. "...so sorry."

"Do not regret," he said. "Regret is not a part of life. This night I begin to live."

Blood coated his hands and trickled down his chest. He glided his fingers through the slick crimson and licked them clean. No aversion.

A manic chuckle burst from his lips and he smiled a grand and wicked smile. He had done it!

What have you done?

"I have lost the battle to freedom," he announced. "Again. No pity, no regret. Bring on the night. Open the world's veins to my lips. I must admit, I rather favor the taste. Roxane?"

Grasping her bleeding wrist she rolled toward him on the bed. Shock widened her eyes. He had not asked permission. But had he not done it with the consideration of a master?

"You should not have..." Her tongue was heavy, made drunk by the throes of passion and loss of blood. "You are not dead?"

"Why in Hades would I be? I've taken the plunge, my pretty vampire slayer. Will you now uncork your precious vial and send me to my grave?"

"This blood..." She clasped the vial lying on the bed sheets.

Both focused on the jiggle of crimson inside the narrow glass vial. Would she do it?

"It...it is mine."

"Yours?"

"It is my blood, Gabriel. I am a witch."

EIGHTEEN

"A WITCH?" GABRIEL SHOT UP FROM Roxane's bed. A bit discombobulated, he teetered. Hell, he'd consumed blood. He had done it!

And yet she sought to bring him down.

"Witch? What further insanity will you concoct to keep me from my goal?"

"Gabriel, it is not a mistruth."

"Too late. I have won."

And he would have his triumph, naysayers be damned. Plucking up his discarded shirt he strode from the room.

Roxane shouted behind him. "You have won nothing but the vampire's curse!"

She lied. It was not a curse but the gift of immortality.

He stopped before his chamber door and pulled the shirt over his head. Frustration building, he kicked the door with his bare feet. "Lies!"

Why this sudden decision to be a witch? If she sought to scare him from vampirism, it was too late.

And yet, he did care. Cared so much he could feel her words drag on his heart. It slowed his steps as he entered the room and stretched out the beats of blood in his ear. Struggling between what he had done and what Roxane had announced—

A witch? Bah! She lied either regarding the vial of blood about her neck or the fact that she was something she was not.

What a moment to try fool him.

He had done it. He'd taken the blood. And, remarkably, he didn't feel shame. Rather, elation coursed through his bones. Light—dare he think it?—and satisfied.

Strolling through the rainbow streaming from above, his palms up, he caught a shower of color. *My first moments as a vampire.* He felt no different. And yet, his entire world would now change. A streak of indigo cut across his skin. A turn of his wrist captured a blob of celadon.

Startled, he shook his hand as if to dislodge the color from his flesh. But he could not put aside the color from his thoughts. *Roxane.* He had done this for her. To give her hope regarding her brother. Why the woman's sudden need to frighten him?

Not that he was in the least frightened.

Hmm... Gabriel stood still. Waiting, wondering. *Is this how it feels? I don't feel different.*

He swiped a hand across his mouth. He studied the liquid glistening on his flesh. Candlelight melted into the grenadine glitter.

A wicked grin curved his lips and he spat out a dose of laughter. Hell, he felt marvelous. He had done it. No going back. No madness or filthy cell for this swish. Damn, *la Luna*! He had won.

"Gabriel?"

The voice of his carelessly discarded victim cut through his macabre joy. He closed his eyes. *How cruel that you pounced upon her like a predator upon prey!*

He had been caught in the hunger.

Must you kill?

No, you can leave them to wake with no memory of your bite.

He should have thought things through, been more cautious. Then, he had not the ability to enthrall. But now?

You should not have bitten her at all.

It had not been a bite, but a slash from the glass shard. And his saliva must have worked to seal the wound. She would be safe. He hadn't planned it. Well, yes, he had. From the moment he'd arrived at his doorstep and sent Toussaint away he had known how this night would play out.

You could have been more considerate. To trick her so?

"Gabriel?"

"Go away."

Apologize, you cur!

A bit late for that, eh?

"I don't understand what has happened—"

"I drank your blood," he explained calmly, pacing beneath the oculus, hands folded behind his back. The loose shirt skirted his bare thighs. "I completed the transformation. I have won the race against madness, only to find you've now gone mad thinking you are a witch."

"I am as I say."

He paused, turning a cold eye on the shivering waif in paisley robe and tangled strawberry hair. She clutched her wrist, blood coating her fingers. And there, the robe was loosely tied, revealing the mark between her breasts. Some sort of witch mark? Surely not a mark of birth, but something unnatural and evil?

"I should have said something earlier."

"Oh really?" Bitter laughter spat from him.

"Yes, but there never seemed to be a right time. Toussaint has all these omens against witches—"

"You were dealing with a man soon to become a vampire and you couldn't just out with it? For example: Pardon me, vicomte, you've been bitten by a vampire. By the by, I am a witch."

"Gabriel, please."

"That mark on your breasts is a witch mark?" Now was no time for this inane conversation. He had stepped over the edge. The selfish need for privacy overwhelmed. To cherish a few moments of consideration for what he had become. "Never mind. You had opportunity to explain; you chose not to. Leave me. Can you not see I've much to contend with?"

He pushed her into the mirrored hallway and slammed the door. A single fist pounded the other side of the door. Spreading his arms out wide, he lifted his head and closed his eyes, drawing the night through his pores in waves of myriad color.

What cruelty to push her away.

What strange happiness to revel in the leap. The stride to the other side. A new world. A new beginning. No *comfort*. Not even the tinkle of gold watch fobs muffled by ells of Alençon lace. He had done it. For good or for ill. To struggle with the wrongs would only convolute the newness of his reality.

A witch? She had best conjure a more believable lie than that. Did Roxane not remember she had convinced him that witches and vampires were enemies? Or was she merely frightened? She had gone to bed with him hours ago, his lover—literally seducing him up from the vibration of madness that had wanted his soul.

Yet, he could not summon regret. It felt alien to consider the emotion. The decision to change had been right.

He turned his hand over, noticing for the first time the cut on his forefinger from clutching the glass. Premeditated escape from madness. A blind leap to savior. He licked the blood from the slash, only to witness it heal. The flesh sewed seamlessly together before his very eyes.

I have lived for over two centuries...

A delicious smile crept across Gabriel's face. *"Bon jour*, immortality."

A sharp bite of pain erupted in his upper jaw. He doubled, falling to his knees beneath the midnight rainbow.

ROXANE STUMBLED INTO HER ROOM and collapsed onto the vanity chair. The posies strewn on the floor had wilted and were stained with spots of her blood. She studied the wound on her wrist. Not life threatening, but it continued to seep. Sorting through her sewing box she produced a strip of linen, the same she'd used to bind Gabriel's wound.

He had drunk her blood!

But the most remarkable thing was that nothing untoward had come of it.

She eyed her reflection, seeking answers. *They are celadon.* She blinked, erasing the need to replace the monster who had attacked her with the kind, charming man she had begun to love. What had compelled him to do such a thing? To, of a sudden, attack her? Though not a violent attack. He'd brought her to orgasm before he'd bitten her. Planned then, yes? He had been so close. The moon promised fullness tomorrow night!

She had not been vigilant in helping him.

You had no intention of helping, only using, remember?

Yes, as bait. And now, what would come of her brilliant plan? How to lure the enemy with bait that had turned enemy as well?

Two men you have failed. She moaned. *Can you love a vampire?*

She had not answered when he'd asked that ridiculous question. It wasn't supposed to be an option. Had he known then that he would succumb this night?

Could she love a vampire? It was doubtful. Vampires were creatures of the night. Witch's bane.

I will follow the night.

Losh!

She turned her wrist this way and that. How had he been able to take her blood without dire consequences? She had performed the ascendant ritual, had gained immortality through the taste of vampire blood—the mark on her breasts had been forged of fire and blood. By rights, one drop of her blood should have obliterated Gabriel.

Unless something had gone wrong. Perhaps the transformation had not occurred? Did he merely play at a silly triumph?

"Damn you, Renan, if you think to toy with me—"

Roxane wrapped a makeshift bandage about her wrist, tugging the knot tight with her teeth, and hastened from her room. She'd not heard him draw the lock across his door.

Aware she wore but a robe, loosely tied, she could not concern herself with propriety. The man had touched, tasted and licked every portion of her body—Tasted?

"Bloody hell." He'd done more than taste. He had consumed her body and soul.

Without knocking, she entered Gabriel's room.

Shoulders squared and arms stretched down and out at his sides, the delicious rainbow sucked him upward. Emerald, fuchsia, and vibrant yellow painted the billowy white shirt that hung from his muscled arms. Strong thighs and calves, bared and taut, took on crimson and verdant ivy. Blood splattered the lace and wrinkled hem of his shirt. Her blood.

Wrapped in his seduction and kisses she had been intensely focused. So close to coming—they had been making love! She had not had time to register the cut to her wrist.

He did not turn to her, only grunted, "Get out."

"Make me."

She strode to the vanity and fingered the powdered hairs of a hedgehog wig that sat upon a sightless porcelain dummy. Coaching her voice to remain calm, she reprimanded. "How dare you use me. Of all the unthinking, cruel—You ask me to love you and then you bite me?"

"You are obviously no worse for wear. Witch."

That single word, laced with venom, thumped in her breast. "So you believe me?"

"Hardly. You are as mad as your brother."

"It is my blood in this vial. It was my blood that killed the vampire who crashed through your window."

"Indeed?" He reeled about and fixed a needle gaze to her. "Prove it. Speak a spell. Command the elements. Bewitch me, witch."

"It—it does not work that way."

"Nothing ever works when it needs to. Why did you not reveal this paramount secret to me before?" Crimson colored his face and eyes, gifting them a bloody glint. "Or was that your plan all along? Tempt the man into becoming a vampire, and then, knowing he could not resist your allure, get him to bite you? And then... Well, what then? Here I am. I stand, Roxane. I have not exploded into a puddle of creature blood. What is to become of your ever powerful theory now?"

"I am as surprised as you." She took a step forward, but relented when he raised a hand. He wanted distance and she would be wise to grant it. Besides, he looked a horror covered with her blood. "I do not believe you are a vampire."

"So you are the non-believer now?"

His smile was anything but charming. It bordered on the smiles Damian wore for his spinning subjects.

He stalked toward her. The sharp glint in his eyes struck out, piercing her in the breast. The swish had become a predator, slinking and working his dark gaze against her.

"You have been so worried should I consume a mere drop of blood. You think sucking out the blood from your veins did not complete the change?"

"It-it could not have. Witch's blood and vampires..."

"Sure death, yes?" He raised a finger between them. "But you forget, witch, I was *not* a vampire before I drew the blood from your veins."

Roxane stumbled upon her own breath. *Losh*. The man had a point. "I had not thought of that." Made utterly horrific sense. "But what makes you imagine it worked?"

AWARE OF HER FEAR, BUT, SHE SENSED, secretly enjoying her trembles and uncertainty, Gabriel pressed the heels of his hands to her shoulders, pinning her to the wall. He drew in her scent as a beast scents its prey.

"Gabriel, please, you're frightening me."

"Not even close."

"Yes, I'm—step back, please."

"If you do not believe the change worked, how then, can you possibly be frightened?"

"Y-you are acting strangely."

"Indeed?" He ran his tongue along the inside of his upper teeth, then stretched his lips open to reveal the new fangs.

"*Mon Dieu.*"

"You plead to God? But I thought witches pagans? Do not your kind worship the Devil? Or some goddess who dances naked in the forest?"

She gasped in a breath as his palm pressed to her breast. "Please, Gabriel."

"So many secrets, witch."

A slap to his cheek took him off guard. But his reaction was not so blind. Capturing her wrist in a tight clutch he growled at her.

"When did it happen? Yo-your teeth?" she hissed against his cheek.

"Moments ago. If you would have granted me the privacy I demanded I might have had time to grasp the magnitude of the occasion. As it stands, you stride in here and boldly wave this flag of blood before me. Shall I test the puncturing capabilities of my new prizes?"

"You cannot take my blood again. It would be madness."

A knee to his groin succeeded in bringing him to his knees. As she slipped from him, he snatched the hem of her robe. Fabric tore, but not without bringing her down. He crawled over her sprawled body, a feral cat climbing upon a pinned mouse.

"You press the bounds of our relationship, witch."

"We have no relationship."

"I thought we had become lovers? That you loved me?"

"You assume very much."

"So you spit that in my face now that I am the monster you love to hunt? What of you? Witch. Are you not a monster as well?"

"I am not! Your grip, it is too tight. You mustn't cut me. Gabriel, please. Be wary of my blood. Remember the vampire!"

A twist of his head and he preened over the stain on the floor. Witch's blood had annihilated the minion. And yet, it had not done so to him. It must be because he had not been vampire when he bit her.

Tears streamed over Roxane cheeks. She touched his chin. He jerked away. "You must never again drink from me," she said on a sniffle. "I don't want you to die. I cannot lose you now."

"And why not? You don't love me. You said you could not love a vampire."

"I-I never answered that question."

"And now? Can you love a vampire?"

Gazing deeply into his eyes, the meaning of *bewitching* grew very clear to her. Falling again, falling evermore and not afraid to surrender.

Roxane tilted her head. "Could you love a witch?"

Stroking his cheek, he softened his stance, his tense shoulders relaxing. She gentled him so easily. "I already do." And he whispered, "God pity us both."

Nineteen

GABRIEL TUGGED THE BLANKET OVER his head and clutched it to his neck. The woven cotton hooded his eyes from the light that seeped through the oculus. He wasn't sure if sunlight would sizzle him to ash. Yet Toussaint had said Mesmer had witnessed vampires walking during the day.

He should slip out from under cover and slide a toe into the light. First sign of smoke he could recoil.

Gabriel eyed the storm of colors raining in from above. Had his sanctity been stolen from him with one drastic act? Would he ever again stand beneath the oculus, bathed in color and serenity?

"The moon reaches fullness tonight, Renan. You will be successful!"

Toussaint's sudden entrance made him burrow down against the pillows.

"Gabriel?" He held a razor and bowl of water arranged on a silver tray that had been only slightly jiggled by his erratic entrance. "Do not tell me you are pouting. You should be elated. Shall I draw the drapes and—"

"No, Toussaint! The light, it bothers me."

"Your eyes still? I wonder what that is about? I can find your spectacles."

"I'm not sure two small lenses of blue glass will serve the purpose this time, Toussaint."

"But why not—" The valet noticeably stiffened. Slowly he turned to squint at Gabriel. The man's mirth slipped down his jaw until it hung open, revealing teeth. "What has happened?"

Rising from his burrow, Gabriel figured he could not lie to his closest friend. Secrets only destroyed lives.

If Roxane had told him sooner would he have avoided her? Hell yes. And yet...

"I drank her blood."

Shaving utensils clattered across the marble floor. Stiff and open-mouthed beneath the oculus, Toussaint mimicked a statue. "You—" He snapped his jaws shut in a repeated biting motion.

"Yes." Gabriel tossed the blanket and shuffled to sit upon a parti-color pillow, still safely within the shadows of the half-tester. He tipped the thick tassels that dangled from the edge of the counterpane and pulled them through his fingers, over and over. "I have become a creature that follows the night and fears the sun. Do I not look one?"

Slowly the valet's hand moved up—as if to make a quick move would alert the beast—until he encircled his throat with shaking fingers.

"Ah yes, I wager you must fear me now. Jump out of it, Toussaint. It is me! I have not changed."

"But you said—Are you having fun with me, Renan? This is not at all humorous."

"You've nothing to fear. Save..." He stretched his lips to reveal the fangs he now considered quite elegant.

Toussaint's squeak could have called dogs.

"Bit of an obstacle at first," he offered with a wag of his tongue at the frightened servant. "If I am conscious of my words and opening and closing my mouth I'll be fine. Only bit myself twice since last evening."

"You're...you're..." A loud swallow descended Toussaint's throat. He clutched his other hand to his neck.

"I am what?"

"Taking this remarkably well!" he shrilled out.

"Isn't so horrible as I anticipated. How is Roxane, by the by? Hasn't fallen dead from blood loss, has she?"

"You bit Roxane? But—"

"She tell you she's a witch?"

"Oh mercy." Toussaint start to sway.

"The chair, man. You'll collapse if you don't sit. And breathe. You'll turn livid from fright."

Gabriel crawled forward, setting Toussaint to a jump and a wide path around the end of the bed. "I am not going to attack."

Grabbing the arm chair and pulling it to the wall— the greatest distance from the bed—Toussaint collapsed onto the plush crimson cushion. "I think I need a drink."

"I thought you wanted this for your dull miserable master? A new adventure to suck the boredom from my routine."

"I think the change has altered your brain. I would have never wished—"

"Well, it is done."

"For what reason? You were so close. Oh, my soul. Was it the madness?"

"I don't believe so. At least, I didn't feel I was on an edge of mental suicide. It was physically challenging, fighting the hunger for blood, but no—I'm quite sure I could have survived to the moon's fullness."

"Then why?"

"There is a reason."

"Such as?"

Lying back, Gabriel turned his head into the pillow. Just go away, he wanted to say. It is done. Why so many questions?

"Very well. I was no help in keeping you from such a decision. Heaven knows I take an interest in the occult. You don't look any different. Are you quite sure, Renan?"

The valet ceased protest when Gabriel once again flashed his fangs.

Despite the gravity of the situation, Toussaint's fears made him smile. That he could produce such a reaction with but a toothy sneer!

"Why the long face, Toussaint? I've become something remarkable for you to study and preen over."

"Much easier to wish for than to actually accept. Was it very painful?"

Now there was the curiosity he expected from his valet. Shoving back the counterpane with a kick, he stretched out his legs before him. "Not at all. Save for running my tongue across these damned teeth the first time."

"And you're quite sure you won't..."

"Regret it?"

"Rage?"

"You mean, attack you without volition? Creep out from the shadows to kill you?"

"Don't say things like that." Again Toussaint clutched his throat. "Are you, er, hungry now?"

"For food? Or something else?"

"I-I'm not sure. What is it you want, Gabriel? Tell me so I can make you as comfortable as possible."

"What do I want?" He moved forward, but the sunlight beaming through the oculus was too bright so he pulled up the counterpane over his shoulders, hooding his head and eyes.

"Does the sunlight hurt?"

"No. But my eyes feel dry and I blink a lot. I don't think I'll burn. On the other hand, I haven't stepped into the sunlight. Everything is so new. I just don't know."

"I seem to recall Mesmer mentioning vampires could walk in daylight. Only, they were not so strong."

"Yes, but what if he is wrong?"

"Perhaps Mademoiselle Desrues could teach you a few things?"

Gabriel speared Toussaint with such a vexing glare the valet actually cringed. "She knows nothing, Toussaint. Only how to drive men to madness and fops to evil."

"You are not evil!"

"How do you know? We, each of us, know nothing."

"It is all in how you look at it. I believe a man can choose to be good or evil."

Gabriel chuffed.

"Come now, Renan, you were born a good man."

"Did such goodness keep the count and countess from abandoning me?"

"They were decent people as well. They choose a different lot. Nothing can change what is inherently you, Gabriel. Do you *feel* evil? Do you feel like killing?"

"No." He sighed and shrugged his fingers through his hair. With a frustrated splay of his hand he said, "I feel no different than I did the day before, or for that matter, a week earlier when none of this had happened to me. I feel like a foppish vicomte. With sharp teeth."

The valet nodded. "You'll have to wield those carefully around the women."

Gabriel curled a sly grin at the man. "Who says?"

THEY HAD MADE LOVE. Sweet passion.

He had bitten her. Terrifying.

He had become a vampire. Against incredible odds.

All plans to help her brother had gone entirely unchecked. Selfish!

What had Roxane done but create a bigger mess? She was now responsible for changing the lives of two men. And of the two she could not determine who was the worse off.

Leaving Gabriel's estate without telling anyone, Roxane had rushed home, not out of fear, but in search of answers. Now, she paged through Granny MacTavish's grimoire to the well-thumbed section on vampires. It listed defensive potions and items used against the creatures: stakes, garlic, wild roses, witch's blood. There was even a notation about giving the vampire a pile of seeds or knotted rope to count to keep him busy.

Prevention detailed the three choices she had initially given Gabriel. But saving a victim from the madness that ensued instead of the vampire's taint was not covered. Nor was reversal from vampire to common mortal possible.

She tapped the book. Just because it was not detailed did not make it an impossibility. There may yet be hope for Damian.

It was too late for Gabriel. He was now immortal. He would walk the earth for centuries.

Would he grow to hate her for the part she had played in his transformation? Would they become enemies simply because that is what they should be? How could either of them ever again be comfortable with the other?

Maybe he had wanted it more than he'd been willing to admit? She recalled the music room, his declaration that he needed nothing, that he was ready for the night. *To follow the night*, he had said. Had she frightened him with her portent of sure madness? She did have a knack for inadvertently influencing the men she cared for. And oh, she did care for Gabriel.

Could you love a vampire?

Of course, for she already did.

Catching her face in her palms, Roxane bent over the ancient grimoire. What cruel irony had her secrets granted? If she had been truthful from the start, Gabriel would have had no inclination to bite her to force the change. But then, would he have sought someone else?

The thought of the vicomte seeking his pleasures— his vampiric origins—with another woman bothered her.

Only me, she thought.

Twenty

TOUSSAINT REPORTED Mademoiselle Desrues had left; things to do at home. While part of Gabriel fretted about her absence, his practical side guessed she needed distance. Toussaint also reported Mesmer had told of a particularly heinous vampire who could travel by day. He had not the strength in full daylight, but he had yet been a force.

Very well, Gabriel had the answer he sought.

He shrugged on a plain black frockcoat of watered silk. He'd foregone the lace for a simpler shirt with a plain jabot tied at the neck.

Tonight he did not want to be noticed. He needed to break free from the sweltering closeness of walls, ceiling and floor. To breathe in the world. To think. To answer the jittery curiosity that stirred him to a fidgety jumble of nerves. To spend some time with the vampire—*himself.*

A twist of his arm displayed a plain hand, shucked of lace. He would meld with the shadows now Leo had been murdered. No longer would he prance about in search of an audience, of approval—

Oh, to the devil!

Shrugging off the coat and practically ripping the shirt from his arms, Gabriel replaced it with a finer piece. Chinese silk, trimmed with lace wider than his fingers. He tugged the shirt over his head, tied the jabot, and replaced the frockcoat. Now he tugged out inches and inches of Alençon lace so his fingers were barely visible.

Just because he'd become a beast did not mean he must appear uncivilized.

GABRIEL WALKED SOUTH, AVOIDING the bustle and gaiety surrounding the royal palace. He'd thought to slip a dagger into his sleeve, for protection. But the idea proved absurd. His walking stick with the concealed rapier would serve. He knew his heeled shoes and lace presented him as a target, as well, the clink of gold watch chains calling to every cutpurse within range.

On the other hand—he ran his tongue along his sharpened fangs and grinned—this target would startle more than a few.

He would relish this new life as he had never before savored life.

Striding confidently, the brisk autumn air acutely twanged at his senses. Every movement, the click of his heels, the sway of his frockcoat, had its own tune, an exact note in his sensory arsenal. Refuse rotting in the gutters speared his nostrils. Faggots stacked outside a garden gate reeked of charcoal. The lingering perfume of a climbing rose closed to the night tinted the miasma with a sweet top note.

Striding the wet cobbles, he adjusted his path to avoid an oncoming carriage. A liveried footmen ran ahead with a torch yelling "Make way!" All were headed for the theatre. Within the hour, streets would be literally emptied, save for the stray child slapping a stick against a wrought iron gate or hanging, fingers gripping tight, from a low cypress branch, not a care in the world.

Gabriel passed the dangling tot, nodding at the child's exuberant smile. Did he not fear the night? Worry that a racing carriage might spin around the corner and clip him? Childhood ignorance granted ineffable bliss. Should something evil happen, only then would the child discover the meaning of fear.

Gabriel had never feared. His childhood had been as lacy and leisurely as Leo's life. The count and countess had spent much time at court, and later in India, leaving him in Toussaint's care. His parents had inadvertently taught him self-sufficiency. And to abandon hope.

He would not fear now. No one could abandon a man of his own making.

But he did fear one thing. That which was now inside him. And the truth behind succumbing to the blood hunger.

He had done this for a woman.

What of the madness? That prospect frightened you, surely?

Certainly. But more so, this venture into darkness had been spurred by his blind love for a woman who may very well consider herself his enemy.

You never told her you loved her. If you do not speak it, it can never become truth.

"I could have spoken it. I *should* have."

Now Roxane would not have him. Her history preached to her of evils and foes. Vampires and witches were enemies. But why, he wondered? So little he knew about this preternatural society he had subscribed to as if merely receiving an annual encyclopedia.

Dodging under a low-hanging metal sign advertising nostrums, he strode to the cool stone balustrade edging the river and leaned on it. He looked down upon half a dozen skiffs and two barges floating the moon-silvered Seine, loaded with cargo from Le Havre or Rouen. Rotting fish filled his senses, quelled only when he tilted back his head to draw in the salty air.

He pressed his palms over his face and rubbed, closing his eyes and for the moment quieting his senses. Inside he had become a beast, a creature of the night that could scent out the indistinguishable with but a sniff.

He didn't feel like a creature. Monsters did not wear Alençon lace. *You bit her and drank her blood!* No, monsters wore ancient velvet and gold trim.

Why had she lied to him? Concealed the truth. Or had she?

At a tap on his shoulder, he twisted. Two men in peasant rags and no shoes flashed their teeth. One slapped a thick stick against his dirty palm.

Expecting the worst, Gabriel calmly propped his elbows on the stone balustrade and crossed one ankle over the other. Leo would never react with such sanguine élan.

"We'll be taking care of your coin for you then, monsieur," the thinner one said. Dirt coated his face so Gabriel could not be certain if he were a Frenchman or a Moor. "Make it quick and my brother here won't find the need to break anything of yours. Bones included."

"And what if I should counter with my own desire to break something of yours?"

The burly one grunted and eyed his brother with a crenellated mouthful of brown stubs. "He's a right lackwit."

"Coming from one who should know," Gabriel countered. "Really, messieurs—and I do use that form of address loosely—I will offer you a moment to dash away and find yourselves a new victim. Before..."

"Before you break something of ours?" Both burst into laughter and the one beating his stick swung it, thrashing the air inches from Gabriel's face.

Gabriel flashed a toothy snarl at the men.

Gape-toothed mouths stretched wide. "He's—do you see that? Look at those teeth! Run!"

The offensive stick landed on the ground before the vicomte's damask shoes. The would-be robbers vacated the area faster than he had thought possible for the accumulation of dirt they carried on their bodies.

Slicking his tongue across his lower lip he tasted the bead of blood drawn by his sharp incisor.

"Fangs," he said to himself. "Who could have imagined? I should start a vogue at Madame de Marmonte's salon!"

The rush of victory lightened his strides. Such a wonder. He looked the part of a monster now. An elegant, deceptive monster, who could easily attract his victims before revealing the truth.

This could prove fortuitous.

A covered wagon, gypsy-like with curved canopy, ambled by, the horses as unenthusiastic as the driver. Keeping a double pace to the echoing horse hooves, Gabriel skipped forward, insinuating himself onto the island's tight streets and seeking the shadows—for that is what monsters did, stalk the shadows.

To his left, Nôtre Dame mastered the east end of the city. It taunted, defying him with a religious sneer.

"Can I?" he wondered, and quickened his pace toward the cathedral, trotting across the tiled courtyard before the church. Stopping, he drew his gaze along the

stone archway coving the entry. To his right, a couple
exited the Portal of the Virgin, their arms draped
together, their heads bowed. Overhead, myriad kings
carved into the jamb invited with silent expressions. Or
did they condemn?

The narthex was quiet, perhaps three or four dozen
candles lit the stone walls with manic flickers. Gabriel's
heels clicked dully on the swept floor. The long, wide
nave was spotted here and there with a bowed head
whispering silent prayers, or perhaps pleading simply to
be heard. To be rescued from their lives.

He clung to a cold marble pillar in the back of the
nave and pressed his cheek to the smooth surface,
relishing the chill. Far down the aisle, the chancel
glittered with a row of tall white tapers. An immense
gold cross mastered the background. The thought to
dash up and cling to the cross struck him. To cleave to
the holy, testing, daring, drawing down His wrath.

Insanity. Blasphemous.

Exciting.

Gabriel curled his head down, his cheek hugging the
cold column. Often, as a child, he had followed his nanny
down the aisle to the second pew up front. She would
bow her head and whisper prayers, often for a time so
long he would nod off to sleep. But occasionally he
would bow his head and whisper as well. Pleas for a little
sister, or a house in the country surrounded by flowers.
The heartfelt plea for his parents' attention. Those
prayers had gone unanswered.

"Will you listen to my prayers now?"

Silence flickered in the myriad candles flames. Tiny
noises formed a symphony of human utterances, throat-
clearings, and shuffling bodies upon the wooden pews.

Walking with purpose he hugged the right side of the arcade, approaching a lavish baptismal font carved with saints, crosses and other gothic apocrypha.

"I am not evil," he whispered, closing his eyes, and this time forcing his very soul into the plea. *I cannot be.* "I will not be. I did this to help another. Can you hear me?" He searched the high ceiling, buttressed with magnificent arches. "Do you curse me now?"

What did it matter?

It mattered so much. For where else would he be granted unconditional acceptance? God could not possibly have abandoned him, for then he could not now stand here in the presence of such holy sanctity.

With a nod, Gabriel decided he would become what he wanted. Life was his to shape. He must use the hands of a sculptor and work well. A careless plunge could result in horror. He must do this right, if not for himself, for the safety of the innocent. The life he had led—his true self—would not be abandoned. The rake was but outer decoration. Inside he knew who he was. Alone, but eager to see that no others suffered abandonment.

He turned and found himself vis à vis the Holy Font. Stepping forward and kneeling before the marble bowl, he dipped his fingers into the pool of blessed water. Before he could bring his fingers to his forehead the foolishness of his act burned through his flesh.

Stumbling to a stone pillar and pressing his fingers between his knees. Wisps of smoke hissed from his skin. Carefully, he pulled them from between his knees. Red boils covered the tips of his fingers. He gaped, his cry of horror a silent wail deep inside his heart.

Rejected by the holy.

He spun into a run and raced from the cathedral and out into the cold, unforgiving world.

TWENTY-ONE

ROXANE SPUN INTO THE KITCHEN and spied Toussaint leaning over the butcher block. He glimpsed her from the corner of his eye, casually went back to his business—then let out a shriek and shuffled around to the other side of the wood block.

At sight of the dagger wavering menacingly before the valet Roxane lifted a brow. "Is that brie?"

The wedge of soft yellow cheese speared on the end of the dagger fell off and landed on the butcher block with a muted thud.

"Wh-what are you doing in here?" he stammered.

"Why are you frightened of me, Toussaint? Will you set that thing down? You look as though I'll lunge for you."

"Er...w-will you?" He kept the dagger in check.

She couldn't resist a smile. "Gabriel must have told you. Is it because I am a witch?"

"P-p-perhaps."

"And what has happened today to make you so fearful of me that could not keep you from me yesterday? I have no intention of harming you, Toussaint."

"You say that, but it'll be too late by the time you've bespelled me!"

"*Losh.*" She went for the cheese.

Toussaint shuffled back against the wall, setting the porcelain cups to a rattle on their iron hooks.

"I don't work spells on people," she said between bites. "I am a simple country witch who deals more with healing herbs and potions than any physical magic. Though I would like to master air magic."

"Oh." The dagger fell to his side. Toussaint rubbed the back of his neck. "But the hex signs. How did you gain the vicomte's home without...? Are they not effective?"

"Very much so. If they were a bit larger and fire forged."

"Fire forged?"

"Fixed with fire to stone. Unless the hex marks are secured in flame they really serve little more than a curiosity. A witch has to step in the center to prove effective."

"I see." Still rubbing his neck, Toussaint turned and pulled open a drawer and shuffled through it.

"So you are startled to defense by the presence of a witch, and yet does not the resident vampire put you to greater worry?"

Toussaint tossed a hunk of chalk from hand to hand. "It does. And it doesn't. Truth? I don't know what to think. Today is not the same as yesterday."

"I should hope not."

Distant music floated into the kitchen. Roxane tilted her head at the remarkable sound. "What is that?"

"Gabriel's picked up the violin today. About time. Bigger, you say?" He wielded the chalk thoughtfully. "And I'll need fire?"

"He's in the music room?"

Leaving the valet to his warding ritual, Roxane gobbled the piece of brie and walked toward the music room. She might worry about what she'd encounter next time she tried to cross the threshold, but she trusted Toussaint would not overdo it, nor would he figure how to effectively fire forge the symbols.

A devilish adagio raced behind the music room wall, thundering in her throat and cleaving to her pulse. His talent was remarkable. Pity Gabriel had not touched the violin since his parents' departure; the man might have played concerts.

The waning afternoon darkened the house, and she could not see candlelight through the glass pane in the door. Did he dance about in the shadows, playing to his dark demons? For the music was demonic. Grating, yet smoothly running from note to note. Evil, yet enticing. It pushed away and at the same time beckoned. A vampire's lament drenched by angst and shadows.

Slipping inside the room, Roxane stood by the door and took a moment to adjust to the darkness. She could not determine Gabriel's position; the whole room bellowed with the cry of his beast. A vampire taunted the strings. A wicked melody, his weapon.

She cried out as something soft fluttered across her cheek. Cinnamon scurried into her senses.

"You like?" came the heavy whisper. He spun away, drawing the bow in another macabre cry.

Clinging to the wall, her fingers tracing the ornate chair-rail, she moved along the room, closer to the window. When she could see her hand before her, Gabriel danced up, sawed the bow in a wicked arpeggio, and then ceased, bowing grandly before her.

"It is...remarkable," she managed. Difficult to keep the strange fear from riding her soul. Her heartbeats raced faster than the music. Had he meant to frighten her?

"Does it put you to comfort?" he inquired smoothly.

"N-not at all. It is violent."

"Yes, isn't it?" His wicked smile tore at the shadows, yet the twinkle in his whiskey eyes softened her fear.

"Why are you playing in the dark? Do your eyes yet bother you?"

"I didn't feel the need for light."

"Oh. Should I—May I light a candle?"

"If it suits you. Do you wish to hear more?"

"Certainly I do. I am pleased you've taken up the violin."

"But for the day."

Roxane touched flint to tinder and ignited three candles in succession on the candelabra upon the pianoforte. "I don't understand."

"This is my farewell recital." He bowed a scale of rapid notes across all four strings and ended with a grand flare. "As I've told you, I once played for my parents in hopes of winning their attention. I fooled myself by thinking that I had succeeded, but I had not. I was merely background noise for their comfort." He eyed Roxane. "It is what they called the opium haze, when they slipped into its settling grip. 'I'm taking my comfort now, Gabriel, do not trouble me.' Or, 'Gabriel, play me to comfort.'"

She stroked his arm, thinking to show him she understood, but he tugged from her with a stride into the center of the room.

"They never really *saw* me. Never heard me. Couldn't swim up from the depths of their comfort to love me. So!"

He swung and thrust the violin across the room. Roxane let out a shriek as the delicate instrument crashed against the wall. Blue splinters, strings, and carved tuning pegs clattered across the harlequin floor.

Gabriel stood beside her, his expression unreadable in the dim light, but the pain in his voice evident. "I don't need their validation," he growled. "I don't need them to come home. It won't restore their love. It won't squeeze the opium from their bodies and make them kind or real or even see me."

She looked from his angry intensity. At her feet a string clawed at the hem of her skirt.

"I need nothing from anyone." He stalked away. "So begins my journey to vampirism. I no longer fear the past. Isn't that a marvel?" He leaned on the pianoforte and pushed the silver candlestick toward her. "Today, I merely am."

Looking as if he'd tumbled from bed more than a smartly-dressed swish, dark, tousled, beraged with a new beast, he winked at Roxane, before setting the bow on the piano.

"You're trembling, witch."

"You frightened me. You destroyed your violin."

"I think I'll play you now."

"Oh?" She clung to his shirt. *Don't fear him. Settle him, calm the beast within.*

Before she could protest she was lifted high and set upon the smooth-lacquered pianoforte. Like a black cat mounting a rocky outcrop, Gabriel climbed the bench to join her.

"It will surely break," she said.

"Never."

"How can you know?" She swung her head to the right. He approached on the left. "Have you tried this before?" A twist of her waist. He'd slipped to her right. "With another woman?"

A hot breath shivered into her ear. "You ask too many questions, witch."

"Don't call me that. I have a name. I have a right to know if I am merely a second in this game of seduction."

"Very well. Never have I made love to a woman on top of this pianoforte. Is Toussaint about?"

"Out securing the perimeter with hex signs."

"Good. It'll keep him busy for a time."

"But the markings will keep me out of your house."

"Not if you never leave." A kiss to the tops of her breasts, and he buried his tongue between her cleavage. "We'll hope he doesn't barge in when I've your skirts over your head."

"My—" Her sight blackened by the billowing silk falling over her face, Roxane felt Gabriel's fingers slide down her hose. He'd found exactly what interested him. And who was she to argue with a vampire?

ROXANE WATCHED THE CARRIAGE roll away from the Renan estate, the springs glistening and the midnight bays shining blue under the moon's illumination. Spittles of foam from the horses' mouth glittered on the cobbles before the hex-marked steps. Just down the street the clatter of coaches jostling for prime space on the linden-lined boulevard de la Madeleine and the yelps of unaware pedestrians signaled the Comédie Française had pulled aside the heavy velvet curtains for the night.

Sitting upon the vanity chair she tossed her hair over her shoulder, propped her elbows on the padded chair arm, and informed the woman who looked back at her,

"He's left for the evening." And she knew that even after the delicious lovemaking session in the music room, he'd left hungry. "He's going to find a woman and bite her. Not me."

The thought made her frown. She didn't want to think of Gabriel touching another woman. He'd promised her he would not—could not—ever make love to another woman. But it was the blood hunger that called to him, she felt sure. And she hadn't decided if she wanted him to bite her again. She should be pleased he sought blood from someone else.

But what was to keep him from answering *all* his desires while extracting blood? Until four days earlier the vicomte had been a confirmed rake. She could not expect him to give up the lifestyle after making love to her but a few times.

But she wanted him to give it all up. To hold her exclusively in his heart.

Because it feels right.

Did vampirism feel right to Gabriel? Might he become a cold-blooded killer like Anjou?

"No."

The vicomte was kind at heart. His philanthropies proved it. Toussaint kept his master's magnanimous accomplishments a secret, but Roxane suspected he had large sums of money, and perhaps gave as much as he gained. Surely the darkness of vampirism would not overwhelm his soul.

If he had a soul now. Had darkness stolen his soul?

I beat the madness. I am free.

Free of what? Had Gabriel merely descended to a new Hell?

He had gone in pursuit of a victim this evening. Knowing so little. He would not know to hide, to blend in the shadows, to be stealthy.

Would he?

Her reflection shook her tousle of red curls. She looked at the ceiling, seeing beyond the wood and the tiles and to the creature that sat in stony silence waiting her command.

She had vowed to protect Gabriel. This night she would.

TWENTY-TWO

GABRIEL STUDIED HIS GLOVES. Alençon lace flowed to his knuckles.

"Vicomte?"

The wench he'd chosen from amongst a throng of pretties removed her laced bodice and peeled away a thread-bare chemise to reveal tiny breasts with wide red aureoles and hard nipples of deepest cherry.

He leaned a shoulder against the wall and removed his tricorn with a flare. The woman arched her back and snaked her body into a sensuous stretch. Appealing, and yet, he suspected, not smelling of rosemary.

With a seductive slide of her hand down her stomach and over her hip, the whore leaned back on the narrow rope bed and drew up her skirts to expose the pad of dark curls between her slender legs. So she was not a genuine redhead. The only true redhead he knew sat back at his home. *Fraises et al crème.* Waiting for him.

Do not mix that pleasure with this necessary act.

"Oh, vicomte," she sing-songed, "come and get me."

His heartbeats shimmied to a tribal beat, lurching into the fray before his rationale could follow. The blood hunger demanded to be fed.

A sniff yielded her salty aroma, reminiscent of the sea and passion. Pain tingled in his mouth, anchored at the root of his fangs. His body knew what it wanted. He had only to agree.

"I had not heard that you are so shy, vicomte. Come."
She patted the bed and followed by drawing her finger
over a nipple. The rosy bud ruched.

Gabriel's pulse increased and his blood rushed to the
fore, not in anticipation of the carnal pleasures, but for
the sensory feast. The sound of her blood sliding through
her veins purled like a brook over smooth summer stones,
tempting him to lean forward and sup.

And yet, he remained by the door, a hand clinging to
the cracked wooden door frame. Outside, the sounds of
minstrels and singers loomed above the note of bustling
shoppers and café-goers. The Palais Royale was the place
to be seen after the theatre. It was also the place to
gamble, to eat, to shop, to rent a room—by the minute—
and to dive into debauchery without fear of drowning.
For someone would pull your head up just high enough to
wrench another *sou* from between your teeth before
pushing you back under.

An ache in his gut, reminiscent of the incessant
hunger pains he'd thought he'd vanquished, made him
grimace. It was more pronounced this time. Not an alien
attack from within, but a feeling, a command to the front.

Very well. He would master this hunger.

He strode to the bed and fingered the diamond
buttons securing his waistcoat.

She will be jealous.

He must erase thoughts of Roxane from his mind.

"I want to look at you," the woman whined and
pursed a pouty moue of carmine lips.

"I'm paying by the minute, dear fuck." He leaned
over her and kissed a rosy nipple. "We've no time for a
strip show. Let's see what we can do about getting you
off."

"You care for my pleasure? You are a unique man— Oh!"

He slipped his finger between her legs and began to kiss her nipples.

I will not kiss her on the mouth, he thought. *I cannot breathe my soul into her. That is for Roxane.*

Nor must he use his teeth. Mustn't risk leaving her with such knowledge.

What to use? Hadn't thought about that.

His eyes landed on the ruby ring he wore. Perfect. While tending the wench deftly, the silver prongs scraped against his prying tooth. The jewel dropped onto the bed near her neck, a solidified droplet of crimson.

Within seconds she was moist and ready to come. He pressed his mouth over the thick vein on her neck and the inexplicable feeling of rightness chased away reluctance. As the pretty whore began to writhe and spill out her pleasure he dug the ring into her flesh and then drank away her giddy passion.

Do not take too much.

The thought discomfited him. He was not a killer. *Could I become a monster?* Had he control over the hunger?

He did not know.

He drank for a few moments. Not so sweet, this drink. Her sighs of pleasure whispered to silence. Her head fell heavily on the flat, musty pillow. And when he felt the pangs of hunger subside, he pulled away. Tugging out his handkerchief, he carefully wiped the few spots of blood from the victim's neck. She did not rouse, but with his direction, she turned onto her side, as if in peaceful sleep. Not dead then.

He pulled down her skirt to cover her exposed pretties—sweet dimple right there—but recoiled from touching her. He had—in all senses—violated her. Would she run to the streets and scream out that the Vicomte Renan had sucked away her blood?

Morbleu! He should have used a disguise, but he was tired of Leo. He would no longer hide. Let the world beware the vampire Renan.

Stepping backward, he stumbled against the door, and it opened out to the hallway. The strains of an ill-tuned hurdy-gurdy jangled up from below. Laughter and shouts for more ale signaled the night had merely begun—debts to be incurred, marriage vows to be broken.

"Come quickly," whispered close by his ear.

Gabriel spun to find Roxane standing there, her face cloaked by the hood of a black velvet cape—his cape. He licked his lips, tasting for blood, and was thankful that he had not been caught with his hands under the wench's skirts.

Rosemary infused his already giddy brain. "Roxane."

"We'll talk later." All business, her manner. "You must flee."

"Flee? Yes. Wise. But..." He turned to the sleeping whore. He supposed Roxane could guess exactly what had happened. "I did not have sex with her."

"You think I care?"

"You don't?"

"Should I?"

"Roxane, why are you being so contrary? I—"

"As I've said, there will be time later to talk. Right now we must be gone from here unless you wish someone to investigate with you in the vicinity."

"Very well." He tugged her hand to make her stay one more moment. A glance to the bed. Snores grated the air. "Will she remember?"

"To judge her appearance, it may be a common occurrence to wake in the Palais Royale sprawled on a bed."

"Roxane!"

"I cannot make promises to anything that is out of my realm of understanding."

The twosome held each other with defiant stares. She had caught him out, but he wasn't so much guilty as relieved. She must know him completely in order to trust him. And love him. Gabriel was the first to soften his gaze.

"Now," Roxane said, "follow me. We'll go out back and onto the roof."

"The roof? But—"

A tug from his stalwart witch whisked him down the long hallway. They cleared the roof. Wide silver urns sported pruned orange trees, sans fruit, but the lush glossy leaves danced in the breeze. Wooden benches were littered with bird droppings, a tipped candelabra sported a broken taper and wodges of white tallow.

A line of stone gargoyles guarded the roof, their massive wings folded against heavy bodies. Gabriel leaned against one and brushed the hair from his face. He couldn't help a proud smile. "My first time with a stranger."

"You'll have to be more careful. Practice concealing yourself. Unless you want to be written up in the *Paris Gazette*."

"Most definitely not. The *Mercure de France* is more distinguished." He noted Roxane no longer smiled.

"You're right, I did not plan this evening well. I strode from my home the elegant monster. I hadn't a clue how I would go about things until I'd gotten her to the room."

"I'm sure I don't need to hear the details." She strolled to the gargoyle next to the one he leaned on and propped her elbow on a wing, her back to him.

"I didn't fuck her," he said.

"I didn't ask."

"But you wanted to."

She shrugged.

"I couldn't. I...you—" He strolled around in front of her, forcing her to look him straight on. "If I could drink only from you, I would. But there is this dilemma of me not being able to bite you. Or so you say. You don't know how badly I want to do it. You tempt merely by existing. The scent of you intoxicates me. You epitomize all I have ever desired. You really are a witch, for I am ever beguiled and bewitched in your presence."

She lowered her eyes, then looked up through lush lashes. "Do you really care about me?"

"Yes. You don't know how I struggled with how to go about seducing that woman."

"Seducing her?"

"How else could I take her blood? I had no intention of pouncing upon her and tearing at her neck." He shuddered. "Sounds hideous to speak it."

"No," she said softly, resolute. "You would consider all the possibilities. It is your manner to think of others."

"I respect you, Roxane. And I don't want to make love to any other woman. I only brought her to a climax so she wouldn't notice when I cut her."

"You cut her?"

"Yes, to bite her would taint her with the vampire's curse. But a cut—"

"How on earth did you guess at something like that?"

"I—" He could not confess he'd spoken to the one man Roxane had been trying to locate. A man who had become a strange ally in his journey to the night. He shrugged casually, tossing a glance toward the moon. "Just a guess. An innate knowledge that accompanies vampirism. *Morbleu.* I am ashamed that you saw me in such a compromising position. You should not have—"

"I cannot say I approve, but I do understand. You need to answer the hunger. It is a part of you now."

"I refuse to kill," he rushed in.

"Of course!"

"So I have to learn to do it on the sly. And if I must seduce, I would never kiss the woman. Promise. Forgive me?"

"There is nothing to forgive."

He reached for the ends of her hair and twirled them about his forefinger. "To kiss a woman is to breathe in her soul. And in turn, give away a bit of my soul."

She bowed her head and he moved in to kiss her, to steal a morsel of her soul and secret it away inside his heart, there, where the other portions resided. Soon he would have all of her, an icy forest so lush it would overwhelm his being. He wanted to own her, to have her, to know she was only his. "Kiss me, please?"

"I can't." Without looking at him, she stuttered, "You will taste like blood."

Yes, of course. "I just wanted to hold you. You ground me, Roxane."

"Difficult to ground oneself when standing so far from it, eh?"

He smiled at her attempt at humor, appreciating the moment of lightness.

"So what are we doing up here? Toussaint waits below. Did you have plans to fly home? Can witches fly?"

"You mean by straddling a stick of broom?"

"I've always heard—"

"What *have* you heard, vicomte?"

"Well, rather it is from the faerie stories I was read as a child."

"I see. Tell me what you know about witches."

Her question piqued his call to challenge. A play at her secrets. For surely she yet held a few secrets close. "Let me see... I am sure witches ride broomsticks and stir in their cauldrons as they cackle at the moon. They are hideously ugly and have warts everywhere, even on their derrieres."

"Oh really?" She stifled a laugh behind a sweep of the cape. "Did you see any warts?"

"It strikes me suddenly that I have not taken the time to really study your bottom. Though believe me it will be first on my list next time the opportunity presents itself."

"What else do you think I should be?"

"It's not what I think you should be. Heaven knows, I've come to a whole new set of beliefs these past days. Vampires exist and witches can be the most lovely things."

"But don't you know?" She swept a hand through her hair and preened luxuriously before him. "It is all a glamour."

"It is?"

She nodded, but her giggles erupted joyously.

Drawing her into his embrace he kissed her cheek through the laughter. "This is not a mask of bewitchery. Your beauty is bone deep. I know." He smoothed a finger along her cheek, soft, like his heart. "My territory, this."

"Mmm, I like being your territory."

He leaned in to kiss her mouth, but recalled her reluctance. So instead he kissed the side of her cheek, a slow and lingering touch. He could sense her heartbeats and—the devil take him—her blood scent infused his senses. But he was full, the hunger sated; easy enough to avoid the temptation.

For now.

"Tell me what else you know about witches?"

"Hmm, well you must have a familiar. I haven't seen a black cat, but can't they change shapes and do their master's bidding?"

"Of a sort. There are feline shifting familiars, but others begin their lives as inanimate object. There is an animation ritual witches use to claim those familiars."

"I seem to recall Toussaint mentioning something about that. But hell." Toussaint had explained how witches use vampires to work an immortality spell. It had involved witches drinking blood from vampires, hadn't it? "You don't need blood to claim a familiar, do you?"

"Not at all. Did Toussaint tell you that? It simply requires a spell. I claimed mine years ago."

"Not a cat?"

"Not at all. His name is Charles."

"He? I'm jealous already. I'd like to meet the fool some time. Does he have four legs, or are we talking the human sort?"

"Hmm..." Roxane bent and looked along the line of the roof—Gabriel wasn't sure what for. "Yes, four legs. And wings."

"Wings, really? So that is how you travel then? Charles flies you about?"

"He does."

He smiled. "Now I must meet this man."

At that, the solid object Gabriel had been leaning on shifted. He lost footing and stumbled to the edge of the roof. Roxane leapt forward and grabbed his wrist, catching him from a sure fall.

"*Morbleu*! What the hell?"

The stone gargoyle Gabriel had been leaning on turned its head and looked right at him.

TWENTY-THREE

MADAME DU MARMONTE EASED herself from the circle of *precieuses* and castaway courtiers discussing the value of the latest color, *boue de Paris*—Paris mud. It neared midnight and her star had not yet arrived.

Clinging to the wall near where a potted fern sprang up gaily, she ignored the irritant leaves tickling her décolletage, and instead fiercely eyed the opposite side of the room. Set in the shadows, the garden door was Leo's preferred entrance. Discreet, yet fragrant.

Was that a *click*? Gold watch fobs?

Or that? A diamond-capped cane punctuating his footsteps?

If everyone would quiet down! But then they too would hear the cataclysmic absence of the vicomte.

The backs of her knees begin to perspire. Her legs started to bend.

"Leo did not show tonight," she gasped. "What will come of my salon?"

Following a vinegar-laced exhale, a most unladylike faint toppled her to a heap beneath the ferns.

GABRIEL EXTENDED A HAND toward the grimacing stone creature in what he hoped would be construed as a placatory gesture. A stony snarl made him recoil, yet no sound came from the beast.

"I would not believe it if I did not see it with my very eyes." He backed away, felt Roxane's body behind him and slipped around until she stood in front of him. A witch shield. To the devil with heroic notions, the stone beast was alive. "Where in Hades did you get that thing?"

Charles roared another silent snarl.

"He is not a thing." She patted the beast between its short stone ears. "And I did not *get* him. Certainly not from Hades. He is a gargoyle. I animated him a few years ago as part of my ascension."

"Ascension?"

"Part of my life-long education in the craft. Witches ascend to various levels. We often study a specific route, such as fire, water, or earth magic. I'm an earth witch. Before my ascension I was required to animate a familiar. Gargoyles make excellent familiars. Don't you, Charles," she said to the beast.

Charles curled his head against Roxane's neck and rubbed as if a cat stroking its master's leg.

"Of course. A gargoyle." Gabriel waved a nonchalant hand through the air. "An obvious choice for a familiar. Mercy."

He noted that as the wings moved the stone seemed to liquefy, and yet when not in motion the thing was clearly solid granite.

Flashes of the night of his attack assaulted with vicious acuity. The duel with the drunk. Anjou's twisted kiss. And the image of a stone beast swooping over the scene.

"I think I've seen Charles before. The night of my attack. How can that be possible?"

"He had flown on ahead of me that night."

"You knew where Anjou would next strike?"

"The general neighborhood. It was only a guess."

"I see." Discomfited, he shrugged a palm over his arm. Still so many secrets.

"We should leave." Roxane lifted her skirts in preparation—to mount? "Come along. You can ride behind me."

"You cannot be serious. Straddle that hunk of stone and wait for it to leap from the building?"

"It is best we leave now while all of Paris is gambling and wenching and has not a care for the shadows that race across the sky. Right here behind Charles's wings. Don't worry, he's very strong."

Gabriel inched forward, his arm extended as if to gingerly test the condition of a sleeping pit bull with a long stick. He touched a wing. "He is stone. And yet, he's very warm. Like he's...real."

"He is real."

"What does he do when he's not transporting you from rooftop to rooftop?"

"He sits upon the roof and waits my command."

Gabriel swung a leg over the wide stone hindquarters of Charles, and circled his arms around Roxane's waist. He had not a moment to adjust to the strange mount when the air whisked through his hair and his yelp got lost in the rush of flight.

THE AIR ABOVE THE CITY WAS SWEET. Roxane drew in a deep breath and stretched her arms wide to take in the freedom of flight. Charles always knew her wishes. She need not speak to the beast for him to understand she appreciated his dedication to her. He was the one stable force that had been in her life for years.

She'd found him sitting atop a dilapidated castle on the opposite side of the forest Villers-Cotteret. He'd looked so lonely perched high in the sky, covered in centuries of soot, dust, and bird droppings. Even from the ground she had seen deep into his carved stone eyes and sensed the inner soul.

On the eve of her initiation into immortality, her grandmother had selected the one who would bring her over—a vampire. It was known he had plans to travel through the forest. Grandmother arranged that the mark would discover Roxane, a lonely innocent by the side of the road.

Roxane had but an evening to bespell the gargoyle and make him her familiar. Drawing herself into a summoning circle, she'd stood upon the thin layer of March snow, skyclad and shivering, but determined.

Smoke of ashwood rose around her and drifted upward to the gargoyle. The spell had been spoken; so mote it be. The gargoyle stretched out a stony wing for the first time since his creation and took to the air. He soared and circled high in the midnight sky. La Luna glittered covetously upon his sweeping wing. Roxane felt their connection. For such freedom he would serve her endlessly.

When the vampire arrived, Charles had indeed served her. The gargoyle made the ritual of immortality much easier. And afterward, when she had lain beside the dead vampire, his chest wide open, and his blood streaming down her chin, she turned to the blazing bonfire. Blood initiated, she cast out her arms and took on the burn across her breasts. Later, she snuggled her head against Charles's wing and fell asleep.

They landed on the Renan rooftop with nary a wobble. Charles touched down lightly and spread his wings to allow his passengers to slide off. Gabriel let go of Roxane's waist—which she feared would bear red marks from his clinging fingers.

The gargoyle nuzzled against her stomach then padded to the roof edge and sat, head down, eyes on the city. Below, people would look up and see a decorative carving. Never would they see the familiar's subtle moves to scan the city, nor would they notice the occasional itch that stirred the beast to scratch his neck.

"That—" Gabriel staggered, then snapped upright. He smoothed a hand over his frockcoat and pressed his colored spectacles up his nose. "—was amazing! Your brother is right about one thing."

"And what is that?"

"You are the mouse that roars. I cannot imagine that I once thought you delicate and frail."

"And I should think twice about my first impression of you."

"A swish?"

"Hardly."

"Well I am, to a degree." He tugged the jabot about his neck, tufting it smartly.

"I'd call you a rake."

"Damn proud of it, too. I've spent some time perfecting an elegantly bent wrist and that idiot mincing walk."

Gabriel could not see her expression, but he sensed her disdain. "What is it?" He rushed to her side, but she pulled her arm from his touch. "Roxane?"

She beat her fists aside her thighs and spun to face him. "I never intended to fall in love with a man like you."

"A swish?"

"No, a vampire!"

Taken by her confession, he marveled at her unabashed confession to loving him.

"We are not meant to be together," she said over her shoulder. "You must understand."

"I understand nothing of late, Roxane." He slid his hands around her waist, and fit his body against hers, setting his chin on her shoulder. "I find myself questioning my every move, my every craving—for it is no longer for food but blood. I feel things that are painful and make me question my sanity. I have never before believed in vampires and witches. And yet, you are real." He kissed her neck. "So real, Roxane. Why must we be enemies? Because some dusty old grimoire declares it so?"

"Because it is my history," she said softly.

"You started out with so much faith, in the both of us. What happened?"

"Perhaps I am tired. I want you to survive this, Gabriel. But you changed the game on me. I was initially interested in a swish of a man, and now, it is a vampire I love."

"Do you know how wonderful it makes me feel to hear you say those words?"

"I should think them utterly common, considering your frequency with women."

"This is the first time they've ever been said with such conviction."

"I mean it, I do love you."

He pulled her out onto the center of the roof. Overhead a million stars sparkled, and all around them the spires of dozens of cathedrals pierced the steely gray sky. The night was still. Even the air up here was of a different universe, another time, untainted by reality.

Roxane laid her head against Gabriel's chest. "I can hear your heart beat."

"Can we do this?"

A relationship had been formed between them, and it went beyond mere companionship or polite friendship. The man had confessed his love for her.

Could she risk loving him?

Had he not been a vampire the answer would be easy. Yes, of course she loved this man. She would marry him in a moment. And in the next moment she would give him a child. Domesticity. Family. Acceptance. Everything he desired.

But could a witch really love a vampire?

"Don't think about it," he breathed against her lips.

"How do you know what I am thinking?"

"The same questions race through my mind. Just hold me. For the moment I feel as if we are the only two people in the entire world. Cruelty does not exist. Nor does fear. Roxane, I want to help your brother."

Mention of Damian dragged a sharp blade through their intimate connection. She broke from him and walked toward the roof door. "I'm sorry, I am very tired."

"I will do anything to help Damian," he offered. "The worry for him taxes you. You need your strength."

"Yes, strength to fight the vampire Anjou."

"Why fight him?" He rushed to lift the door for her but blocked her descent. "You don't need him anymore, you have me! Why do you think I—"

She glanced at him, panic paling her eyes.

"I can help your brother now, Roxane."

She opened her mouth to reply, but said not a thing. Slipping around him she stepped quickly down the stairs, his black cape billowing in her wake.

He did not call after her.

Twenty-Four

"YOU WANTED ME, RENAN?"

"Yes, I need to go out, Toussaint." Gabriel startled at his valet's appearance. Hadn't he just returned from distributing Gabriel's idea of alms? "You are disheveled, man."

"Huh." The valet patted his wrinkled shirt front and noted the misbuttoned waistcoat.

"Your hair is all ascatter, and is that lip rouge on your neck?"

Toussaint slapped a hand over the incriminating evidence.

"I see. Just come from Ninon's, yes?"

The valet nodded meekly.

"Toussaint, I believe you are leaving behind more than mere money."

"The woman likes to chat. It is very difficult to get away."

"I see." Difficult to get away? Surely, with his pants around his ankles. "Perhaps your lover will enjoy a return visit this evening."

"Whatever for?"

"You got the package I requested?"

"Right here. Took a bit of sleuthing to dig up such garb. Does this mean you'll be visiting Mademoiselle Desrues at her home?"

"Yes, I sent her after the grimoire. I wish to learn all it details about the vampire. She hasn't returned. Perhaps speaking spells?"

"So what is the plan?"

"Well, there is this silly costume. But first, I must make an obligatory visit to the Palais Royale. I'm feeling a bit peckish."

"Of course. I'll bring around the carriage."

"Do tidy up a bit first, you wouldn't want to appear lazy to your lover. Quickly. I've an appetite brewing."

ROXANE STRODE AROUND THE CHALK circle she'd marked on the hardwood floor before the hearth. Amber flames flickered and shot out fire sparkles. Skyclad, her body sucked in the heat. It felt delicious, rousing, and forbidden. She settled onto her knees in the center of the circle and lit the five white candles she'd placed around the chalk border.

The star-like placement of the candles would invoke peace and sanity. It was a ritual she followed on evenly-numbered days. As she had done every other day for two months.

It was all she could do, for her brother's madness lived in his soul. She could not influence souls. Her grandmother had taught her the human soul was not something to dally with, being the very essence of a man's life. It was good and bad. Dark and light. It was all that we are and all that we will become.

She knew there were some witches who practiced dark magic and could manipulate a man's soul; such power frightened her.

If only she could do more for Damian.

By now she should have returned to the vicomte's with the grimoire, but she needed time. Distance from the man who tempted while he also frightened.

Did Gabriel comprehend what it meant to live with a black soul? No redemption for him. No heaven.

Bending forward she blew out the candles and carefully scooped the scattered dragon's blood petals into her palm.

A knock at the door startled her to her feet. Brushing the petals into the fire released a pungent gust of floating ash. Naked, she stood in the center of the chalk circle, momentarily discombobulated. Who would call so late?

Another knock moved her. She tugged her gown from the chair and ran to the door and gripped the pull. "Who's there?"

"Renan."

She glanced around the room. The chalk circle on the floor was partially distorted from her scramble to the door. She'd alluded that she had plans to cast a spell for Damian before she had left this afternoon. He already knew she was a witch.

Of course, right now she was a naked witch.

Again the knock. "Roxane?"

"Yes." Pulling the heavy velvet gown over her shoulders, she was thankful the ancient garb did not require lacing or pinning. A gift from her great, great grandmother, she oft wore the gown when casting; it grounded her spells with the wisdom from the ages.

Fluffing out her hair, she opened the door. Gabriel stood in a long black redingote, a tricorn set upon his dark hair. A wigless head. No lace? And where was the requisite walking stick?

His dark eyes fixed to her from above the narrow blue spectacles, granting him a roguish appeal. Not that the man needed any help with accessories for that.

She smiled at the sight and stepped back. "Come in."

He did not enter so much as magnetically attach himself to her.

"This gown!" He threaded his fingers through hers and held out her arms from her body as his eyes dripped over her from head to toe. "Why, it's positively medieval. Where did you find it?"

"It was my great great grandmother's." She touched the embroidered leaves that danced about the wide neckline. "It has been in the family for some time. It's threadbare and simple—"

"It is divine, Roxane. The emerald color makes your eyes darker. Like jewels. And your hair"—he twined his fingers through her unbound tresses—"it falls over the velvet as if an exotic fabric. Monsieur Bousset would gain a fortune if he offered the like in his shop. Lovely, just lovely. You are truly the ice-forest queen."

"I am quite sure you say as much to all your women."

"Hmm, perhaps." He turned and strode a few paces toward the door. "But would I do this for any woman?" He flipped the openings of his great coat and flung it to the floor behind him to reveal—

"*Losh!*"

REMOVING HIS REDINGOTE *WHOOSHED* a draft up behind his legs. Gabriel managed a regal posture. The look on Roxane's face was worth the humility.

"You're wearing a plaid!" she declared in glee.

Toussaint had worked wonders in conjuring the costume in record time. Gabriel obliged by turning, kicking out his heel, and posing. The kilt was actually very freeing. He favored the unique feel of fabric moving loosely over his flesh. Everything beneath swung so...freely.

He slipped a finger behind the fur-edged sporran and waggled it up and down. "Bet you want to know what I keep in here, eh?"

"Actually—" she slipped a hand down his plaid thigh "—I'd love a peek *under* the plaid."

"The woman is a brazen."

"I can't believe you did this, Gabriel. What possessed you?"

"You did once tell me you desired a Highlander. Here you are. One French Highlander, in the flesh."

"For me?"

"There's not another soul in this world I'd allow to see me in such a costume. A little breezy down there, though not entirely uncomfortable. What do your countrymen do about their, er...danglers?"

"Not sure."

"Good." He kissed her nose. "I'd hate to hear you have the answer to that one."

"I will discover what you've done with your danglers."

"I wager you will. But first..." He crossed to the hearth and looked over the chalk marks on the floor. Guttered candles circled the drawing and a trail of ash swept up and into the hearth. She'd been casting a spell, no doubt about it. "Any luck?"

"I cannot touch my brother's soul. And it is his soul that requires saving."

"Did you check on *my* soul in your book?"

"Didn't have time. I was planning to bring it to you—"

"No worry. We can inspect it later."

He'd come here with debauchery in mind. No need to stray from his intentions. He spread his arms to display the fabulous costume. "Are you up for a little play?"

"Sure." She sunk in the chair. Folds of emerald velvet curled about her limbs. Gloom misted upon her sigh.

"You, my lady, sound positively eager."

"I want to find that bastard, Anjou—"

"You don't need him anymore."

She turned on him, wonder in her tearing eyes. So she had not figured it all out, even with his remarkable clue last eve.

Gabriel splayed his hands before him. "You think I couldn't have made it to the full moon? But one day remained."

"But—"

"You don't believe I could have made it without going mad? I do."

"Then why did you succumb?"

"I sought the challenge. A new beginning, perhaps." He picked at a tuft of beaver fur rimming the curved edge of the sporran. "That wasn't the only reason I chose to complete the transformation."

"Gabriel, you can't mean... I had thought your suggestion last night—"

"A farce? I overheard you telling Toussaint you required a vampire to transform your brother in an attempt to cure his madness. Do you still want to try?"

"You drank blood...to help Damian?"

He nodded.

"I don't know what to say. You..." She pushed fingers through her hair, and spun away from him. Should she not be stepping into his embrace? Why could she not accept what he offered? "You sacrificed your mortal soul for Damian!"

"Yes, well, at the time, I wasn't aware of that small detail. Though I am still not sure I am without said soul. I don't feel lacking. Only your dusty book can tell." He toed the thick volume.

"I'm sorry, Gabriel, I should have told you more, but I never expected—"

Feeling her pain with every shivering word, he kissed her, silencing further protest. "I do not want you consorting with that killer. You cannot trust him to help you and your brother. Did you actually believe that you could somehow entice Monsieur Anjou to help you?"

She embraced him and laid her head on his shoulder. Her body loosened and hot tears dripped through the thin white Holland shirt Toussaint had insisted the Highlanders wore with the draped plaid that ran from shoulder to waist. Spreading his hands over the burnished green velvet and around her waist, he felt her curves fill his palms. How she filled his empty heart. He could feel Roxane's relief, yet tainted with tendrils of pain. And he could hear her blood, rushing throughout her body. But the only temptation was that to make her life better.

"You've sacrificed much," she said, looking up into his eyes.

He bent to kiss the palest, sweetest lips he had ever kissed. She opened her mouth and dove inside him. `Twas as if he were being invaded, taken over, his castle gates plundered. Roxane laid siege to his heart. And he surrendered.

"Take it all," he whispered. "Master me. Spill your luscious colors over me."

"Make love to me, Gabriel," whispered against his open mouth. "Right here, on the floor. I will get a blanket."

"Unnecessary. I believe for all the plaid I'm wearing we'll have an ample nest to roll about."

"Let me help." She unpinned the silver leaf broach at his shoulder and, walking around behind him, began to unwrap the ells and ells of blue, green and crimson plaid. "Like unwrapping a gift!"

He twirled out of the plaid, his shirt falling to his thighs and his sporran hanging to conceal what lie beneath. "Och, my lassie, er...well, something like that. Come, vixen, care to take a peek behind the sporran now?"

Dropping the plaid between them, Roxane took to that offer with a delighted giggle.

He spun and upended her over his knees. "But first—Time to check for warts."

"What?"

"On your derriere, my love." She whimpered as his palm glided to her bare bottom. Smooth and soft, and so in need of a sucking kiss. "No warts. Are you sure you are a witch?"

"I am."

"Then prove it. Bewitch me."

Twenty-Five

True, she was half Scottish, thanks to her maternal side, but when in her lifetime had she ever helped a man *on* with his plaid? Gabriel stood with arms out to the side, patiently enduring Roxane's perplexed study of the situation. She held a clump of plaid, half-wrapped around the man's waist. Did not this tartan come with instructions?

"You know," he said, "you speak Scottish in your sleep."

Roxane gaped. They had dozed after making love. "What did I say?"

"How the devil should I know? I don't speak the language. Whatever it was, it seemed to please you."

She felt a blush heat her skin. Maybe she had been whispering sweet nothings about their lovemaking. She'd not known she did such a thing. Surely, he teased her.

"There must be a trick to this far more canny than magic. I've never seen a man put on a plaid."

"Only take one off?"

"Shush, you swish, I was a virgin when you had me."

He turned and kissed her, playfully tweaking her cheek with his palm. "Promise you'll have no other man beside me?"

"You mean our sleeping together is not to be construed as a marriage proposal?"

He gaped.

She had expected such a reaction. But it didn't bother her. Roxane had chosen freely to sleep with one of Paris's most infamous rogues. Far be it from her to expect to tame him in so little time. But, if given opportunity, she did favor continuing with a more permanent form of bewitchery.

"Would you have me as your husband?"

"In an instant."

"You would?" His eyes switched between hers in such nervous surprise, it made Roxane smile. Perhaps not so much surprise as sheer terror.

"I do love you, Gabriel."

"And I love you."

Slipping an arm around her waist he tugged her to him. Dark, his whiskey-brown eyes, but they twinkled with bits of mischief. She touched his upper lip, ran her finger along his soft moustache.

He playfully nipped at her fingers. His voice, soft and husky, touched her very soul. "The past few days I've been struggling with whether it was love or simple lust."

"Lust is never simple."

"True. I only realized it last night when I walked into this room and saw you standing in that lovely dress." He pointed to her grandmother's gown, heaped on the floor before the hearth. "You are the most vivid color in my life. I would be honored to be your husband, Roxane. Will you be my wife?"

So unexpected, yet desired.

He lifted her chin. "Have I completely befuddled you, then? *Mon Dieu*, you don't know how I yearn for domesticity."

"I have my suspicions." For she had remarked the simple man behind the lace and wigs. "You want to be noticed."

"Only by you."

"To never feel abandoned."

"To love and be loved. To have a family. To have a partner, a wife I can shower with pretty things and show off at the theatre. Can you be my wife? Would you choose to live with your natural enemy?"

"A vampire and a witch." She draped the plaid over his shoulder and turned to face the simmering coals in the hearth. Mountains of ash glowed red around the base like a guttered volcano. "It is quite the farce. At some point you are going to crave blood, and the only one around will be me."

His embrace sent a shiver through her system. Strong arms spread around her torso and his hands gently cupped her breasts. "I would never harm you, Roxane."

"I know you would not." A moment to linger in his truth. A lifetime to breathe his presence. It could not be. "But as your wife, would I be expected to allow you to go off in search of whores that you would pay to bite?"

"I—er... That's not fair, Roxane."

"Yes, it is." Bending to pick up the emerald gown she pressed it to her breasts and turned to him. "If I don't question now, it'll be too late when the answers are given. I do love you. But could I really live with knowing that you embraced other women—"

"To survive!"

She nodded. Sighed. Why was she asking the tough questions? Why not rejoice, celebrate the love they shared and seal that by posting the banns?

"Well..." he thought about it, finger to lip. "I could bite only men?"

Roxane quirked a brow.

"Just a thought. I would do what I could to make it easy for you, but there are some sexual feelings involved."

"I had guessed that."

"I never did tell you how it felt when Anjou attacked me. Vulgar. And yet, he made me—"

"Want the bite?"

"Yes." *You will be loved.* "I loved him for that moment."

"That explains some things." About Damian as well. "You were mumbling nonsense after the attack."

"Shameful things."

"Damian said much the same. I know that your female, er, *victims* would mean nothing to you but a means to an end. But we must face reality. I could unintentionally harm you, Gabriel."

"So my pretty witch believes her blood to be so sweet as to be irresistible?"

"Do you honestly believe the blood hunger will always allow discretion?"

"Of course not."

"You have shown me you are not as you appear on the outside. The lace is just a costume, a façade. You are a fine man, Gabriel."

"Just not husband material?"

"I didn't say that."

"You are frightened of marriage?"

"Not at all. I—"

"Say you will have me, please?"

She searched his face, finding genuine need in the depths of his dark eyes. So soft, so tender, utterly compelling. He wanted to be loved. A simple request. An honest desire.

But she, a vampire's wife? And he, a witch's husband. What a farce!

And yet, they both understood one another

"I love you?" she murmured.

Gabriel tilted his head. "Are you asking me or telling me?"

"If you think it can work, I want to give it a try."

"I've witnessed more enthusiasm from a man riding the tumbrel to his end."

"I'm sorry—"

A knock on the door drew both around. Roxane shrugged at Gabriel's silent query. She tugged his plaid down and tucked it in at the waist. A terrible mess of fabric, but it did cover all the dangly bits. In turn he pulled the gown over her head.

"Who is it?" she called.

No answer.

Roxane opened the door, and her world became more complicated than she could ever imagine. "Father."

THE MAN SHE CARED SO LITTLE FOR stood in the doorway waiting to be invited in. As if only yesterday she had danced about his legs, begging to be swung by the arms in a circle. As if mother still lived. As if he had not fled their family a decade earlier.

Dressed in fine satin and looking a courtier for his white bagwig and red heels, Xavier Desrues had improved his couture since she last remembered him wearing a simple shirt and chamois breeches.

She felt the warmth of Gabriel's hand slide down her back as she contemplated her options. She did not despise Xavier so much as to appreciate he had gifted her with this fine apartment. But this gift—and the city— had lured Damian to destruction.

No, that wasn't right. Damian had found madness on his own. Xavier had nothing to do with the vampire Anjou's attack.

"Roxane?" Gabriel whispered in her ear, nudging her to surface from her muddled thoughts.

"Father." She signaled he enter with a bow of her head. "I had not expected your visit."

"Apparently," the man said as he eyed her gown—the hem was rumpled and crunched—and then he took a long look over Gabriel. "Won't you introduce me to your companion?"

Clutching for some piece of fabric to cover her— hide her from the condemning eyes of her father— Roxane slipped her fingers through Gabriel's warm hand and coaxed him around to her side. She winced to think what a sight they made. She in grandmother's ancient gown and he in a tangled plaid and no shoes, with tousled hair.

"Father, this is Vicomte Gabriel Renan. Gabriel, my father, Xavier Desrues."

"Ah, vicomte." Xavier bowed curtly. "I believe I have heard of your reputation."

"All of it earned, I'm sure," Gabriel offered. "I have heard very little about you from your daughter."

"To be expected. Neither did I say what information I have on you is favorable."

Gabriel bristled. "I care little what you think of me, Monsieur Desrues."

"Well then, let us cut through the surface niceties and get to the point, shall we? What the hell are you—a rake of the first water—doing in my daughter's home dressed like a savage Scot?"

"It is not your concern, father."

"Roxane." Xavier's jaw tensed, but his eyes remained gentle, submitting. Ever quiet in his control, she remembered futilely. To walk away from his family without warning had been the cruelest form of control. "I accept the fact that you despise everything about me. And I know you can never love me the way a daughter does her father. I've missed many years of your life, which I regret. But know this, I have never stopped loving you."

"You have a strange way of showing it," Gabriel interjected.

"And I will know"—Xavier glared at the vicomte—"what one of Paris's most infamous rakes is doing in your home with you dressed in—whatever that is—and he looking as though he's tumbled from your bed!"

Gabriel splayed out his hands. "I have tumbled from your daughter's bed."

Xavier gripped the hilt of the rapier fastened at his hip.

"Father, no!"

"I have also just proposed marriage to her," Gabriel continued. "I love your daughter, Monsieur Desrues. Please accept my apologies for our appearance. Though certainly, I am to understand, Roxane would have never expected your visit."

Xavier lifted his chin, his eyes not leaving Gabriel's. Roxane could feel the heat simmer between the two of them. She sensed that if she put her hand between their line of sight it would ignite.

"You plan to marry this rake?" Xavier asked her, not hiding his obvious contempt for the vicomte.

"I don't know."

Gabriel bristled. "You don't know?"

"You have only just asked."

Lifted from his spell of anger, her father directed a much softer gaze at Roxane. "Forgive me, sweet one."

She lowered her head at the moniker. Distant memories rushed back at his favorite nickname for her. "Another dance with papa, sweet one?" Once upon a time they had been so happy.

Why had he abandoned them? Did he not understand, no matter his reasons, the pain could never be justified? The loss without answer. The constant questions. Had he at least given a reason before walking away her soul would be all of one piece now.

Now Roxane felt her connection to Gabriel deepen. She squeezed his hand. They had both been abandoned.

"It is your life to live," Xavier finally said. "I will not ask further. Though I would request you find a robe."

"Certainly."

Thankful for a reprieve, Roxane rushed to her bedroom, followed closely by Gabriel. A moment to breathe, to regroup and accept that her father was here, looking exactly the same as he had the day he left—if that was possible. His hair had always been short and spare, and acorn color. Green eyes, like mother's had been. And a soft smile that seemed harder to find now. It was as if he had not aged a single day.

Shrugging her arms into the tattered blue duster, she turned and found herself in Gabriel's arms. "I'm sorry, I had not expected him."

He kissed her on the nose. The touch lifted her from the abyss of tense confusion.

"Let me adjust your plaid." She spun under his arm and tugged at the long ells of fabric.

"He doesn't look so terrible."

"My father is not a terrible person. It's hard to explain."

"He abandoned you when you needed a father most."

"Yes."

"He broke your mother's heart."

"Completely."

"He led your brother to Paris, and ultimately, to madness."

"Father was not to blame for Damian's attack."

"Exactly."

She found herself in Gabriel's gaze. Not condemning, but compassionate. They were two alike. And yet, two who stood at very opposite sides of what could and could not be. "Can you forgive me the lack of compassion for your own abandonment?"

"Neither of us were taught compassion by our parents."

"My mother did," Roxane said. "But after father left, well, she did not live long after that."

The threat of tears was imminent. So much to contend with. Gabriel, her lover. Gabriel, her supposed enemy. Damian, a lost soul. And now, her father—a dangerous hit to her bruised heart. "I've been through so much emotionally these past few months."

"I understand."

"Yes, you do." For all she yet had not learned of Gabriel's bruised heart, she did know their pain was similar. "When my world first fell to tatters about me, I had my brother to comfort me. What did you do, all by yourself?"

"There was Toussaint. That man has caught me in more than a few sudden hugs—he initiating, of course. I'll be damned that the man always knows when I need that silent comfort. He has seen much."

"Mercy, what a mess we two are," she said on a silly trill that tried to grasp mirth, but could only touch devastation. "My father waits."

"Will you be able to face him?"

She nodded. "You won't leave me with him?"

"Of course not. I am yours to beckon, my brazen little witch. Just pull the draperies, or your father will find it odd if I wear my spectacles indoors."

ROXANE IMMEDIATELY PULLED THE curtains shut. Only then did Xavier turn and face the twosome who stood before the glowing ash in the hearth.

"I had come to see if Damian might like to attend the theatre with me this evening," Xavier said. "Is he about?"

"Er—" Thought of confession frightened her as much as having her father in her home did. "Actually, Damian has been out the entire night. I'm not sure if he'll return until late this evening." She'd never lied to her father. But Xavier did not deserve to know, not yet. Not until she could find a way to make everything right. "You expect to walk back into our lives as if nothing is amiss?"

"Is there a better way to retie a loosened past?"

"Yes. No. I don't know. I've never abandoned my family!" Roxane bowed her head. What had she expected of the man? She needed time to sort her thoughts.

"I have my reasons. Yet I cannot explain them."

"When will you?"

"Sooner rather than later?" Gabriel challenged Xavier.

"Yes, soon. I promise. When I can sit down with both you and Damian."

"Damian is not here. He's...in love." She winced at the lie.

Xavier whistled. "Both my children in love? How splendid. Is she lovely?"

Roxane shrugged. "Of course."

"Titled?"

She swept a look to Gabriel.

"It is rumored," Gabriel offered with the same painful expression that held Roxane in check.

"Well, well." Xavier paced to the hearth and toggled the pendulum of the brass clock that had not been wound since the night of Damian's attack. He looked over the chalk markings, seeming unfazed. "This news fills me with joy. I insist the two of you—rather, both couples—accompany me to the theatre tonight. To celebrate?"

"But—"

Gabriel spoke over Roxane's imminent protest. "We would be delighted, Monsieur Desrues. Though I cannot vouch that we will see Roxane's brother before then. Love has a tendency to change the hours of the day to serve only desire."

"Very well. I should be thankful one of my children is willing to rekindle our relationship."

Roxane bristled at his suggestion. She wanted to scream, to shout, to stomp and pout. To rage at the man. To make him see her. Look at me, I have changed. I have survived! To make him feel the pain of loss she had felt so many years ago.

She had gotten over that loss. But now, with Xavier's re-entrance into her life, the scab had been peeled away to reveal a seeping wound.

TWENTY-SIX

"HE'S GOING TO ASK MORE about Damian. I should have never lied like that!"

"The truth would have only frightened him. Besides, I sense you want to help Damian before revealing to your father all that has gone on."

"If that is possible."

Gabriel stroked her hair and kissed the crown of her head. "Your brother and father are much alike, yes?"

"Very much." She shed the robe and strode to the hearth to toe the remnants of the chalk circle. "They are both fops, living for the chase and women."

"Sounds more rakish to me."

"You and your definitions."

"I thought we had gone beyond labels."

"So had I."

"Yet still you label your father and brother?"

Bending, she plucked up a stray flower petal and pressed it beneath her nose. Turning, she smiled with her memories. "Damian is the sweetest, most genuine man. He would throw himself before a cavalry to save a loved one."

"And your father?"

"He was once a kind man, always laughing, playing with me. I followed him about the gardens as if a puppy dog. Damian would often yip teasingly at me." But for all the good, the darkness would never recede. "Father left my mother without explanation. She died because of him!"

"Roxane, don't get upset. I know this is painful. But the man could not have been the cause of her death."

"He was!"

"Tell me about it. Please?"

She sniffed and settled into his arms. "My mother drowned. I found her lying in the meadow surrounded by yellow coltsfoot and clutching the grimoire. She had bespelled herself, grandmother said."

"I don't understand. Did she fall into a lake, a pond? To have drowned?"

"After father left, she was not the same. Mother drew away from Damian and me. She cried constantly. I mean it—literally, her face was never dry. Grandmother said she had placed a spell upon her soul with her sadness. Doom nested in her being. She was a water witch; forged in water, she could only be destroyed by the like. She literally drowned in her own tears, Gabriel. It was horrible. She died of a broken heart."

"Does your father know?"

"I would not give him the satisfaction of knowing how he left our mother. He believes she drowned in the usual manner."

"Do you think that is fair? Should not the man know? If he never explained his reason for leaving maybe he was forced?"

"He walked away of his free will."

"According to the eyes of a child."

"I was sixteen. Old enough to understand."

Yes, old enough to know when one has gone beyond concern in the eyes of a parent. *Adieu, Gabriel, we leave you with the house and your inheritance. A good life for you.*

"When a man leaves should he not be obliged to, at the very least, offer parting words? I want to love him, Gabriel, truly I do. Because that is what you do—you love your parents unceasingly. But where is the sanity in such complete and utter abandonment?"

There was none. Xavier's leaving could not be justified from this side of the coin. Roxane's feelings were real and true and they touched Gabriel in that hollow core of his being. A part that rarely allowed in hope.

"So your mother was a witch?"

"Yes."

"Did your father know that?"

"Yes, of course." She sniffed back tears. "As well, he knew that I was."

"Damian is not?"

"It doesn't take with the men as easily as the women. Male witches are rare. I was born into my magic."

"Perhaps the truth will bring out the unspoken secrets from Xavier."

"What truth?"

"Of his leaving his family. It cannot be as simple as wanting to live in Paris. I do not accept that."

"You've known the man less than five minutes and already you take his side?"

"I stand beside you, Roxane. Always." So tender his gaze; a vampire's gaze. Seductive and primal, yet genuinely touched by compassion. "But I sense that a decade of separation has widened the chasm between father and daughter. Did you ever ask him?"

She shook her head. "I've never had opportunity. He chose to widen the distance with his indifference. And now look what I've done. To make him believe his son is in love with a duchess!"

"We did not specify her title."

Roxane moaned miserably. His embrace did nothing to dispel the queasy roil in her gut. She wished she had a spell to erase the past twenty-four hours—no—for then she would erase the delicious lovemaking with her French Highlander.

Could she get through this evening sandwiched between the father she did not understand and her new vampire lover?

"Tell me your thoughts."

"I am thinking I am heading straight to Hades for my lies to father, and for taking up with a vampire."

"This coming from a witch? Are we not both destined for hell?"

"We are not evil, Gabriel."

Turning, she retrieved the heavy grimoire and returned to Gabriel. They settled onto the chair and together paged through the book, scanning the ink-drawn pictures and touching the fragments of raven's feather and dried nettle and various bits of broken glass and torn fabric.

Roxane read the words her grandmother had written, "The vampire sacrifices his mortal soul for immortality."

"I see," he whispered.

"I know your heart, Gabriel. You are a fine, good man, that is all that matters."

"Sure."

So little belief in that one word. It was a horrible truth to learn. There was no way to make it any less by detouring him from reality.

"Is he like me, your brother? A man without a soul, or is it that we still have souls only they are dark now?"

"I believe he still has one, tormented as it is."

"So why would you want to rescue your brother by darkening his soul?"

Roxane gaped, closed her mouth, and said, "You make it sound twisted. I only want to help him. I have struggled with this decision, Gabriel. Would not a dark soul be far better than madness?"

"I'm not sure."

"Damian has his lucid moments."

"Who is to say madness is not the very definition of an evil soul? Those men I saw in Bicêtre, their eyes did not possess life."

"Yours do."

"We will help your brother get back the light in his eyes." He embraced her and kissed her forehead. "We can bring him to my home. Toussaint can help watch him."

Gabriel looked out the window. Certainly drinking blood had been a finer trade for madness. But would such a hunger eventually drive him toward the same madness Damian Desrues lived?

AFTER WAITING AN HOUR AT THE THEATRE, Roxane decided Xavier would not show. Just as well. She had no desire to face him after the lies she had conjured. Until truths could be spoken, she preferred her father to remain at a distance.

Gabriel had suggested they go for a walk. Just the thing to clear their minds and settle their tensions.

She had not before been to the Tuileries. Always Damian would remind her they had not the courtly presence to secure pass through the gates. Though she had known Damian dreamed of strolling the militant hedgerows as much as she. A framed print of the garden held a place of honor on the hearth in their country parish.

Now she fluttered her fingers across the stiff boxwood. Perfect planes shaped the shrubs into exact angles, curves and arabesques. Her skirts dusted the grass, sweet with fragrant midnight dew. The scents stirred in her wake reminded of home.

The night guard had recognized Gabriel—as Leo— immediately, and admitted them. Roxane was thrilled to find they had the entire garden to themselves. Though she could not determine Gabriel's mood. He hadn't spoken more than a few words during their walk. It was as if his thoughts were a star's journey away. Certainly, with good reason.

The oil lanterns dotting the stone paths burned low and put out an acrid scent. Spinning in the aisle of a curved hedgerow, she lifted her arms and tilted back her head. The moon was not in sight for the clouds. Perhaps that was the bitterness that kept Gabriel at a distance and lingering in the grotto on the other side of the double broderie. He ran his palms over the tops of the boxwood, counting, an absent distraction.

She would let him stew.

Life had once been simple. Unfettered by worry, by wanton greed or fear. Lilac, roses, and rosemary surrounded the parish. A garden of simples hugged the east side, while a potagerie paralleled the south.

Roxane gulped in deep breaths of the verdant air.

Loosening the tight laces that crossed down the front of the red velvet bodice—her nicest for the theatre—her lungs expanded and rejoiced at the freedom. The night breeze kissing the bare mounds of her breasts felt exquisite. Her nipples tingled and hardened.

Plunging to her knees, her skirts spreading in a ruby wave about her, she pressed her fingers into the grass. Cool dew licked at her wrists. Scent of the untainted, the pure and unspoilable, enticed her to lean forward to brush her lips across the grass tips.

"Take me home," she wished aloud. "Make life simple once again. Remove the taint from my life. I pray to you, earth goddess. With this earthen kiss grant a beginning to a new life. So mote it be."

Not a spell, but a form of wishcraft that required exquisite timing and determination. *It will come to pass.*

A black shadow grew across the bejeweled grass. Roxane turned and rolled onto her back, smiling up at Gabriel.

"Do you know, there are eighteen boxwood shrubs down this aisle, and a matching eighteen across the way? One-hundred and twenty-two lindens line the pond back there. And the stones, I should really look into their numbers..." He turned and started toward the stones.

Roxane grabbed his ankle. "Come, sit by me. We'll count the stones later."

"But..." She tugged and he relented, sitting by her and trailing a finger through her hair. "Remember Toussaint's net? We vampires like to count, to our detriment. Did your brother go mad from the hunger before the moon reached her fullness?"

"No, the madness accompanied the arrival of the full moon." She twined her fingers into his. That brought him down to lie on his side facing her. "Do you hunger now?"

"Yes."

"How often does a vampire need to drink blood?"

"Not sure."

"Do you feel instinctive about it?"

"Yes. No. I'm not sure. Well, yes, I know the feeling when it arrives. Deep and ingrained, if you can believe that. I guess it is something I will become accustomed to."

"Do you wish to leave? To find an, er...manner to quench your hunger?"

The sudden heat of his mouth on her breast chased away her troubling query.

"I'm hungry for this," he murmured against her flesh as he tugged the ribbon laces even looser. "What have you been up to, running about untethered?"

"The urge came upon me."

"Mm, I'm familiar with urges, you saucy nudist. But you're not alone now. In fact, I have it on good authority that you hold company with a dangerous creature. The mythical vampire. Are you frightened?"

"Should I be?"

He tweaked her nipple, and she arched her back in response, lifting her breasts high and entreating him continue. She did not fear him looking upon the fire mark; it was who she was. Circling her nipple with his tongue, he sucked and laved at her flesh. "We might be discovered."

"Good."

"Oh? You are a voyeur then?"

"Voyeurs like to watch. I think to *be* watched might be exciting."

"I'll keep an eye on you." The nearby lamplight reflected in his eyes. Two wide glowing fires burned in the centers of his dark irises. They matched the blaze that flickered inside her. "This mark of ascension is gorgeous. You are gorgeous." He slipped a hand down her thigh and pulled up her skirts. Her lace petticoat rustled like the linden leaves overhead. "I want to watch you come, lover."

His hand slid across her thigh, up, warming a path to her belly. A commanding move that drew pleasurable moans from her throat. Roxane parted her legs and felt him enter her with a single finger.

"*Mon amour,*" he breathed. "You're so ready."

"You make me ache, Gabriel." Two fingers danced inside her, exploring, mapping Renan territory, then slipped up to tease at her aching clitoris. "Yes, right there—no, don't stop. You tease me."

"Merely prolonging the madness," he whispered.

She could sense the irony in his voice, but closed her eyes to darker meanings. Fire coursed through her veins. Dew dripped from her flesh to splat upon the midnight-sweet blades of grass.

Pulse beats quickened, synchronizing between them and huffing out in wanting gasps and moans and whispers for more, more—"More," Roxane cried.

"I've a spell of my own, witch," he whispered. "You like it?"

"If this is the vampire's thrall, I gladly sacrifice to have it. Oh!"

Silently she succumbed, floating upon the madness of pleasure he offered. Little frantic pulses tugged her limbs and shivered through her being. Delicious. Splendid. The rush of desire would not relent.

"I want to feel you." She slid her hand down the buttoned satin waistcoat and to his breeches.

Gabriel muttered, "That's not a stake in my pocket."

She laughed, despite his droll humor. But too quickly her laughter segued to uncontrollable gasps. Her body convulsed, mining the edge of release. So close to flight.

A fang grazed her nipple and she flashed her eyes wide. "No, Gabriel!" She jerked upright, pushing him away with a palm to his forehead.

But he resisted her and seized her hand, pinning it behind her back. Flickering light glinted on the sharp fangs that skimmed his lower lip.

With her free hand, she touched one. He grinned. His other hand, still caught between her legs—a flick of one finger shot a shudder through her system.

"What shall it be?" he wondered in a deep voice laced with whimsy. "Pleasure or pain?"

"Don't do it, Gabriel. I choose pleasure." She squeezed her thighs about his hand. Vibrations of her flight hummed, taunting, cleaving for release, to glide as if floating. "Please?"

"What if I wish to chance it? Once already I have tasted your blood."

"Why must you speak like that? I don't want to lose you. I love—"

He gripped her neck, choking off her words. The finger between her legs slipped out and across her thigh.

Roxane swallowed. His fingers clenched her throat. The sensations still roiling in her loins were difficult to hold on to. What was he up to?

"You will *not* love me, don't ever say it." He bared his fangs in a wicked sneer. Moonlight glinted upon his truth. Gabriel's eyes sought hers, bouncing from one to the other. "I am a beast. I do not want the burden of such emotion."

"You cannot speak my mind for me. It is the blood hunger talking. You are not like this, Gabriel. Stop!"

That burst of fear changed the malicious glimmer in the vicomte's eyes. As if suddenly realizing his slip into malice, his face softened, his mouth falling open.

He nestled his face into her hair, his jaw resting on her shoulder. A beast subdued? She mustn't test, for fear of his fangs. One bite would see him dead.

"Please don't love me, Roxane, for you are the very death of me."

Bittersweet truth.

"Must I be satisfied with making love to you, but never *having* your love?"

"Yes, that is how it must be. It is the only choice I can offer you."

"What has become of your proposal to marriage? Must I accept becoming your wife without the love? What of your desire to have a family?"

"Roxane." A humorless smile. "Be satisfied with what I can give you. You've no worry that I'll take up with another woman. I want only you."

"You want this." She gripped his wrist, dragging his fingers to her mons.

"Oh, yes. Sweet witch, dripping for me. Moaning for— But I want all of you, Roxane."

"What if I refuse to give all without your love? Without the promise of a family and marriage and a normal life?"

"Normal? You ask that of a vampire, witch?"

He had a point.

She hated to hear him talk like this. It was not Gabriel drawing this negative argument, it was the urge for darkness, the need for sustenance. "Very well." She spoke the lie easily. Things would never be simple. She would never truly know happiness. "If that is all you can offer, I want it. Fuck me, Gabriel."

"My sweet little witch."

And her body reached the pinnacle she had touched. Gabriel bewitched. He commanded. He devastated. Climax rode a silent wave through her every bone.

And when the two lay still within the shadows of the garden, her lover whispered, "I love you, Roxane."

All she had wanted to hear meant so little now.

"I hate you, Gabriel Renan. I hate you for your lies and your truths." She pulled herself up. "Take me home. To my house, not yours."

Twenty-Seven

THEY LET OFF ROXANE AT HOME. She did not turn to Gabriel nor did she bid him *au revoir*. It mattered not, for his skull yet echoed with her vehement diatribe.

I hate you, Gabriel.

How was that possible? After they had made love in the shadows of the Tuileries? *Morbleu*, he may have been abrupt with her. Indeed, it had been the hunger talking. But he'd confessed his love!

And had then taken it back.

The horses snorted; their hooves pawed the cobbles. Toussaint waited for a signal that they leave.

"Go," Gabriel said on a sigh.

"Home!" Toussaint bellowed at the driver.

"The Palais Royale," Gabriel called to correct. He ignored Toussaint's appalled gape and stared out the window.

I HATE YOU, GABRIEL.

Roxane had every right. First, he asked her to marry him, and then he promised her he could never love her.

Well, he couldn't. His love would only hurt her. Vampires and witches were no mix.

He must do what he had planned. Save the brother from serving as endless liege to the mad men of Bicêtre, then be done with Roxane. A vampire vicomte was not what was best for a simple country witch.

"We're here."

"Very good. Don't wait, Toussaint. I'll walk."

"But—"

A flash of fang silenced the servant.

SATED, GABRIEL DRAGGED AN ARM across his mouth. No blood on his shirt; he was learning delicacy. Swaggering into a grinning stride he mentally congratulated his neatness.

Breathe now. Be alone. Dive into this new life. Understand it, so it will not bring you so far into the shadows you can never emerge.

He walked around a blurry haze of light reflected on the ground. Glancing up he spied a window that released candle glow to the outside world in the shape of a cross. He stood outside a little chapel.

"Be alert," he chided the giddy new beast inside him. "Or soon find your death."

Footsteps echoed. From around the corner walked a man in blue damask and tricorn.

Him.

"We missed you at the opera," Gabriel called.

Xavier Desrues did not appear in the least startled. "I was otherwise occupied."

"Roxane expected as much."

The man strode a wide circle about him and the cross-shaped glow on the cobbles. He drew black gloves through his fingers, stroking, slightly menacing. "So you've fucked my daughter and offered the requisite marriage proposal. Quite the gentleman you are, vicomte."

"I've no dispute with you, Desrues. I've no intention of judging, for your life is your own. As well, Roxane's life is her own."

"So if she chooses to run about with a known rake I should stand back and allow it to happen? You are foolhardy if you think I care so little about my girl. Yes, we have our differences. I'll be damned if she blames me for her mother's death. I blame myself every morning that I rise. Roxane has suffered for my indiscretions. But I'll not allow you to make her life the worse."

"I've no intention of doing any such thing." Gabriel stepped forward. The cross glow touched his flesh. He recoiled at first sense of heat. "I love your daughter, Monsieur Desrues. I crave a life of domesticity with her and our children."

"You'll grant me the benefit of doubt, since I am aware of your reputation."

"Mere surface glamour. I am not the man you see."

"So, you are a liar?"

Gabriel punched a frustrated fist through the air and paced away from the dangerous light shaped of the holy. "You've every right to hold me to the highest standards, for she is your daughter. No man should be good enough for her. Especially not a—" *Vampire*, he thought.

Xavier's damask heels clicked toward Gabriel. The man, much younger than he should appear, angled a hard gaze at Gabriel. "Would you walk away from her if I insisted?"

It is what he should have done all along, the very moment the ice queen bewitched him with her celadon gaze. But what man could resist her allure? The hope of love...

"Yes," Gabriel offered.

"Then I insist."

"But—"

"Ah." Xavier waved a finger between them. His eyes castigated. "I knew there would be a but. There always is."

"Do you honestly believe that you, a man who has walked back into Roxane's life for but a few moments, can know her heart?"

"I can never dream to guess at the machinations of my daughter's heart. Much as I would give my life to do so."

Separated by the cross glow, the men faced each other in a duel of wills. "Do you trust you are doing the right thing by asking me to walk away?"

"I know the hearts of men of your ilk. You are her enemy, vampire." Xavier pulled a wood column from inside his frock coat. The point was sharp as a rapier. "Walk away, and I'll not stake you through the heart."

"You speak madness." But while Gabriel protested he fought to conceal his surprise. First encounter with opposition—and a knowing opposition at that. "What do you know about me?"

"I know you are a vampire."

"How?" Shocked at the truth, he tilted a wary eye on the stake-wielding bastard. Had the man seen the smoke rise from his hand when he'd briefly moved it into the cross-glow? "Vampires are myth."

"It is the myth that keeps them safe. You wonder how I know? It is apparent."

"It is? How?" Gabriel spread his arms and looked down over his body. "Please tell me, because I am new at this, and if I am sending a signal or flashing a warning I probably need to be aware of it."

Xavier smirked and strode carefully around the distorted shape of the cross. "Oh, you don't flash."

"Are you a witch, like your daughter? Is that how you know?"

"You know my daughter is a witch, and yet you risk your life by being with her?"

"I was not a vampire when first we met. I had no idea she was a witch, until..." No sense in telling the father he'd made his daughter a victim, his very creator.

So he had wronged Roxane. Had taken the blood from her without permission. *You used her to serve yourself.* Indeed, he should, and must, step away.

"She holds far more power over me than I do her."

"How did the two of you find each other?"

"She found me. Right after the attack on me."

"Ah, yes. Friend of yours?"

"Are you mad? I would have never asked for this!"

Xavier nodded as if considering. "I see you decided not to resist the blood hunger."

"I decided—" Gabriel paused. He wasn't sure how much the man knew. Roxane felt sure Xavier Desrues did not know about his son's unfortunate slip into madness. He couldn't tell all his reasons for succumbing to vampirism. "It's a hell of a better option than madness."

"So I have been told. But enough chatter." Xavier twirled the wooden stake expertly. "Leave, or you're a pile of blood and ash."

"Not until you give me some answers. You know what I am, and I will consider stepping back from your daughter at your request, but I still don't know what you are. Or if you are more a danger to Roxane than I can ever be."

"You accuse me of wanting to harm my daughter?"

Gabriel reared from the raised stake. He was just getting the knack of vampirism, no sense in so quickly bringing the party to an end. "I want to know where you stand in the whole scheme of things."

"I am merely a concerned father."

Who had happened to guess Gabriel was a vampire? Of course the man had come from a family of witches; he would have knowledge of the supernatural.

The stake remained in the air, threatening. Gabriel raised his hands to placate. Had he the strength to take the man down? Of course. But jumping his lover's father would never redeem him in Roxane's doubting heart.

"Very well then," he conceded, lowering his hands. "I will not go to her."

"You had better not."

"But I cannot prevent her coming to me."

"You will, or you will not live to dream about having a future with Roxane."

"You're a hell of a mystery, Desrues."

"And you are dead if you so much as breathe my daughter's air."

And what would the man make of the vampire Anjou if he knew what he had done to his son? Together the father and daughter could work to destroy Anjou. But they wouldn't have a hope without Gabriel to coax Damian up from the madness.

"I am leaving." Gabriel stepped back. "But I'm not giving up on your daughter, or your son."

XAVIER DESRUES HELD THE STAKE aloft as he watched the vicomte's hasty retreat into the shadows.

His son? What in hell had the bastard meant by that? What had Damian to do with this?

Releasing the breath he had held during the entire encounter, Xavier stumbled backward, thinking to catch himself against the outer wall of the cathedral. His hand slashed through the golden light that had kept the vicomte nervously at bay. A spiral of smoke sizzled from his fingers. He clutched them to his chest and coiled, spinning and stumbling, seeking the darkness.

His cruel darkness.

Twenty-Eight

GABRIEL HAD TOLD XAVIER DESRUES he would walk away from his daughter. He should not have made such a promise. It would be the honorable thing to do. A choice that would keep Roxane from a future that promised only pain.

How to do it without hurting her more than he had to? Without hurting himself?

She had made it clear she hated him. Or could it have been a senseless tirade, a result of her affronted morals? She cared for him still. She must. As he did her.

But to keep her safe, he must push her away.

"I'll figure a way," he hissed. "I'll...put her under my thrall and make her believe she doesn't love me." Like a drug, the thrall would turn her to indifference. Give her heart new hope to love another.

He charged through his bedchamber door and Roxane spun around at his entrance. Azure, violet, and narrow streaks of rust infused her flesh. Crimson rained upon her hair, dramatically brightening it in bloody rivulets around her face. Around the circumference of her skirts sat fat white candles, guttered and hissing smoke, freshly blown out. A dagger glinted in her palm.

"What the hell are you doing?" he demanded. "Are you placing a spell upon my home, my private chambers?"

She spread her hands before her in a placatory manner, but didn't offer an argument. She had not a lie to cover her tracks this time.

Gabriel narrowed his gaze on the woman. So lovely. So deceptive. Speaking a spell against him? What had he seen in her that he'd thought for one moment he could love her?

"I-I can explain," she started.

The glint of a dagger caught his eye. He could not be sure if the line of red purling down the edge of the blade was merely color from above or blood. Until he scented the witch's blood.

"So you challenge me with your deadly blood?" He paced closer, circling the candle-enclosed perimeter. "You needn't stab me with that weapon, merely a touch will incinerate the vampire, yes?"

"I've no intention of harming you, Gabriel."

"Why not? You hate me."

"No."

"You said as much. What better way to rid a nuisance from your life than to be done with me?"

"Don't get too close—"

"Why not? Prolonging the inevitable? Or have you not finished your spell?" He kicked and sent two candles flying. Wax sluiced the marble and solidified in streaks.

"Please, just listen to me," she cried. "I don't want you—"

"I know you don't." Resolute, he wrangled his anger. He had come to place distance between them. She was making it remarkably easy. "And I don't blame you. We are black and white, we two. So opposite and dangerous to one another."

"We share the same pain!"

That he had confessed his darkest shame to her crushed him now. Truly, she had bewitched the truth from him.

How to enthrall a witch? He hadn't a clue, and yet, likely he did. It was all in the eyes. He'd controlled the whore at the Palais Royale with but a look and a whispered suggestion.

He lowered his head and looked up through his lashes at the impudent witch.

"Gabriel, I—" She touched her mouth. Wide celadon eyes danced with his. "Where have you been? I've—Why are you looking at me like that? Gabriel?"

He drew in a breath. Concentrate. There must be a way to see inside her, to take control. "I will find your core, witch."

"What are you—"She stepped forward, but paused. Smoke hissed up from a candle, coiling wispy tendrils of sulfur between them.

He felt a tug inside his gut. As if he had grasped upon a speeding soul and his connection had halted it cold. *Yes, fall into my gaze.*

Roxane's hands fell to her sides. The dagger slid down the length of her skirt and clattered upon the marble floor, spinning once and stopping against a candle. A slash of blood sliced the white wax.

Her mouth pursed and loosened. She muttered a faint "No."

Lifting a hand toward her, Gabriel pressed his will out from his fingers and imagined it entwining about the witch's shoulders and arms.

Her arms snapped tight to her sides.

Empowered by the witch's sudden loss of control he lowered his hand, sending determination down and around her legs. Her skirts swished and closed tight about her legs, the motion causing one of the remaining three candles to flicker out in a wink of sulfur.

Unceasingly, he held her with his eyes.

Emboldened by this newfound skill, he tilted his hand and curled his fingers upward.

Enrobed within the stream of kaleidoscope colors, Roxane's body rose. Her head fell back across her shoulders. Slowly her body turned, a limp doll commanded by his thrall.

With but the power of his mind he had commanded another. The thrall was his to own. He stepped close to study her. Held on the air, a curiosity that couldn't possibly be evil. Could not be the enemy.

"I will keep you," the child inside of Gabriel murmured. Thought crashed into plot mode. "With you in thrall, I can keep Anjou away from you once and for all. Then I, and only I, can help Damian. It is what is best, Roxane. You must trust me. I love you. I want to make the world right for you."

He spun to leave the room and Toussaint, eyes wide with wonder, stepped through the doorway. The valet must have witnessed the entire thing.

"You did it," Toussaint said on a gasp.

"Indeed, it is the thrall. Quite the spectacle, eh?"

"Now you will let her down?"

Gabriel smirked. "Not yet. I've an errand to perform."

"But you remember what Mesmer said about the thrall. For every moment that a witch remains in such a state her immortality slips away."

"Nonsense, Toussaint." Gorgeous, the witch suspended beneath his sanctuary of colors. An angel mid-fall. He would prevent her from hitting the unconsecrated ground. "Roxane is not immortal. She is a mere earth witch. She has not mastered time."

"We don't know that!"

"Oh? So you assume this meek and delicate creature has consumed the beating, bloody heart of a vampire in order to attain said immortality?"

"Well..." Toussaint shrugged.

"Exactly. She'll be fine until my return." Gabriel strode out of the room. "Don't touch her!"

TOUSSAINT SWUNG HIS HEAD TO study the woman who literally floated in a slow coil beneath the stained glass oculus. That Gabriel had been able to do such a thing was a marvel.

And yet, he feared for the woman. Gabriel's anger blinded him to all but his own troubles. The vicomte could have no clue what sort of danger he had introduced to Roxane by putting her in such a state.

He stepped forward, gingerly touching a toppled candle. Had she been up to witchcraft? Had Gabriel been justified after all?

He dared to poke a finger against her skirts.

Propelled by a sudden force, Toussaint flew across the room. His shoulders and back cracked against the wall. He hadn't time to thrust out his arms to catch his fall. He landed, face down upon the marble floor.

He lifted his head from the hard marble. The witch remained untouched, enthralled within Gabriel's cruel whim.

"I won't let the darkness take you, Renan," he croaked.

Twenty-Nine

"SOMETHING IS NOT RIGHT," Toussaint pleaded as he swept Gabriel's cape from his shoulders. "She is weak."

Gabriel dashed up the stairway and into his room. Darkness kept him from immediately placing Roxane.

"The lantern!" he called to Toussaint.

No vivid colors lighted the enthralled witch. A thin streak of light from the street lamp outside the window cleaved between the drawn velvet draperies, slicing a clean line down the center of her twisted skirts. Still in thrall, Roxane was bent backward, arms and legs slack, as if a ragdoll strewn over a narrow table.

Close enough to smell the rosemary, but not touching, Gabriel held his open palms over Roxane's stomach. Warmth permeated his flesh. The flow of her blood sounded in his skull. Slow, not a normal pace.

Was she truly immortal? That would mean she had taken part in that horrid ritual! A witch must drink the blood of a live vampire to gain immortality. This gorgeous, delicate woman—how had she done such a thing? He shook his head.

Perhaps the thrall affected a mortal witch equally by draining her life force?

Either way, this was not what he had intended. What a bastard he had been. He did not hate Roxane or wish her death. He had only thought to detain her while he sought the vampire Anjou. His search had turned up nothing.

How to reverse this cruel thrall?

A shower of color swaddled the suspended ragdoll and Gabriel's hands. Overhead, Toussaint's footsteps pattered across the roof. He heard the valet say, "Take it easy, boy." Charles must be wary of his mistress's danger.

"What have I done to you, my beautiful Roxane? I did not intend to harm you. I just wanted to—"

To what? To contain her. To punish her for her lies, for saying she hated him when he knew she did not. What sort of evil thing had he become that he sought to punish? He was no man to be so vicious to a woman. Even if she was a creature who should be his natural enemy.

"Not enemies," he whispered to the frail beauty. "Never. I love you, Roxane. How do I stop this? Can you hear me? Can-can I touch you?"

His fingers brushed the pink satin skirt. He *could* touch her. Lowering his other hand to her stomach, he looked her up and down. This contact did nothing but stop the slow circling of her body.

Before he had felt her succumb, he had stepped into her very core with his concentration. Could it be so simple as returning that willpower to her core?

"Look at me." He lifted her head. Her eyes remained closed, the ice queen sheltered from the vampire's storm. She was so weak. "I did not wish for this, you must believe me."

Compelled to a greedy embrace, he accepted her weight into his arms. Plunging to his knees, he followed Roxane's body down and cushioned her descent to the marble floor. Guttered candles rolled away from their embrace, strewing soft wax trails out like rays of a wicked sun.

The dagger Roxane had held lay at the end of one of those wax runnels, dried witch's blood taunted from the blood groove.

Let me explain...

Mayhap she had been speaking a spell to protect him from Anjou? Or for her brother?

"Come back to me." He lifted her wobbly head and pressed his lips to her cold flesh. One arm outstretched, her pale fingers curled upon the marble. Vermillion haze splashed the underside of her arms.

Tears streamed from his eyes and pooled at the corners of his lips. After decades of fierce refusal to show emotion he could not contain the ache. Gabriel swallowed his salty pain and hugged Roxane to his chest, rocking her.

"Come out of it, my love. I release the thrall!"

Her body jerked and shuddered. Fingers clutched at his shirt, tugging the tired lace jabot free from the bow.

"Yes," he gasped. "I release you, Roxane. Open your eyes. Come back to me!"

"G-Gabriel?" A sigh spilled from her mouth and over his lips. "I...I was lost."

"No, you were right here in my bed chamber." She tilted her head but did not open her eyes. "I'm so sorry. I put you in a—"

"—thrall." She swallowed and opened her eyes. The ice queen, so sad—had she been defeated? A blink released a single teardrop down her cheek and splat upon his hand. "You've taken so much...from me," she managed.

Depleted, she laid her head against his shoulder and closed her eyes. The fingers that clutched his shirt opened and slid down his chest.

WHAT A FEW GOLD COINS COULD bring to him astonished. Henri checked the ropes secured about his prize's wrists and ankles and stuffed his handkerchief— smelling of clove—into the boy's mouth. The blood tempted. But he had far grander plans for this simpering idiot.

He was pretty and young. A hell of a lot more naive than Xavier had been. *Master*, the boy had called him as he'd fallen to his knees in the midst of the rabble that had wandered the dust-dry exercise grounds of Bicêtre.

So he remembered him?

"Ride on," Henri called to the driver.

SETTLING ONTO HIS BED, with Roxane in his arms, Gabriel eased against the pillows. Still weak, she allowed him to move her about.

"Tell me I have not irrevocably harmed you, Roxane, please. I will plunge a stake into my heart if I have done anything to hurt you. I did not know. I could not have guessed."

"I will...live," she said, a sigh hushing her breath across his throat as she clung to his shirt. "Just not...forever."

"You had immortality?"

Her nod moved across his chest.

"And now it is gone?"

"Not sure. Have no idea how long it requires to steal it away. I am weak."

Her head heavy upon his chest, she sighed. Gabriel stroked her hair, toying with the curls. It was impossible to keep his thoughts from going to the place of horror Toussaint had described from Mesmer's explanation.

"So you...performed the ceremony to become immortal?"

"Yes."

Her confession stirred the blood in his head to a woozy spin. That this seemingly simple, unassuming woman could have done such a thing. To a vampire. A man like him. For her own gain.

As you took her blood for your gain?

No, to help Damian.

And yes, for himself. For the passion and life ever after.

"Forgiveness is not mine to beg." He kissed her forehead. Her fragile hand landed on his, a withered flower upon hard stone. "You must rue the day you met me. If I would have died that night of the attack, you might have had your brother back by now."

"Or I may have been killed by Anjou. Don't say such things, Gabriel. Just hold me. I feel as though I am...yet slipping. I don't feel safe."

"But you are." Hope was that she truly was safe in his arms, but truth told she was probably in more danger with him than out alone in Paris. Even his accidents could prove dangerous. "So sorry, Roxane."

"I should have explained everything to you. I secreted my truths. I had initially thought to use you to get to Anjou."

"I will be whatever you wish me to be. Your lover, your bait—"

"Don't speak like that. My heart has changed. I love you, Gabriel."

"You should not love me."

"It is not that I should not, but that I *wish* not to. Only because I don't want to cause you any more pain. If you were not mine..."

He closed his eyes and kissed the crown of her head. True words that made his heart swallow. "I love you, Roxane. Forgive me."

GABRIEL WOKE AND LOOKED OVER the wilted flower he had lain beside through the night. The draperies were drawn, but he sensed it was morning. He could not see Roxane's face in the hazy light, but he could hear her soft, shallow breaths. Untroubled sleep, he hoped.

Thank whichever God would listen for that.

He kissed her forehead and she stirred. Slender fingers entwined within his. Drawing his lips down her nose and to her mouth, he felt the curve of her smile.

"I feel as though I've walked against a raging windstorm," she murmured.

He fought renewed tears, "I could have killed you."

"You did not know," she said, her eyes still closed, but her head turning to find his mouth. She kissed him. Such mercy. "You had to see if you could do it."

"I did not think the thrall would harm you. I would not have left you if I had known."

"Where did you go?"

"To find Anjou and—hell, I wanted to kill the bastard. Give you no reason not to choose me to help your brother. It was selfish of me. The evil has cleaved to me. The remnants of my soul are turning black, Roxane."

"Don't say things like that." Her fingers fell upon his mouth. Still so far from her strength.

He clasped her hand in his. "It is truth and it frightens me. Would I have killed Anjou if I found him?"

"You would have ended a life that has taken so many others."

"Do not in any way make me heroic. I am like Anjou."

"You do not kill for blood."

"I am a novice. As my heart blackens so will my ways."

"Stop it."

"What?"

"Playing the tragic victim! You are a good man, Gabriel. You will remain so, I know it. I won't have you thinking any other way. Promise?"

"You do not cease to startle me. Even after all I have done to you, you remain kind and open to my black heart."

"It is like breathing, Gabriel."

Her simple kindness killed him. For she loved her own death. "I must know, the thrall. Did you lose your immortality?"

"I suspect so."

"You can restore it?"

"There is but one way to do that."

"You mean..."

"Yes."

He kissed her mouth, soft and warm. In her celadon gaze he saw his reflection. Did he reside there or was it merely a trick of the light?

"If I could give you my heart, I would."

"You already have. And I did not treat it with the respect you deserve."

"Nonsense," he said. "I should not have been so judgmental. Can you forgive me?"

"I have. But can you ever trust me now?"

"Why not?"

"I will always be looking at you as someone who can give me the immortality I have lost."

"Ah. And I have offered my heart to you. Literally."

"I could not take it."

"I don't imagine how you could have ever performed such a ritual."

"Charles helped. I won't elaborate."

Nor did he wish to hear anything so vulgar cross his lover's pale lips.

He nuzzled into her neck. The pulse of life tempted him to press his lips there, but he kept back his desires, and instead kissed softly, his lips hiding his fangs.

"Oh, lover."

He slid his hand down her stomach. The chemise tickled her knees as he inched it up with his fingers. The pillow cupped her head as she pressed back, riding the sudden pleasure of his touch and moving it throughout her body.

THIRTY

THEY STAGGERED FROM BICÊTRE as if refugees allowed out into the light for the first time. It was not a sunny day. Thunder clouds sweatered the sky. The atmosphere felt heavy, foreboding with a crackle of lightening across the sky.

Stunned, Roxane turned to Gabriel. "How could he have escaped? Where would he have gone?"

"I'm not sure. We will find him, trust me."

The administrator had reluctantly confessed to Damian's absence—an escape unnoticed by anyone on duty during the late hours yesterday.

"He could not have gone far."

"Paris is but leagues away," Gabriel said. "Can he ride?"

"Very well."

He gripped her by the shoulders. "We ride to your apartment and check there."

DAMIAN HAD NOT RETURNED TO the garret on the rue Vivienne. Roxane strode the room looking for signs that her brother had been there, but everything was to its place, scattered as that was.

"We'll go to my home and—"

"He would not go there," she stopped Gabriel abruptly. "He doesn't know you."

"True. But we need all the help we can summon. I can send Toussaint out in search. I will search the city as well."

"Yes, thank you. I'll stay here in case he returns. You'll send Toussaint with news if you find him?"

"Immediately." He kissed her. "You should eat, you're shaky and chilled. We will find him."

"I pray he has not gone to Anjou."

"He would not."

"You said there was a bond," she asked. "Between you and the man who bit you. That you...loved him?"

"Only in that moment of the bite. Don't fret, Roxane, we will find him."

AFTERNOON STIRRED ROXANE to impulsive jitters. She could not sit still waiting. Nor did she want to risk going too far from the apartment. Weak and jittery, she needed something in her stomach. Perhaps a meal would calm her. And maybe a walk down the avenue to look about for Damian.

Weary and defeated, she arrived at the Pont Neuf and thought to forego the bridge, packed shoulder to shoulder with hawkers and strollers and children.

She would never find Damian in this bustle of humanity.

She clutched the vial hanging around her neck, but her fingers closed about nothing. She had worn the glass vial since the day she had arrived home to find Damian lying on his bed, bleeding and jabbering about a creature with dark eyes and a sharp, seductive kiss.

Roxane had thought her decision correct by influencing Damian to hold out for the moon. Three weeks he'd waited. She could not guess why he'd succumbed to madness quicker than the signs began to show in Gabriel. Damian had never received magic. Only the females in the Desrues family had. He'd never said anything to her, but she'd felt his jealousy through the decades. Magic had bonded her with her mother.

Thick, frothy elm trees lined the riverside, providing much needed shade. A vendor called out his refreshing wares. Slipping two sous from her purse, Roxane purchased a lemon ice. Finding a stone bench beneath a tree, she sipped the tart ice from the rind.

Just float, she coached. Do not sink.

When a carriage rolled close to the bench she had to tuck her legs to avoid getting crushed. The black coach stopped, effectively pinning her in.

"Driver, move on!" she pleaded, but the cloaked driver remained impassive, his head facing forward.

"Mademoiselle Desrues."

The voice inside the carriage seeped out the window as if a black fog. A shudder rode her spine. Clutching the window, she stood and peered inside the carriage's dark shadows. The windows were shaded with heavy fabric and so she did not see more than two pairs of legs until the voice that had spoken leaned forward.

She clutched for the vial, then swore softly—not there. What could she use? She pressed her thumbnail to the blue vein on the underside of her wrist.

"Hold your artillery, witch," Anjou hissed. "I've something you'll want to see before you splatter me with your blood. If you make one move to cut your flesh, I will slash his pretty throat."

The glint of silver flashed near Anjou's head. His arm was draped about something, and his other hand held a dagger to a man's throat.

A scream lodged at the base of Roxane's tongue. "Damian."

Her brother had been cruelly bound about the mouth and his hands and legs. His eyes were maniacal, his stifled mumbles pitiful.

"What do you want?"

"You, witch. Dead."

A thin crimson line blossomed under Damian's chin. Not a fatal cut, but enough to warn.

"You'll let him go?"

"Of course. Step up inside. We're going for a ride."

Having no choice, Roxane stepped up into the carriage and sat opposite the two.

Anjou kicked the door and the driver started onward.

GABRIEL PACED THE FLOOR OF his bed chamber. It was difficult to concentrate on his hunger when there were more important worries. Had Roxane found her brother at their garret? He needed to be out in the city, searching. He'd taken the coach down the rue St. Honoré, and circled the Palais Royale three times.

Toussaint had taken the left bank. If the valet did not return soon he was prepared to go out again. Not for sustenance, but for a different kind of blood—vengeance.

The front door creaked open. He raced down the hallway to find Toussaint standing meekly in the open door, his head bowed, and hands folded before him.

"What is it, Toussaint? Did you find Roxane? Her brother?" He skipped down the stairs and scanned the carriage, the horses pawing the ground and lather glistening on their withers. No witch, no madman.

"She didn't make it home," Toussaint whispered. "She was..."

"What?" Tears glistened on the valet's face. "You spoke with Roxane?"

"No. I saw her as I crossed the Pont Neuf, but it was too crowded to get to her. I saw her buy the lemon..."

"Toussaint!"

"I think she's been taken."

"Taken?" He slammed a fist to the door frame over Toussaint's shoulder. "I don't understand."

"I saw her sitting in the shade eating a lemon ice. A carriage passed before where she was sitting and when it moved by, she was gone."

Gabriel closed his eyes and winced. There was only one person who had reason to take Roxane—but that made little sense. The vampire would not risk kidnapping a witch. Would he?

Unless he found a way to keep Roxane from dousing him with her blood. Easy enough. Just keep her away from sharp objects by binding her hands.

Morbleu, had the vampire kidnapped Roxane in an attempt to lure Gabriel to him?

There was no reason for Anjou to fear him; he was now of his kind.

Of course, Anjou did not know that.

"Quickly, Toussaint. My coat and...a rapier, instead of my walking stick. We must ride now."

Toussaint rushed inside and, Gabriel, left alone on the step, craned his neck back and stared up at the dark sky.

"I wonder." Staring up this side of the house, he spied two of the drain spouts. Would Charles know where his mistress was?

UP ON THE ROOF, HE WASN'T SURE how to communicate with the stone beast. But it was obvious from Charles's open-mawed silent yowls he sensed something was not right.

"Can you find her? Can you scent out your mistress?"

How to communicate with a chunk of stone? He tentatively touched the stone wing and felt the flow of...life? "She is in danger."

"No thanks to you!"

Gabriel swung around to find Xavier Desrues lurching up behind him with hell in his eyes and a stake in hand.

"I see my daughter's familiar has taken up residence," Xavier announced. He wielded not only a stake but also a dagger in the opposite hand. "That insufferable beast."

"Where is Roxane?" Gabriel glanced to Charles, who again cawed silently but insistently. The beast wanted Gabriel to pay attention, to understand—but what?

"Listen, Desrues, whatever it is you have against me, it will have to wait. Your daughter is in danger."

"Petty tricks. I'll not leave until you are dust, Renan." Xavier lunged, nicking Gabriel's hand with the dagger.

"We don't have time for this! Do you not care about your daughter? Or your son, for that matter?"

"What of my son?"

Roxane had insisted he not tell her father about Damian. But if the man could help his son? No time to hide the truth.

Xavier lunged and pinned Gabriel against Charles's massive body. "Don't try to fool me with lies, vampire. I want the truth."

Gabriel wrestled with the dagger but could not get it from the man. He stroked backward and heard the blade cut through—not flesh, but stone. Charles moved, knocking Gabriel to the ground. The familiar sliced out a wing. Xavier stumbled backward, grasping his cheek. Blood spilled down his neck. But when he pulled his hand away a macabre grimace exposed glinting fangs.

Gabriel gasped. "You're a—" The wound healed. "You and Anjou? Allies?"

"You're not very quick on the uptake are you, vicomte? Sorry, but I won't have my daughter's heart broken. As well, you are in Anjou's way. I'm here to remove you. Permanently."

"If I have put myself in that bastard's path it is only to save your daughter."

"Anjou is not after Roxane. He knows the danger in dallying with a witch."

"You don't know, old man. He tried to kill your son. He'll not blink an eye at killing Roxane."

Xavier ran across the roof.

Gabriel ran toward him. He kept his eye on the stake, raised high. Their bodies collided in a crush of bones and racing blood. Gabriel gripped Xavier's hand, wrestling away the stake. But he could not hold his ground, the force of their collision shook his equilibrium. He stumbled backward, Xavier in his grasp. The old vampire let out a shriek as they fell together.

THIRTY-ONE

A GUTTURAL CRY CHUFFED FROM Gabriel's lungs as he fell one story and landed on the floor of his bed chamber. Xavier's body cushioned his fall. Multi-colored glass rained about them. Shards tore his flesh, letting out his blood in agonizing streams.

Xavier's face poured up tears of blood. He was out cold.

Thundering beats crackled overhead. A shard of emerald glass clung to the lead frame of what had once been the gorgeous oculus. Charles peered down through the destruction.

"Do you think you can find your mistress?"

The beast stomped a foot, shaking the entire room to a rattle.

Gabriel would take that as a yes.

ROXANE HADN'T A CLUE WHERE the vampire had taken her, save that she had spied the city walls when he'd shoved her out of the carriage and forced her inside a three-story house. The darkness caused her to stumble, but she did not walk into any furniture.

'Twas as if a dungeon here in the dark, dank, earthy room. An iron torch flickered on the wall to her left, another across the room filled the air with a smoky brume. A tattered chaise and a half-tester bed with strewn sheets sat in one corner. No windows. No ventilation to let out the choking smoke. Did the vampire live in this squalor?

The manacles that secured her were attached to the wall by heavy, rusted chains. She moved her wrists, wishing her hands were narrower so she could slip free of the iron bracelets. Her feet were not bound, but it mattered little. With no way to get free she was at the vampire's mercy.

After securing her, Anjou had slapped her face with his open palm, and then left her alone to wonder if the scratching in the corner were a rat or something worse. For as much as she called to Charles, she was too far away for him to hear her mental plea.

What plans had that bastard for her brother? Poor Damian! How had Anjou gotten him out from Bicêtre? In her next thought, Roxane knew it took but a bribe to rule that asylum. Each day visitors arrived to gawk, to marvel, and to purchase inmates for use in all manner of twisted rituals.

She wracked her brain for a spell. An earth witch could not cast a spell through iron. But maybe there was another way. She could coax the flame in a torch, but if she were not exact she could start the faggots stacked near her feet aflame. The last thing she needed was to be trapped in a room aflame.

Concentrating, she mentally lifted one of the logs. It dangled top to bottom in the air above the stack. Blowing out a breath, she released hold and the log landed on the floor. A direct hit to the head might take out the vampire, but it wouldn't kill him.

Beseeching the goddess, Roxane bowed her head and began to chant.

WHAT THE HELL TO DO WITH the idiot and the witch?

Henri d'Anjou paced the darkened carriage run paralleling the side of the house he had claimed weeks earlier. The owner had not minded. In fact, the shoeless nothing had left this world with not a whimper of protest. 'Twas good fortune it was so easy to dispose of bodies. Les Innocents was being dug up and quick-limed to cover the remnants of plague. One additional body to the stack of bones and partially decomposed was never noticed.

Pity the younger Desrues man had not died. Anjou had left him bleeding, fully believing him dead. Had the witch brought him back to life? He wasn't sure that was possible. He believed in black magic, but Roxane Desrues was too weak for such powerful sorcery. She had yet to lift a finger in her own defense. Not that he'd given her opportunity.

Strange how life worked a man's world into such small rotation. Henri had not known, at the time, that the pretty taste was Xavier's son. Xavier would not forgive him the truth. Hardly a pity, for Henri had already booted out the sniveling old bundle.

Of late, all his troubles could be traced to that meddling witch!

Meddling, and oh, so dangerous. She had but to cut herself and his breaths were numbered.

Henri yanked open the carriage door. The stench of urine crept out in a miserable wave. The madman pounded his forehead against the padded velvet seat. Child-like whimpers decorated each miserable beat.

Through it all the scent of blood rose to tempt Henri closer.

He reached in and jerked the younger Desrues out by the ropes binding his wrists. Light from an oil streetlamp highlighted the blood smeared across the man's forehead. Henri bent and licked the enticing treat.

Enough to satisfy. For the moment.

"BLOODY CREATION!" Toussaint literally slid into Gabriel's bed chambers—blood and glass spattered every surface—barely stopping himself from collapsing on Xavier Desrues's inert body. "What is the calamity?"

"I've had a bit of a disagreement with Monsieur Desrues." Gabriel shook off the shards of colored glass from his shirt. He stood, apparently unharmed, adjusting his jabot.

"That is Roxane's father?" The valet bent over the sprawled body, his shoes crunching glass. "Is he dead?"

"Unfortunately, he is immortal."

"What?"

Gabriel smirked at the frightened rise in the valet's voice. "Another vampire, Toussaint. Can you keep an eye on him for me?" He tilted his head and looked to the ceiling, seeing beyond to the quiet sentry who waited. "Charles and I are off."

"But I—" Toussaint looked from Gabriel to Xavier to the glass littered about. "This man...vampire? Does Roxane know? How will I—You're going to leave me alone with him?"

"Grab a stake, Toussaint. Tie him, or secure him in some manner. Don't allow him to leave until I've returned with Roxane. And if I should not return..."

"You will!" The valet drew up his shoulders and nodded decisively. "I will take care of this matter. You can rely on me."

"I know I can, Toussaint. Off to find the woman I love."

THE HEAVY IRON DOOR THAT secluded her from light and fresh, smokeless air creaked. In stumbled a tangle of limbs and sodden clothing. Falling, Damian caught himself upon his bound forearms and rolled to his back. The cloth binding his mouth had slipped to his chin and giggles erupted near her feet.

Anjou barely avoided stepping on Damian's toes as he paced near the end of the tester bed. The torch flamed wildly behind the vampire's mass of curly black hair.

"It is the witch!" Damian announced amidst his giggles. "The bloody witch!"

"I see your brother admires you," Anjou stated coolly. "It is amazing what the moon will do to a man, no?" He bent to Damian and gripped a thatch of his tangled hair. "Why don't I kill him now for you, save him years of suffering?"

"Don't touch him," Roxane warned. She looked upon her brother's wasted form. The cloth bindings were loosened, though he was still contained. Yet should he concentrate he might wriggle free. "You did this to him."

"Oh no, it was not *my* choice that saw the idiot to Bicêtre. He was dead when I left him in his bed."

"You are a stupid creature! Following your vicious attack he had merely passed out. He bled, but not enough to bring death."

"Take the blood!" Damian shouted, and continued the chant.

Anjou strode to Roxane and lifted her chin with his finger.

"Take the blood! Take the blood!"

The pale-eyed vampire grimaced, revealing the tip of one sharp incisor. To look him in the eye felt as if she stood on the precipice to Hades.

He nodded toward Damian. "Shall I? He seems to want blood. If I transform him, do you guess we'll have a mad, blood-sucking fiend on our hands, or might he be restored to his former self? A pretty boy he was..." The vampire swung a lingering gaze at the squirming man whose chants had mellowed to frantic whispers. "I considered making him my own. A toy to keep close. A replacement for one of whom I've grown tired. Shall I tell you a tale of my lover fair? Claimed many years ago. Stolen from his family?"

"I don't want to hear tales of your twisted life."

"But you may have an interest."

Roxane struggled with little result. She bit down on her lip—and tasted blood. Why hadn't she thought of that before?

She spat. Anjou raised an arm before his face in defense. Her spittle landed on his sleeve. "Bitch!" He jumped over Damian and clung to the opposite wall. "He dies!"

"Come and claim him if you can!" she called defiantly.

The vampire remained by the wall.

Sucking at her bleeding lip, she worked the spittle in her mouth. She would bite herself silly to save her brother.

"Damian," she said, keeping an eye on the leery vampire. "Damian, loosen the ties around your ankles. You can do it."

"Don't listen to the witch, boy," Anjou hissed as he stepped forward.

Roxane lifted her chin and spat again, landing the projectile but a foot from the vampire's feet. Anjou reacted quickly, lunging for a log on the stack of faggots. He thrust it at her, hitting her in the gut. The blow expelled her breath and bloody spittle down the front of her gown. Another log rapidly followed, bruising her shin, and another landed on her knuckles. She cried out, punctuating Damian's frantic hisses to "Take the blood."

Suddenly her vision burst into a brilliant flower of amber flame. Anjou taunted her with the torch, stabbing it close. "There is but one way to kill a witch," he declared, holding the flame down near the logs stacked at her feet. "Care to guess?"

"You'll never find Gabriel without me."

"I no longer need the vicomte. He poses no threat. I'm damned thrilled to claim a witch and her idiot brother. I've already got the father. A complete collection!"

"The *father*? My—Xavier?"

"Oh indeed, such a delicious vampire that man could be if only he'd shrug off his mortal misery. Always lamenting his lost family. But you didn't want to listen to my tale of lust, love and woe."

"F-father?"

"Burn the witch! Burn the witch!"

Anjou chuckled. "Pretty sycophant. I will keep him to myself after we've roasted his sister to ash. I'd like to experiment with his transformation. Should it restore his senses, well then, what a lovely treat. If not, a minion for my ranks."

Roxane dodged her head to avoid the flame's heat.

"Not so daring now, are you?" Anjou returned the torch to the wall and lifted Damian's head by a scruff of his dirty hair. He pulled out his dagger and touched it to the man's neck. Damian gripped the blade, slicing through his fingers. Anjou smiled cruelly at Roxane. "You make it too easy, witch."

Roxane had but one option. She prayed it would work.

"Tell me about my father!"

The vampire lowered the dagger, yet held Damian securely. If she could occupy him... Anything to buy time. Could Gabriel be looking for her?

"You and Xavier have..." She hated to think it. "...been together a long time?"

"Xavier is my lover. Has been for over a decade."

"Over a—" That must be the reason her father had left her family. For this bastard? "Did you take him against his will?"

"You would like that, wouldn't you?" He scratched his chin with the side of the blade. A smirk worked his devilish features. "To believe the man was merely a victim in life's miserable game of fate?"

"He would not have left his family otherwise. He was—is—a good man!"

"The man loves me, witch, get that into your skull. Xavier Desrues could not resist the gift of immortality I offered. Once mine, he decided against returning to Villers-Cotterets. Didn't want to endanger his wife and poor children. If they knew their father had become a monster—well!"

Xavier had been attacked by Anjou. He'd had no choice but to keep away from his family. It made sense. Poor father. All these years—if only she had known. Might the truth have saved her mother a broken heart?

"He has been with you in Paris all this time?"

"Enough chatter."

Anjou approached her as a stalking panther. A deep darkness set within his eyes raised the shiver bumps at the base of her neck. And yet, a glint of something else lived in the dark orbs.

She squinted. What did she see there? Love? Greed? Obsession and command.

Anjou whispered, "Yes, witch, fall."

Fall? What did that mean? Where? She was manacled—She could not fall. The only means to fall was there...

...deep within Anjou's soul-raped eyes.

Roxane felt her eyelids grow heavy. She blinked. Why was she suddenly tired?

"Can you see what it is you believe in?" Anjou cooed. "Look deeper, Roxane."

Her name floated through her mind. Rox*aaaaane*. So pretty. Dancing like a butterfly over a meadow of lavender.

"Yes, that's it."

And she felt her body stiffen. Inside, her blood hardened, momentarily, then grew thick and heavy, as if a paste. As her last conscious thoughts blurred she realized her defeat. The vampire's thrall overwhelmed.

Thirty-Two

HENRI PRESSED A FINGER UNDER the witch's chin and lifted her with ease, trapped within the thrall, bound to the wall like a mermaid to a ship's prow. The manacles were unnecessary now, but he wouldn't forego the additional security.

He stroked the soft mounds of her breasts rising from her dirty pink dress, avoiding the spittle of witch blood that crept down the fabric. The satin pushed up her bosom and the lace bordering the neckline invited him to slip a finger behind the bodice, and pinch her nipple.

He had an aversion to women—men were not so catty as females—but in fact, this woman smelled of rosemary and fresh air, and sweet, sweet blood.

Yet, there, the pattern of fire—ignited by vampire's blood—burned into her flesh. Bitch.

He jerked away, clasping a hand to his chest. A sensory thrill shivered through his system. "You tempt even in thrall, witch."

"Take me instead."

Had an angel fallen to land behind him?

Henri turned to find the tattered madman supporting his slight weight on one hand, his head tilted to reveal a bare neck. Such a pretty column for lace. And sharp kisses.

Seemingly lucid, the man stretched out his other hand and touched Henri's shoe. "You are...my liege."

A wistful sadness flushed Henri's being. A faithful subject sought his embrace.

The witch left to wither in thrall, he bent and pulled Damian to him. Pale parched lips opened to his kiss. He had forgotten the sweetness of this one.

THE KISS SUMMONED DESIRE TO the surface. So sweet to be commanded by the vampire.

Master.

To be drawn into his realm of tempting kisses. To toy with life and death.

Not so insane now.

Know what I want.

Roxane is in peril. Cannot survive on her own.

If he could detract Anjou from Roxane perhaps the vampire would glut his thirst on him, allowing his sister a chance for escape. Either way, Damian would succumb. To death. And this lucid nightmare would finally be over.

CLINGING TO THE GARGOYLE'S NECK, Gabriel prayed the beast could read his thoughts as it did Roxane's.

The familiar circled high above the Marais, swooping low over the remnants of the city's stone barricade, and skimming the sails of a nearby windmill before careening sharply and repeating the process. *Morbleu*, but the city looked a cartographer's map, so tiny had everything become.

"Where is she?" he called. "Can you sense her? Does she call to you?"

Another swoop over a windmill that edged the city and Gabriel lifted his feet to hook his toes over the gargoyle's tail. He'd almost nicked a sail. Did the beast toy with him? Or was he scenting out his mistress, homing in on her location?

Suddenly Charles plunged. Gabriel's head aimed straight down. He clung with all his might, yet felt his body slipping, sliding forward upon the stone beast. And when he thought to become a victim of a gargoyle suicide, the familiar pulled up and soared through the air, a feather upon a wave.

His heel skidding across a ridged stone spine, Gabriel struggled for hold. An abrupt bank spun Charles in a spiraling descent toward the ground—Gabriel spiraled left.

The gargoyle swooped into the dark, close quarters of the city and landed on the cobblestones of a narrow passageway with a stone-upon-stone, pebble-crunching thud.

Slipping off, Gabriel stumbled forward and caught himself against the greasy wall of a limestone house. Right below the kitchen window, to judge from the crust of foul odors beneath his palms.

He clapped his palms together and strode out from between the close buildings toward the open street. "Time to slay the vampire."

Thirty-Three

STANDING IN THE COOL BLACK ROOM, Gabriel stilled. The place was bare of furnishings. Lamplight glistened in a bare corner dirtied with centuries of dust and grime. Yet, did he—yes—he heard the rumble of voices. Below him.

Picking his way forward he navigated blindly toward the narrow beam of light that clued him to a door.

He kicked the iron door and choked as the entry of fresh air sucked out the smoke into his face. He immediately placed two figures in the center of the room and strode inside.

"A party? And no one thought to invite me?"

Anjou pulled himself up from leaning over Damian. A cocky sneer lifted his lip. "On the contrary, so kind of you to have arrived, vicomte. You are the prince of all gatherings, yes? But it is gauche to bring weapons."

"Better gauche than dead." Gabriel extended his arm, aiming the rapier at Anjou's heart.

Now he spied another figure to his left. Heavy manacles held Roxane's arms down near her hips. Her eyes were glassy. Hell, the bastard had put her in thrall. She hadn't much time.

"Release the two of them. It is me you want," he demanded.

"You value yourself highly, neophyte."

Roxane had told Anjou about his transformation? That left him nothing with which to bargain.

"She blabbered at first threat," Anjou hissed.

Gabriel kept the blade en garde. The vampire did not move, but mastered the center of the room.

"And how does one kill a vampire?" he prompted. Damian groveled at the ancient vampire's feet. "A stake through the heart?"

"I have heard it serves the purpose. But you must know your toothpick of a blade will do no more than pain."

"It appears to be keeping you back. If you don't mind, I'll hang on to it—"

Anjou moved like the wind, slapping the hilt from Gabriel's hand. The man's shoulder plunged into his gut. They landed on the floor. Breath chuffed from Gabriel's lungs. Briefly he touched unconsciousness. But with a shake of his head he came to and struggled with the man who tried to strangle him. Could taking away his breath kill him? Unlikely.

"It might put you out for a while," Anjou hissed, as if he'd read Gabriel's thoughts. "But it will not kill you."

Drawing up his knee, Gabriel finessed a kick to the vampire's groin. He gasped in smoky air as Anjou rolled off him. But he continued to roll, and before Gabriel could pull himself upright, Anjou grabbed the torch from the wall.

"Do you know the only way to kill a witch, my fledging foe?" Anjou swept the flames before Roxane's skirt. Dirt on the hem kept it from bursting to flame. Captured in thrall she remained unaware.

"What do you want?" he insisted. The rapier lay near Anjou's feet. He had no weapon to hand. The logs below the torch were too thick to serve as a stake, only a funeral pyre.

Anjou thrust the torch toward the shadows in the corner. The light fell upon Damian, who, bound by wrist and ankle, sat pounding his forehead against the wall. Dirty fingernails scratched bloody runnels down the stone wall.

Anjou's lips curled into a hideous grin. "I want him."

"Unthinkable," Gabriel said. "Take your leave of Paris and I'll consider you a man granted his greatest desire. That is all I will offer."

"Leave Paris?" Anjou paced center of the room, the torch blazing at his shoulder. "This is my city. I have reigned here. And to know that the two of you live, minions of my blood? Too risky."

"You started this!"

"The witch would not allow me to end it. She showed up before I had finished the task. Explain to me why you care so much for this...thing." Anjou stretched the torch toward Roxane. "She is your death. Ah! I begin to understand. You possess some twisted carnal fetish that makes you toy with your own death as you climax above her. Tempting, I must admit. I've had liaisons with the enemy. Forbidden fruit is so delicious."

A giggle from the shadows rippled through Gabriel's blood. Unhinged, that voice.

The words the vampire spoke may very well be true. He dallied with danger.

No. *You love her. You have breathed her into your very soul, damned as it may be.*

He had sacrificed his mortality—perhaps his very soul—for the Desrues siblings. And he would see Roxane safe. As well, her brother.

He eyed the rapier, which lay but a reach from Anjou's shoe. To his left, Roxane hung suspended. The ice queen had been usurped. So beautiful. Tragic. A spark sizzled at her hem and flame began to eat the tattered threads of her gown.

There was one sure way to kill a vampire—witch's blood. He risked his own life. But to grant Roxane freedom?

A man has to believe in something.

Gabriel believed in Roxane.

He squinted to study the witch. The vial Roxane always wore around her neck was not suspended from the delicate gold chain. Where to get the blood? *So pretty, it stains your lace and seeps your very life...*

"Roxane," he called. "I love you!"

"Such theatrics!" Anjou declared with a dangerous sweep of the torch near Damian's head. "The thrall masks her senses, vicomte. She wilts as we witness."

"Hold!" Gabriel pressed the vampire to silence with a stiff palm out before him. He would have this moment to make her understand. "You do know, Roxane, that I love you? I would do anything for your happiness. Sacrifice...myself."

The stillness was cut by an outburst from Damian. "Take the blood!"

Gabriel bowed his head. Take the blood? Indeed.

Using the moment to his advantage, he plunged against Anjou's body. The torch flew to the wall, landing dreadfully close to Damian, who began to chant, "Burn the witch! Burn the witch!"

Gabriel felt flame singe his back and knew the madman had somehow gotten to the torch and whipped it across the room. It landed before Roxane's feet. Anjou slammed a fist against his jaw. Blood spittle, sweet in his mouth, slid down the back of his throat. He struggled with Anjou, finding the old vampire's strength greater than his own. It mattered little. He merely needed to position him a few paces to the left—

Damian's maniacal laughter filled the room. Gabriel thumbed the cold, steel rapier blade. Flames burned near his head, the sound of crackling fire punctuating the cacophony of madness. He slid his fingers through the hilt and, using the moment Anjou took to recoil for another imminent punch, he rose. Anjou followed, wielding a fist.

Roxane's skirts had taken the flame. She remained livid, oblivious. Gabriel kicked away the torch.

Anjou's defiant stare glittered in the flames, devils dancing in his eyes. "Such a dilemma," he said. "Do you save the woman, or yourself?"

"Not a dilemma at all." Gabriel swung his arm, drawing the rapier across Roxane's arm, feeling resistance as steel cut into her flesh.

Her scream would be the last thing he heard. And it cut much deeper than any blade ever could.

"I love you," he whispered, as he felt the spray of witch's blood splatter his face.

Thirty-Four

BITTERSWEET JOY WASHED through Gabriel's heart when he saw Roxane's blood splatter Anjou's shoulders and neck. Grenadine death cocktail. For all vampires present.

Anjou clutched his burning flesh. Yowls of agony clambered the walls.

It happened quickly. The witch's blood sizzled over Anjou's neck, working an acidic path up his jaw. It entered his flesh and gushed through his veins, racing up and down and filling his body. The explosion was sticky and wretched.

Gabriel turned his head into his elbow to avoid the rain of vampire. A heavy splat of blood and flesh hit his back. Droplets sprinkled his forehead.

One vampire had been finished. As for the other...

Roxane's sobbing ripped through the dull horror. The vampire's death had released the thrall.

Gabriel twisted at the waist and leapt toward the fire. He clamped his arms about her legs, using his body to smother the flames eating her skirts. Vicious heat gnawed through his shirt and burned his torso. But he clung, knowing he would never again touch her, or hold her—for he tasted her blood in his mouth, could feel it slide down his face—

Any moment now.

Rip me asunder. I die loving you.

Flame ceased to burn. Perhaps he had already disintegrated and could feel no pain? A blessed death if that be truth.

Still clinging to Roxane's hips, he huffed in a cloud of smoke and coughed. He did not spit up blood or feel his body tear apart, or...melt.

He dragged a finger through the blood on his face. Not his own. Not Anjou's, for he had turned his face away. Scent of witch. His *fraises at el creme* lover.

When would it happen? When would he combust into a puddle of bloody jelly?

He smeared a palm across his face. Roxane's blood touched him everywhere. And yet, to look upon his hand, the whorls and lines infused with crimson, he did not feel the burn. No pain. Just...hunger.

Swiping his tongue across his palm filled his mouth with rich, sweet blood. The blood hunger stymied him.

"Gabriel? You are alive?"

Would it not come?

He hugged her legs so tightly he knew it must hurt her. But he could not believe it. He lived! He'd had no qualms to sacrificing his life to save hers, and yet... he had been rewarded with life.

"Gabriel, stand up. My blood," she gasped. "It did not burn you? Let me look at you."

Pushing up from the scatter of blood-soaked faggots, he rose and quickly licked the wound on Roxane's arm where he had dragged his rapier in a sacrificial slash. Saliva would heal her.

Securing hold against the wall behind her he stretched higher, kissing her neck, sooted and stained with her tears and blood. He bracketed her face with his palms and kissed her deeply. Inside her kiss he found a perfect untainted moment of bliss. Pressing his body to hers they could not be closer.

Yet they could be closer—Roxane's blood pulsed within his veins.

"Your blood, when I first drank from you..." He kissed her effusively, so thrilled he was to be alive and holding her. "...it is inside me yet. It has made me immune to the danger." Another kiss. "Yes?"

"That is *my* blood all over your face?"

He nodded. "I am free, Roxane. Free to love you with my sharp kisses. How do you like that?"

"You did not know that before you cut me."

He shook his head. "Forgive me, I tried not to cut too deep."

"Gabriel, you sacrificed yourself to save me."

He shrugged. "What did you expect from a lacy swish?"

"Oh, I love you! Please, can you get me from these manacles? My arms hurt dreadfully. Where is Damian? Is he safe?"

"Huddled in the corner. Is there a key?"

He followed Roxane's gaze to the puddle of blood on the floor behind them. Fabric and any metal that had been on the vampire were mired in a goop of pulpy, crimson muck. Only great strength would see Roxane free from the irons.

"I've an idea." He kissed her again, then dashed out the door and down the hallway.

"Gabriel?"

"Right back, love!" he called.

The elation of having survived lightened his strides and returned a much-needed smile to his face. A thousand suns could not beat him down this day!

Arriving at the window that had served as entrance, he stuck out his head. High above, a stony visage watched over the city. "*An evant*!" he shouted. "Your mistress needs you!"

Gabriel dodged as Charles took matters into his own hands—er, wings. Glass shattered, scattering inside the window sash like a crushed sweet. The limestone wall crumbled in a powdery haze of stone and pebbles. The gargoyle's every step punched into the wood floor.

"Careful!" he warned as the gargoyle neared the dungeon door. "She's to the left."

And so Charles smashed through the wall on the right and bit into the manacle around his mistress's wrist. The iron sliced open and her arm dropped to her side. Charles bit off the other manacle and Gabriel caught Roxane's weak body as it tumbled into his arms. He settled to the floor and swept a hand over her body.

"Are you all right?"

"A bit shoogled, but I'll make it. Damian," she whispered.

"Still in the corner." A dark figure coiled into a squatted ball silently rocked.

"Charles, will you?" Roxane asked.

Charles lowered himself before the man in the shadows. A soiled hand thrust out and trembling fingers touched the beast behind its stone ears.

"He knows him," she reassured.

Damian climbed onto Charles's back, clutching the beast's neck and wrapping his legs around his back as if a child clinging to a huge family pet, seeking safety—and finding it.

CHARLES PRECEDED GABRIEL AND Roxane to the vicomte's home . They ran up to the roof to find Damian sleeping peacefully in the gargoyle's protective shadow.

"The window." Roxane stepped to the edge of the shattered oculus.

What had gone on in her absence? She hadn't felt as though she had been with Anjou for long. But the thrall had drained her. Now she wobbled and gasped as Gabriel clutched her from behind.

"Step back," he whispered. "You're still weak."

Thankful for his solid, sure presence, she settled into his embrace. Here was home, in his arms. "What happened here?"

"I had an accident," he offered and turned to Damian. "We should get him inside. Surely the poor soul has been through much."

"Thank you." She threaded her arms about his shoulders.

A kiss bonded them beneath the midnight sky. They had survived the ultimate test to their love—the blood sacrifice—nothing could separate them now.

FORCING HIMSELF TO LEAVE Roxane's arms, Gabriel lifted the thin slip of a man clothed in rags and smelling of his own filth and carried him downstairs to the guest room. Crisp linen sheets received Damian's body with a welcome that Gabriel hoped would comfort. How to chase away the dark demons of madness?

If Anjou had bitten him again had he begun the change? What hell reeked silent havoc behind the man's closed eyes?

He examined Damian, tilting his head to study his neck and under his chin. "Anjou didn't have opportunity to bite him."

"Help me, Gabriel," Roxane whispered against his neck. She threaded her fingers through his and tilted her head to rest upon his shoulder. "I want to make things right for my brother."

"Do you think he could manage a lucid moment? If we questioned him perhaps he could make the choice himself?"

"I think that option was stolen by the moon."

"Witch," Damian spat. Awake, he struggled upright on the bed to crawl across it and sprawl before them. The liege lord of Bicêtre had been released to reign over Paris. "Take my blood, vampire." Seduction coated his voice. The devil danced in his eyes. "It has begun. Do not deny me again."

Roxane shuddered, but felt Gabriel tighten his grip on her hand.

"It is not your brother who speaks to us now."

"Then who is it? He is in pain."

"Burn the witch." Damian curled to his side and balled his legs up to his chest. He closed his eyes. "My faithful! Where are my faithful?"

Roxane settled cautiously on the bed before her brother. "I love you, Damian." She made to touch him, but at his flinch, drew back. "I will never deserve your forgiveness, and you mustn't worry to grant it. If I could take back the days and make you whole I would."

"Witch," muttered out from the man's tucked head.

"If you allow the vicomte to bite you..." She looked to Gabriel. In his eyes she found compassion so rich, so vast she wanted to dive in and lose herself—and bring

Damian along. "Take the blood," she whispered. "Pray it makes you whole."

Damian rolled to his back and stared up at her with his pale green eyes. Celadon. Indeed, an ice forest waiting for its prince's return. For a moment Roxane thought she saw understanding. Acceptance.

Damian nodded, and stretched a hand toward Gabriel.

She moved aside as the vicomte, in tattered lace and bloody attire, bent over her brother and lifted his thin shoulders.

"Forgive me," she heard Gabriel whisper.

Damian let out a moan as the vampire's bite pierced his flesh. His fingers clenched and unclenched and he kicked at the mattress, but he did not struggle. Soon he wrapped his arms about Gabriel and clutched, clinging, worshipping...becoming.

Had this been Gabriel's moment? The attack under the stars interrupted by his valet? So intimate, the twining of their bodies, the drawing of blood. The gift of the night.

She felt her lover curl fingers around her wrist. Damian lay quietly gazing up at the ceiling. Blood trickled from two perfect wounds on the side of his neck. Her lover's kiss.

A shiver traced her arm as Gabriel kissed her wrist. "He must drink from you," he whispered. "Grant him the immunity that will protect a brother from his sister's deadly weapon."

"I—" She tugged away and clutched her wrist at her breast. "I don't know."

"Roxane..." he nuzzled his nose aside her ear. She scented the blood on him. Anjou's blood, her blood,

Damian's blood. "Make him safe. Bring your brother back to you."

"P-promise?"

"I can promise only that you are with two men who love and need you."

Now was her chance to right the wrongs served Damian. Murmuring a blessing for success, Roxane pressed her wrist to Gabriel's mouth. He drew a fang across her skin, opening her vein in an icy slice.

"To life," he said as he directed her hand to Damian's mouth.

"And love," Roxane said as the pull of her blood tugged at her very being.

"I DON'T WANT TO KNOW."

Roxane roused from a drowsy sleep. Wedged between Gabriel, who snored softly, and Damian, whose leg twitched in his deep sleep. The voice had come from the open door. There stood Xavier Desrues, wearing Gabriel's robe, looking as if the cat had gotten him.

"My son is safe?" he asked.

Roxane nodded.

"And you?"

"I should explain—"

"No." Her father put up a hand. "I trust you and the vicomte. Toussaint tells me Anjou is gone?"

She could only nod, for she knew now her father had loved the man, no matter his twisted mien. And if Toussaint had been speaking to Xavier, then she needn't worry for him. Not at this moment.

Xavier tilted his head and closed his eyes. A smile crept onto his pale mouth. "It is good to be with my family."

"It is." And she laid her head aside Gabriel's shoulder and drifted to sleep.

EPILOGUE

IN TWO WEEKS GABRIEL'S LIFE had spun completely around. No longer did he stand facing the cruel mockery of his past. Now, he stared straight ahead at a future that promised much adventure, love, and probably a bit of danger. (Toussaint took immense pleasure knowing that.)

He was ready for a new life. The witch and the vampire had found their comfort, twined within one another's embrace.

Xavier stayed on at the Renan estate. He wanted to gain the time he had lost with his children—and would. But presently he dealt with Anjou's massive fortune. Together Xavier and Gabriel had plans to build a grand children's home. In fact, last week the *Mercure de France* reported an anonymous donation to erect that very charitable home. Xavier's influence at court would prove Gabriel's boon.

Damian had improved remarkably, and was almost himself. He followed Gabriel, learning all there was to know about his new life. Gabriel every day learned new things himself, so he felt the student guiding the fledging. They often sought advice from Xavier, who could surrender to the vampire's way, for now he had all he wanted in life.

Damian was more lucid than mad. His mental state could only improve. But there were still nights Gabriel and Roxane lay in bed listening to the pounding against the wall. Damian forgave his sister, in fact, he'd apologized for the cruel words and epitaphs the madness had worked against her. Gabriel prayed for the day Roxane would forgive herself for her brother's condition.

Now he and Roxane visited the country often. They had plans to renovate the parish and raise their children far from the stifling confines of the city.

Yes, the future glowed brightly. Gabriel smiled from behind his blue spectacles. He had many lifetimes to hone his skills and become the exquisite beast he strived to become.

But his lover would enjoy a mere mortal lifetime.

Now, he held her as they lay in bed, naked, after love making. His muscles were languid and warm. Rosemary and cinnamon shrouded the room with their mixed essence.

"Roxane, love, tell me you can get your immortality back?"

She nuzzled against his chest and darted a tongue at his nipple; it hardened at her command. "It is possible. I would have to perform the ascension ritual again. Not a pleasant act by any means."

He kissed the crown of her head, nuzzling into the strawberry softness. "If I found you a vampire, would you do it? For me?"

"You want me to commit such a bloody act?"

"If it will see you by my side forever, yes. But I won't force you to do something that would make you uncomfortable."

"Let me think on it."

"Fair enough."

He turned his head and stared up at the ceiling. The gaping circle where the brilliant oculus had once reigned had been boarded over. Xavier had already invited a glasscutter to dine with the family to discuss an even more brilliant replacement. The entire rainbow must be restored.

"There is Madame de Tencin's salon tomorrow night," he said. "I've a new damask frockcoat I've been dying to show off. Perhaps I could show off my fiancée?"

"Gabriel, you know you just put a frockcoat before me?"

"I did?" He smirked. "I did."

"Ever the swish," she said, and nestled against him. "My vampire swish."

The End

To read about Gabriel and Roxane's daughter, Jane Renan, look for FROM THE DARK at your favorite online retailer or used bookstore.
For more information about the characters in Michele Hauf's world of Beautiful Creatures, go to Club Scarlet online at:
clubscarlet.michelehauf.com

COMING SOON…

An anthology featuring four of the paranormal romance genre's award-winning and bestselling authors.

Patti O'Shea ~ Lori Devoti
Michele Hauf ~ Sharon Ashwood

Get ready to **Crave The Night** with dark, seductive tales of vampires, werewolves, faeries, and demons.

Available in digital and print editions at your favorite online retailer.

www.SwellCatPress.com

45719813R00189

Made in the USA
Middletown, DE
12 July 2017